Goblings Attack!

Slimy flesh bubbled from the ground. What had once been ten thousand goblings was now one hideous amalgamation, a creature of nightmares that could only exist through darkest sorcery.

The field exploded, and the beast revealed itself in all its terrifying power. The horde towered one hundred feet high. Tendrils shot out and dragged men to gruesome deaths. The air filled with screams and crunching bones.

I strode through the rush of fleeing soldiers. The horde swept forward, a ravenous tower of phantom flesh, its countless eyes studying this morsel standing before them. For a moment I thought it might have sensed my trap, but I was too tempting a snack. With a hungry snarl, the horde rushed forward and engulfed me....

Tor Books by A. Lee Martinez

Gil's All Fright Diner
In the Company of Ogres
A Nameless Witch
The Automatic Detective
Too Many Curses

A Nameless Witch

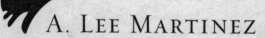

A. Lee Martinez

TOR®
fantasy

A TOM DOHERTY ASSOCIATES BOOK
NEW YORK

This is a work of fiction. All the characters, organizations, and events portrayed in this novel are products of the author's imagination or are used fictitiously.

A NAMELESS WITCH

Copyright © 2007 by A. Lee Martinez

A Tor Book
Published by Tom Doherty Associates, LLC
175 Fifth Avenue
New York, NY 10010

www.tor-forge.com

Tor® is a registered trademark of Tom Doherty Associates, LLC.

ISBN-13: 978-0-7653-5458-7
ISBN-10: 0-7653-5458-6

First Edition: May 2007
First Mass Market Edition: September 2008

Printed in the United States of America

0 9 8 7 6 5 4 3 2 1

I was born dead. Or, to be more accurate, undead. Not that there is much difference between the two. It's just a matter of degrees really.

When I say undead, I do not mean vampyre, ghoul, or graveyard fiend. There are many versions of unlife. These are only the most common. My state was far less debilitating. Bright lights bothered me to some noticeable degree, and I preferred my meat undercooked. Once reaching adulthood, I'd become ageless. Most means of mortal harm could not truly hurt me, and I possessed a smattering of unusual gifts not known among the living. Yet all these advantages came at a high price.

Exactly how I came to be born undead is a long, complicated story not really worth telling in detail. It involves my great-great-great-great-grandfather, a renowned hero of the realm, and his conflict with a dark wizard. This wizard, his name is lost to history so I just call him "Nasty Larry" for convenience' sake, had raised an army of orcish zombies to ravage the land. Now everyone knows orcs are terrible things, and zombies aren't much fun either. Mix the two together and you get an evil greater than the sum of its parts. Naturally, a legion of heroes was assembled, and the requisite last stand against doomsday was fought and won by a hairsbreadth. My great-great-great-great-grandfather slew Nasty Larry, cleaving his head from his shoulders with one sweep of a mighty broadsword. Nasty Larry's head rolled to his slayer's feet and pronounced a terrible curse, as decapitated wizard's heads are prone to do.

"With my dying breath, I curse thee and thy bloodline. From now until the end of time, the sixth child of every generation shall be made a gruesome abomination. A twisted, horrible thing that shall shun the light and dwell in miserable darkness."

That bit of business finished, Nasty Larry died. According to legend, he melted into a puddle, the sky turned black, and—if one could believe such tales—the land within a hundred miles turned to inhospitable swamp. That was the end of Nasty Larry's small, yet noteworthy, influence on my life.

I often wondered why my parents chose to have a sixth child, being forewarned as they were. They had many excuses. The most common being, "We lost count." Second common, and far more acceptable in my opinion, was, "Well, none of our family had ever had six, and we thought it might not have taken." Perfectly reasonable. Not all curses grab hold, and one couldn't live one's life fretting over every utterance of every bodiless head one ran across.

Being undead was not all that horrible a curse. Unfortunately, this was not the end of my worries. For besides being made a thing born to dwell in darkened misery, I was also made, in the infinite wisdom of fate, a girl. These two conditions taken individually were minor handicaps, but toss them together, and you would understand the difficulties I experienced growing up.

There are kingdoms where a woman is prized for her mind, where she is more than a trophy or a poorly paid housemaid. Kingdoms where the chains of a thousand years of chauvinism have finally rusted away. I was not born in one of these kingdoms.

I was not very popular among the male suitors of my village. It was nothing personal. Husbands just prefer living wives, and I met so few potential spouses locked in my parents' basement. At the age of eighteen, I was already an old, undead maid sitting in a darkened cellar, waiting to die.

Of course, I don't die. Not like normal people. Certainly, old age wouldn't accomplish the task. So I settled in for a very long wait. I figured it would be another fifty years before my parents died and one of my brothers or sisters would inherit caretaking duties of their poor, wretched sibling. One of their children would take over next. And so on. And so on. Until one day, they either forgot me, or all died, or maybe, just maybe, an angry mob would drag me from the shadows and burn me at the stake. Not much to look forward to. But no one is master of their fate, and my lot was not all that terrible in the end.

All that changed with the arrival of Ghastly Edna. That wasn't her real name. I never learned it. I just called her "Ghastly Edna" because it seemed a proper witch's name. She was a grotesquely large woman, bearlike in proportions, with a pointed hat, a giant hooked nose, and a long, thin face. Her skin, while not truly green, possessed a slick olive hue. Her nose even had a wart. Ghastly Edna's only flaw, witchly speaking, was a set of perfectly straight, perfectly polished teeth.

The day I met Ghastly Edna changed everything, and I remember it well. The basement door opened. I scrambled to the foot of the stairs to collect my daily meal. Instead, she came lumbering down. Her bulky frame clouded the light filtering behind her. She placed a callused hand under my chin and smiled thinly.

"Yes, yes. You shall do, child."

Ghastly Edna purchased me from my parents for a puny sum. I'm certain they were glad to be rid of their cursed daughter, and I couldn't honestly blame them. My new mentor whisked me away to her cottage in the middle of some forsaken woods far from civilization. The first thing she did was clean me up. It took six long hours to wash away the accumulated filth of eighteen years and cut the tangle of hair atop my head. When she finally finished, she stood me before a small mirror and frowned.

"No, no, no. I do not like this. I do not like this one bit."

The effect this had on my self-esteem was immediate and crushing. I'd always know myself to be a hideous thing. Yet Ghastly Edna was no prize beauty herself, and to evoke such a revolted tone could only mean that Nasty Larry's curse had really had its way with me.

"You're not ugly, child," she corrected. "You're quite"—her long face squished itself into a scowl—"lovely."

I had yet to dare look in the mirror for fear of being driven mad by own hideousness. Now I chanced a sidelong glance through the corner of my eye. It was not the sanity-twisting sight I had expected, but still a far cry from lovely.

"But what about these?" I cupped the large, fatty mounds on my chest.

"Those are breasts," Ghastly Edna said. "They're supposed to be there."

"But they're so . . . so . . ."

"Round. Firm." She sighed. "That's how they're supposed to be. Ideally."

I found that hard to believe, but I wasn't about to argue with the person who'd rescued me from my solitary existence.

"And that bottom of yours." She mumbled. "You could bounce a gold piece off it."

"But the skin is pale," I offered, trying to please her.

"It's not pale, dear. It's alabaster." She circled me twice, looking more disappointed with each passing moment. "And I don't believe I've ever seen eyes quite that shade of green. Or lips so full and soft. And your hair. I washed it with year-old soap, and it's still as soft as gossamer." She drew close and sniffed. "And it smells of sunflowers."

"What about my teeth? Surely they're not supposed to look like that."

She checked my gums and teeth with her fingers. "No, dear. You're quite correct. They're a tad too sharp. But it's not an obvious flaw, and besides that, they're nice and white. Good gums too. The tongue has a little fork in it, but only if you're looking for it."

She ordered me into a seat, still naked and slightly damp from the bath.

"Are you certain you spent all your life in that basement?"

I nodded.

"No exercise. Dismal diet. Dwelling in filth. Yet somehow you come out like this. Not even half-mad as far as I can tell."

"You mean, I'm not cursed, ma'am?"

"Oh, you are cursed, child, and undead. That much is certain. Curses come in many forms however, and not all are as bad. Especially death curses. It's tricky enough to cast a decent spell when you're still alive. But throwing one out as you're expiring requires a certain knack. Apparently, the wizard who cursed your family was not as in control of his magic as he should've been. The undead part came through, but the hideousness element didn't quite make it. The magic must've had a better idea as it sometimes does."

She handed me a towel. "Cover yourself, dear. I can't bear to look upon you anymore."

I did as I was told.

"That's the thing about death curses. One really shouldn't employ them unless one feels they can pull it off. It just makes the rest of us look bad."

She spent several minutes rocking in her chair, mulling over the situation. A dread fell upon me. I didn't want to be sent back to my cellar if I could help it. Given no other choice, I'd accepted my fate. Now my universe was filled with other possibilities, and I didn't want to lose them.

Ghastly Edna snapped up from her chair.

"Well, dear, the magic called me to you. Far be it from me to contradict it. Your loveliness just means you'll have to work harder at your witchery. A handicap yes, but not an insurmountable one." She peeled the wart from her nose. "False, darling." She winked.

She proceeded to wipe the greenish makeup from her face to reveal skin that, while rough and haggard, was not especially hideous. She removed six layers of clothing to show that her hunch was nothing more than an illusion of well-placed fabric. When she removed her hat, I realized that Ghastly Edna was a large and ugly woman, but not at all witchly without her full outfit.

"We all need a little help, dear. You just need far more than I. Now let me see what I have here that might do the trick." She began digging through various moldy trunks filled with equally moldy clothing.

My heart leaped with joy.

Ghastly Edna spent the next six months acquainting me with the ins and outs of witchly wardrobe. Wearing just the right outfit was fifty percent of a witch's business, she explained. She was not exaggerating. It took a great deal of work to make one look as bad as was expected. Especially for me, my mentor pointed out, as I was afflicted with a form most unsuitable for a witch.

Once I'd mastered the art of looking witchly, she proceeded to teach me the black arts: necromancy, demonology, the forgotten language of unspeaking things, and forbidden nature lore. The powers of magic that had drawn Ghastly Edna to me had not been mistaken, and in due course, I mastered the craft of the witch.

And for a while, I was happy.

Until the dark day when they finally killed her.

Exactly how long **I** lived with Ghastly Edna, I couldn't say. It was forever autumn in those woods, and as a side effect of my ageless nature, I do not measure time well. I assume Ghastly Edna did grow older, but as she was a wrinkled, old witch when I'd first met her, she didn't get more wrinkled, at least not noticeably so, over the course of my tutelage.

However long it took, it was soon after I'd learned everything she could teach me that she woke me early one morning. The morning light perturbed the undead in me, and Ghastly Edna respected this. I knew right away something was wrong.

"No questions, dear," she said. "I need you to go to the lake."

I stirred from my bed. "But, mistress . . ."

She put her fingers to my lips. "Shush, child. I don't have time to explain, and even if I did, I don't have to. You'll do as I say."

I nodded.

"Very good. Now you must go and bathe yourself in the lake. And I'm not talking about merely your face and hands. I mean, your entire body. I know the light will bother you, so you can wear your hat to shade your eyes. But otherwise, you must strip off every other stitch. After you've gotten yourself nice and clean, you must hurry back. I'll be dead by then, and we'll have one last talk before I go."

This final piece of news stopped me cold.

"But . . ."

"I said, shush, child. Now get dressed. We'll have time to talk when you return. But you must hurry to the lake." She lumbered from my small room, barely squeezing through the door. "And don't bother with the whole outfit. Just your hat and your black dress, that one with the loose skirt."

I always did as Ghastly Edna told, and today was no exception. As I got dressed, I couldn't help but think about her death. Not for a moment did I doubt it was going to be. She often spoke of the future and other things that she could not know. It was the magic. It talked to her, and as far as I could tell, it never lied. It was not fate, she'd explained once, but rather the past yet to be. Not to be confused with the future that might come or the present that never was. Subtle distinctions I'd never truly understood, but Ghastly Edna had reassured me this was not my fault. It could not be properly explained by her. Only by the magic, and the magic had never talked to me. Rather, I'd yet to hear it.

I slipped on my dress. It was comfortable cloth cut in a most unflattering way. It failed to hide away all the unwanted charms of my unwitchly form, but it was better than nothing. Normally, I wouldn't dare be seen outside without a tattered cloak and a frumpy shawl. I scowled, pressing a palm against my flat stomach. I'd been working to develop a flabby belly and chubby behind for as long as I could remember. The curse kept them tight and toned, no matter how much I ate.

"Hurry up, dear," Ghastly Edna said.

I grabbed my hat, tattered and pointed with a wide brim, and headed for the door. On the way out, I stopped and watched my mistress, her back to me, fussing over the stove.

She did not turn around. "And take Newt with you. He'll soon be yours anyway. Might as well get used to each other."

I still couldn't bring myself to leave. Not that I thought staying would do much good. If the magic said she was to die then I couldn't stop it.

"Be off, child." She glanced over her shoulder. "Don't make me box your ears."

"Yes, ma'am."

The hard light burned my eyes. I tolerated it, but its rays prickled my skin. I shivered beneath a warm breeze. I pulled my brim over my face and gave myself time to adjust to the morning.

I called for Newt.

"You don't have to shout," he said from the cabin roof. "I'm right here."

"We have to go to the lake."

Newt cocked his head to one side, squinting one eye at me. "What?"

"The mistress ordered it."

He cocked his head the other way. "What for?"

"She didn't say. Just that we must hurry."

"We?"

"You're to come with me."

"Are you certain?"

Ghastly Edna shouted from the darkened cabin. "Go on, Newt! Do as she says!"

"Oh, very well."

Newt was my mistress's familiar. Familiars come in countless varieties: demons molded into animal shape, enchanted creatures, dreams made flesh, flesh made dream. Ghastly Edna had created Newt by enchanting a waterfowl with intelligence and speech and then grafting a pinch of pure demonic essence. The end result was an ill-tempered duck, unhappy with the entire world and quite willing to share his unhappiness.

Being a duck was what he was most unhappy with. Not just a duck, but a white duck. Brown feathers trimmed his wings and ran down his back, but they failed to make him more sinister. Even if he'd been midnight black, I don't think it would've helped. Ducks, even demon ducks, just aren't terrifying to look upon.

He hopped off the roof to land beside me. "Let's get going then. If we must. You'd better get dressed."

"I am dressed."

"I think not. You're barely covered at all."

I explained that this was all Ghastly Edna allowed me to wear. He quacked his displeasure. We walked the path down to the lake. Newt had a peculiar way of walking. His bow-legged swagger seemed more ridiculous than a traditional waddle. I'd told him once, and he'd told me to mind my own business. So I did. Even if he did walk like a bird with a rash between his legs.

When we got to the lake, I hesitated to do as I was told. I'd spent most of my life in the dark. I'd bathed in the lake many times before, but always at night. Not that the sun was a true danger. I just wasn't used to it. It was so bright, and I would be so exposed.

Newt sighed. "Get on with it, would you?"

I pulled my hat tighter on my head and slipped off my dress.

Newt sighed again. "Dark gods, girl, you're beautiful." It was not intended as a compliment.

I quickly immersed myself up to my chest, hiding from the warm sun beneath the cold water. "It's not my fault."

"Have you tried eating lard?"

I nodded.

"And it didn't do anything?"

"Nothing does anything."

He paced back and forth a safe distance from the shore. He didn't mind water, but only in shallow tubs and puddles.

"Self-mutilation. A nasty scar or two couldn't hurt."

"I don't scar," I replied sadly. "I considered sawing off a limb once, but the mistress said it would just grow back. She says as long as I live, I'll look like this."

"Bad luck."

Newt pushed his wings up in a duckly shrug. In this particular matter, he could sympathize. Just as I was too pretty to be a witch, he was too white and fluffy to be a creature of fear.

My bath didn't take long. I was just emerging when Newt raised his head and glanced around the woods. "I think there's somebody out there."

"There's nobody out there," I replied, even as I slid on my dress to cover myself. It hid little. The cloth clung to my damp skin.

"I think there is," he said.

I joined him in scanning. At night, I could've seen everything. During the day, my eyes suffered. I didn't see anything or anyone, but I felt something. I wondered if this was perhaps the magic finally talking to me. Ghastly Edna said that it talked to everyone, but most were unwilling to listen.

"I think we should get back," I said.

I refused to allow myself to run back to the cabin. I wanted to flee to my sanctuary from the light and phantom eyes. But I was not about to give in to the dread. The farther we got from the lake, the better I felt. My sense of foreboding ebbed, then rose as the cabin came into view.

"That was a complete waste of time." Newt stopped and peered at me. "Are you crying, girl?"

I wiped a tear away. I didn't want to go back. I told myself if I didn't go on, if I just stayed put, then Ghastly Edna would never have to die. I knew it wasn't true, but it was the only thing I could do.

"Why are you crying?"

I pushed away my tears. Witches weren't supposed to cry.

"What is it?" Newt demanded.

"She's dead."

"What?"

"I should've stayed."

"What are you talking about?"

"She's dead."

"Why would you think that?"

"Because she told me she would be."

Newt spread his wings in alarm. "She told you! She didn't tell me! Why didn't she tell me?" He dashed toward the cabin in a speedy, flapping skip. "Why didn't she tell me?"

I ran after him, overtaking his short strides and reaching the cabin before him. I threw open the door and stepped inside.

Ghastly Edna lay on the floor, a sword blade buried deep in her back. A scraggly man, hairy and dirty, poked around the cupboard. He turned, revealing a scarred face.

"What have we here?"

He leered. I'd never been leered at before, and I didn't like it.

He rubbed his grimy hands together. "My, what a healthy young girl we have here."

A second brute emerged from my room. "Hey, look what I found. I think someone else lives here."

"I'll say."

The brute laid eyes upon me and wiped his mouth. The two killers advanced, no doubt intending to force themselves upon me. Newt strolled in between my legs. He took one brief glimpse of Ghastly Edna and turned on the killers. His eyes glinted in a way I'd never seen before.

"What'cha gonna do, girl? Sic your bird on us?"

Newt bellowed a monstrous quack, deep and bestial. It wasn't very scary, but as scary as any quack could be. The demon rose within him, and he pounced. A storm of webbed feet, slashing bill, and slapping feathers tore into the killers. They ran screaming out the door. Newt chased after them, squawking curses. I left the murderous scum to their executioner and checked on Ghastly Edna.

I pulled the sword out of her and rolled her over. She looked so peaceful. It was almost a shame to bother her, but it was her last order.

My ability to talk to the dead was a gift of my curse. Witches knew ways to speak with the deceased, but it was complicated magic. On the other hand, I could awaken the soul of a fresh corpse with just a touch. Provided the soul was still in the flesh. The spirit usually remains for a few minutes, just to be certain that the body has really expired. Ghastly Edna, knowing I would be back, would certainly still be waiting.

Newt strolled back into the cottage. He was covered in blood, none of it his own. He left scarlet, webbed footprints behind him.

"They're dead."

I was not as comforted by this as I would have thought. The killers being dead didn't bring back my mistress.

"You should've seen it. I speared out the big guy's heart

and showed it to him before he died. And the little one, sliced off his head with three slashes of my bill. I don't mean to brag or anything, but it was something to behold." He grinned, but the grin vanished quickly. "Ah, damn it. I can't believe she's dead."

"Quiet. I need to concentrate."

I laid a hand on her stomach and dug around for Ghastly Edna's soul. I wasn't certain I could do it. I'd only practiced on animals up to now: rabbits, squirrels, sparrows. But my first person wasn't much harder. It took only a moment, and there was no resistance.

Her eyes snapped to life. "Hello, child."

She squirmed stiffly on the floor.

"Be a dear and help me up, would you?"

Getting her to her feet proved difficult. Her corpse and her spirit were barely connected now, and she hadn't been very graceful when alive.

She wiggled her fingers mechanically. "Excellent work, child. Now help me to the table."

On rigid legs, she clomped to the chair and sat down. Her knees cracked. She patted the chair beside her.

"Quickly now. My body is a leaking vessel, and we haven't much time before I must take more permanent leave of it."

I sat, and Newt hopped on the table.

"Dear boy, you're a mess."

"I am anointed in the blood of your murderers. You have been avenged."

"Hardly." Ghastly Edna smiled. Or perhaps the left side of her face twitched without her knowledge. "Those two were merely the tools of another. But I appreciate the effort just the same. It's the thought that counts." Her face went blank again for a moment. "Now the girl and I have matters we must discuss. Things you need not hear. Besides, you're dripping all over my floor. Go outside, and clean yourself up."

Newt, like I, didn't question Ghastly Edna. He quacked, turned up his bill, and left.

I took Ghastly Edna's hand. She'd always been ice cold to the touch, even alive, and I'd found comfort in that before. But not today.

"I should've stayed."

"Then you would have been killed as well."

"But they were just brutes . . ."

"Brutes or not, a witch was to die here this day. That was what had to be."

"The past yet to be," I said.

"Close, but no. This was the present that would be, but need not be as it would."

I didn't understand, and this last bit of confusion weakened my will. I started to cry. Just a few tears. I expected Ghastly Edna to chide me for the display, but she brushed the tears from my cheek. She ended up poking me in the eye too, but this was merely an accidental twitch of her inflexible arm. The jab made me cry harder.

"The time has come, child, for you to strike out on your own, find your own destiny. I know you're scared, but you'll find the world is not so frightening. And you've got a lot going for you. You've a good heart and good sense. This undead business is rather minor really, and you're an accomplished witch. Accomplished enough to overcome your unfortunate physical defects."

"I don't want to go. I want to stay. Here. With you."

She laughed. Her bouncing corpse nearly toppled from the chair. "Unfortunately, I must be leaving soon. And so should you. Things change, dear. Even for the ageless. You can't hide away from the world forever. I know you'll do fine. In fact, I know you'll do me proud."

She winked. Her eye held shut.

Her voice became a whisper. "Before I leave, I offer you these three pieces of advice. First, be wary of mortals. They may be small in power, but they are large in number.

"Second, remember that people, human or otherwise, are, with rare exception, basically good at heart. Treat them as you would be treated, and you'll almost never go wrong.

"And thirdly, and this is something you should never forget, feed a troll and you'll never be rid of it."

She laughed again.

"Almost time. When you leave this place, follow the trail around the lake and through the hills. When you reach a fork in the path, you'll have a choice to make. Head east and you'll take the first step toward truly avenging my death. Or dying horribly yourself. Or possibly both. The magic is not entirely clear on this.

"Head north, on the other hand, and you'll find a life of quiet contentment and simple pleasures. More happiness than most people happen on, but less than you might find to the east. Even with that horrible death possibility. On this, the magic is quite clear.

"I wish you well whatever choice you make. Now, give me a hug before I go."

Years of living with Ghastly Edna left me ill-prepared for this last instruction. Displays of affection were not, strictly speaking, against the witch's code, but she had never been very affectionate. Not in a touching, doting way.

"Come now, child. I don't have all day."

I wrapped my arms around her ample frame for the first time ever. She was a large, lumpy woman. I'd never realized just how lumpy. She hugged me back with the one limp arm she still had some power over.

"I love you," I whispered.

It was another first.

"I know, dear. I love you too."

She shivered as her soul slipped from her flesh. I felt it go. It floated down to the cool embrace of the earth where any good witch's soul went.

I couldn't bring myself to let her go. I held her corpse tight, and even if it was an unwitchly thing to do, I cried for a good long while.

Newt *splashed around in* a barrel of fresh rainwater. Though he disliked his waterfowl origins, he was duck enough to enjoy a good bath. I shaded my eyes from the light of day.

He stopped preening his wing long enough to raise his head and ask, "Well?"

"She's gone."

"I assumed as much, but what did she say?"

I told him of the path and the choice I must make.

"That's it?"

"No. She also told me to be careful of feeding trolls."

"That's just common sense." He briefly dipped his head below the water. "Anything else?"

"She said she loved me."

Newt frowned. "That's it?"

"Yes."

"Nothing for me?"

I shook my head.

"That's a fine thing." He jumped from the barrel and shook dry. "I was her familiar. I'd known her a good many years longer than you. And she breaks witchly protocol by admitting she loves you and doesn't even say a word to me. Not an 'I'll miss you' or 'Thanks for the years of loyal service.'"

"Sorry."

"That's quite all right. I'm used to it. Life of a familiar. Always get taken for granted. Still, I'll miss the old bat."

My eyes followed the trail of blood from the cabin door to the corpses of Ghastly Edna's killers. Newt had finished them off before they'd gotten twenty paces. I was surprised they'd made it that far, given the severed body parts Newt had sliced away. An ear here. A nose there. One forearm had been torn away with enough force to fling it onto the cabin's roof. The bodies were hardly recognizable, hacked and mutilated as they were. I was impressed with how thoroughly Newt had done away with them in such a short time.

"You did an excellent job," I complimented.

His inner demon flashed a pleased grin, hampered only by his lack of teeth. "They're the first men I've killed. I slew a bear once. And a couple of badgers too. Purely for reasons of self-defense, I assure you. These two were a good deal easier. If I'd been here, I could've saved her."

I didn't contradict him, but I didn't think this true. Something told me Ghastly Edna's death couldn't have been averted. Perhaps it was the magic that told me this. Perhaps the simple logic that my mistress wouldn't have sent Newt and I away if we could have been of some help.

A witch was to die here this day. I supposed this meant that if I'd stayed behind, I would've perished. I couldn't know this for certain, but I suspected it was true. Ghastly Edna had sacrificed herself for me.

Again, I wondered if the magic told me this. I listened. Hard. All I heard was the wind rustling the leaves.

"So I guess I'm yours now," said Newt.

"Yes."

"What now, mistress?" He chuckled lightly at the title. I ignored that for the moment.

I glanced back to the darkened cabin. It was the only home I'd known since crawling from my parents' musty cellar. But now it seemed an empty box without Ghastly Edna's cool, comforting presence. Leaving it behind would not be so difficult. Only fear of what lay outside these woods held me back.

"Fear is not a bad thing," Ghastly Edna had once explained. "Among everyday creatures, it is a great motivation. Fear of being eaten, or of not getting enough to eat, are why men gather together in villages. Villages which become towns. Towns which become cities. Cities which become countries. Countries which become civilizations. Remember this, child. Even the greatest kingdoms are founded, however distantly, on fear.

"But we are witches, and we are not of civilization. Not the mundane civilization of men at least. We understand fear. We know when to listen to its whispers and when to ignore its shouts."

Remembering this put a smile on my lips. Ghastly Edna was not gone. She was always with me now. If it wasn't technically magic, it should have been.

"We leave within the hour. Get your things together."

Newt quacked. "Things? What things? I'm a duck."

I ignored him again and went inside to prepare. I stuffed as much as I could into two old satchels. Mostly clothes, a handful of herbs, a small box of witchly implements, the locket my mother had thrown lovingly down the stairs on my fifth birthday, and a moldy squirrel hide Ghastly Edna had tacked on the wall to brighten my room. Witches travel light.

I spent the rest of the hour getting dressed. I buried myself beneath layers of clothing. Any traces of the svelte creature underneath were soon obscured to my satisfaction. I put on my crooked, pointed hat and smeared some soot on my face. I grabbed a broom and held it, handle down, as if necessary to balance my weight. For a finishing touch, I wrapped a billowing vomit green cloak around my shoulders. I measured myself in the mirror. It was adequate, but I would never be as good a witch as Ghastly Edna.

I cast one last glance at my mistress, sprawled facedown across the table. I was proper this time and didn't weep.

I limped from the cabin. There was no one around to appreciate the act, but it was good practice. Newt waited by the door, and a pack of wolves had gathered around the mangled bodies of Ghastly Edna's killers. They had not been drawn here by the scent of blood.

The leader, a thick brown hound, approached. "It is time for another to return to the earth."

Talking to beasts was the first trick Ghastly Edna had taught me. "She's inside."

"Very good."

The leader barked, and his pack filed into the cabin. The sounds of tearing flesh issued forth.

"I would ask a favor of you. Please do not eat those two." I nodded toward the dead killers. "They do not deserve the honor of your stomachs."

The wolf bowed his head. "As you request, but you need not have asked. They are false flesh, not true men at all."

"What do you mean?"

"Just as I say." He shrugged. "I cannot explain. I am, after all, only a wolf, and can only understand the world through a wolf's eyes. And nose. They do not smell of men. Or of anything natural. I would not eat them if I were starved half to death."

A good witch heeds the wisdom of beasts, and I thanked him for his insight.

"You're quite welcome. My sympathies for your loss. Now if you'll excuse me, I'm famished."

"Certainly."

He strode inside and joined his family in their meal.

I checked the bodies. They looked of real flesh and blood. But then again, not quite. It was hard to tell with the condition Newt had left them in, but I trusted the wolf's nose. Something larger was at work here than two thugs happening upon a cabin in the middle of nowhere. Something more sinister.

"Perhaps you should try to raise them," Newt suggested.

"Too late for that. Their souls must be gone already. Even if they remain, you left little to work with."

"Sorry. Guess I got a little carried away."

"Quite all right."

He milled about in an embarrassed fashion. "It's the demon in me. I can't always control it."

"I understand."

"I'll try to be more careful in the future."

"Very good. Come along, Newt."

I limped away from the cabin and my old life. And I didn't look back.

We WALKED IN SILENCE. The woods were deathly quiet. There was no wind off the lake, no singing birds, not even the rustling of leaves. The forest mourned Ghastly Edna. Neither Newt nor I broke the silence. Only after the wind returned did we know it respectful to speak.

"Nice limp," he said.

"Thank you."

"Have you decided yet? The path, I mean."

"I haven't really thought about it."

"No rush, I suppose."

We walked awhile more without speaking. I didn't think about the fork ahead. It was a decision I wasn't ready to make.

"What would you do?" I asked.

Newt stopped. "You're asking my opinion?"

"Yes."

He squinted at the sun. "Strange. All those years, the mistress never asked my opinion on anything. It was always 'Newt, do this,' 'Newt, fetch that,' 'Newt, find my woolen socks.' But never once did she ask my advice."

"You're my familiar now, and I'm asking for it."

He rubbed his bill with the tip of a wing. "I don't know. Give me a minute to think it over."

We walked around the lake and into the hills, knowing that each step brought me closer to a decision I was no more ready to make than before.

"I'd go west," Newt finally said.

"That wasn't one of the choices."

"Exactly."

I got an inkling of why Ghastly Edna had never asked his opinion.

"That's me though," he said. "I'm part demon, and demons despise being told what to do. They aren't very fond of fate either. And they greatly enjoy being contrary for its own sake."

"I'm not a demon. Nor even part demon."

"True enough. In which case, if I were not part demon,

and a witch, and in your position, I suppose, taking everything into consideration, then I would go east."

"Any reasons?"

"Seems a simple decision. North, you'll find happiness. Nothing against happiness, and there's no rule saying a witch must be miserable. But, ultimately, it isn't a very witchly reason to do anything. But east, you'll get a chance to avenge your mistress. Vengeance. Now there is a witchly motivation."

"Or horrible death," I added.

"Exactly. A horrible death seems a goal every witch should aspire to. In fact, it seems to me that too many people are neglectful of their deaths. It is the last act of their lives. Give me a memorably gruesome demise over a long, boring life any day. Just ask Skewered Bob."

"Who?"

Newt hopped in front of me, turned, and walked backward. An impressive feat for a duck.

"You've never heard of Skewered Bob?"

"No."

"He was a soldier. Fought in some battle somewhere. No one remembers who was battling who or why anymore. Don't even know anything about old Bob's life. Other than this was his first real battle. A small skirmish of no real importance. The kind that pops up all the time over land rights or a maiden's honor or some other triviality."

He waved a wing. "Like I said. Unimportant. So Bob, he's just a young grunt, one of dozens of boys looking to kill each other. But Bob's so eager, he wants to be at the head of the battle. Like he's a great hero or some such nonsense. He's so enthusiastic, in fact, that when the bugler blows the assembly call, Bob thinks it's the call to charge. So he dashes onto the field, all by himself, and he's so eager to slaughter his enemies that he doesn't even realize until he's halfway there."

"What happened?"

"These were military men and great believers in excessive force. So a rain of arrows comes down on Bob's head, and he's thoroughly punctured. Pierced from every possible angle and two or four impossible angles as well. Falls dead to the ground on the spot."

"And the battle?"

"Who knows? Who cares? Of every man that fought on that field of honor, amid all the bravery and blood-soaked savagery, only Skewered Bob is remembered. Not because he was a great hero. Not because he fought well. Not even for his foolhardy courage. But because he was wise enough to die in memorable fashion."

Newt flapped his wings and skipped a few steps. "You see my point? Obviously, Skewered Bob wasn't all that bright. Had he not died as he had, he would've no doubt lived a perfectly dreary life, hardly worth remembering. But now he's famous. He lives forever."

"I'd never heard of him," I remarked.

"Now you have, and one day you'll tell somebody else, and his name will go on."

"How do you know he even existed at all?"

"I don't. But that's not important either because even if he didn't, even if he's just a story, then he only illustrates my point further. A horrible demise, even an imaginary one, beats an ordinary, real life."

"There's more to life than being remembered," I said.

"I guess."

"And I am capable of living forever. In theory."

Newt shook his head. "That doesn't mean you shouldn't give the matter serious consideration. Just in case."

I tested a more exaggerated limp. It slowed my walk and gave me time to think. Much of what Newt said made sense.

Ghastly Edna spoke from my memory. "You must remember, child, that death is not something to be frightened by. Everything dies. Well, not everything, but most things. And this is as it should be because if everything lasted forever, the world would soon become a very boring place. Death is merely nature's way of mixing things up.

"Not that there's anything wrong with living forever. I myself wouldn't care to, but I suppose it wouldn't be all that bad. Just remember to keep yourself busy, and I suspect forever will pass surprisingly quickly. Time is like that. Even endless lengths of it tend to go by faster than we'd like when we're enjoying ourselves."

Ghastly Edna was right, of course, but I had to admit a small and unwitchly fear of death. It was difficult enough for mortal creatures to face death's inevitable kiss when they knew it must come. But endless centuries lay before me, and oblivion was a companion I could easily avoid with care and foresight.

When the fork in the path finally sprang up before me, appearing as if by magic around the curve of a hill, I'd made my decision.

"Well?" Newt asked.

I held little fear of either death or eternity. And I did not crave the promise of quiet contentment. Ghastly Edna had not been the kind to bear a grudge, even against her own murderers, but I was not so witchly. If it was within my power to avenge her death, then I really had no choice but to do so. And though I did not wish to die myself in the process, it was just one possibility of many. And it seemed to me that no matter how it came out, the many possibilities of the east were far more interesting than the singular fate to the north.

"We go east."

Newt muttered. "I still think we should have gone west."

And, once again, I ignored him.

*T*he *path joined up* with a road, and I decided to follow it. I'd made my decision at the fork, and I assumed my fate would now find me. Everything outside the forest was one vast, foreign land. Newt had lived most of his life by Ghastly Edna's side as well and couldn't offer anything in the way of advice. But all roads lead somewhere, even if it isn't always someplace worth visiting.

After finally leaving behind the hills, the edge of the world I had known, an apprehension fell upon me. And a sadness for my lost mistress. And an exhilaration for whatever lay ahead. A strange, heart-fluttering mix.

Newt stopped. "Can we rest? My feet are killing me."

I kept going. "Time enough for rest later. After the sun has set."

The bright orange globe was an hour from sinking below the horizon. I planned on stopping and watching it go. I'd always liked the sunset. Not just the pretty colors of the sky, but the soft dark of early night. The light of day was obnoxious and hard. It burned away the mystery of all it shone upon. Dusk was subtle and gentle. The world always looked a little brighter beneath the gliding shadows.

Newt groaned. "We've been walking for hours."

"And we'll walk until I say otherwise." I didn't care when

we rested, but Newt was my familiar. It was important to establish my authority now, while our link was new.

He jogged after me. "Easy for you to say. For every step you take, I take four. And I've got flat feet."

"So fly. I don't mind."

He quacked in an annoyed manner.

Magic is not a something-for-nothing proposition. The enchantments on the duck gave him intellect at the cost of instincts. He'd forgotten how to fly. He could get airborne in a pinch. These were always short flights, no higher than the cabin roof and for brief seconds, awkward displays of clumsy flapping wings and muttered vulgarities. The remembrance made me smile.

"Can't you do something? Something with your magic?"

"There is something, but you won't like it."

"Anything's better than taking another step."

"As you wish. First, raise your right leg."

Newt did so.

"Now, put it back down, and raise your left."

He did so reluctantly. "Are you certain this will work?"

"Quite certain. Now put down your left leg, flap your wings three times, and quack once."

He tilted his head skeptically.

"Trust me."

After he'd done as instructed, I held up a hand, fingers bent clawlike. I circled Newt while mumbling in witchly fashion. Then I scooped him up, tucked him under my arm, and started walking.

"Is that better?" I asked.

He squirmed. I knew very well that he hated being carried. He considered it undignified, but he didn't complain. His feet must have been very sore.

"What was all that business with the leg raising and wing flapping?"

"Practice. A witch should always keep you guessing. Did it work?"

He shifted to a more comfortable position. "It was very peculiar."

I blushed. Being peculiar was something all good witches should be. Anyone could act mad, but it took a special knack to be strange without overdoing it.

The road led from the hills to another forest very much like the one I had just left, yet different. Ghastly Edna's woods had always treated me well, and we'd become old friends. This new forest was a stranger. So I paused to introduce myself.

"Hello. Very pleased to make your acquaintance."

"What?" Newt said.

"I wasn't talking to you."

A squirrel scrambled across the road. It bounced to my feet and placed a walnut before me.

I bent on one knee, collected the walnut, and scratched the squirrel on his head. "Thank you. I have nothing to offer in return."

"Your presence alone brightens the woods, child. But if you keep to this road, you will find a blight in this forest. We would be most grateful should you remove it."

"Of course."

The messenger of the forest scampered away.

"We can't even eat that," Newt said. "You'd think the woods would pay you something more practical."

"It's not a payment. It's an offering."

"I'm just suggesting that perhaps something more substantial wouldn't be out of line. A fresh rabbit wouldn't be asking too much, would it?" He licked his bill.

"It didn't have to give me anything."

"Exactly. And nothing would have been better than a nut. This is just drawing attention to it."

"You're missing the point."

"Apparently. So can we stop now?"

"Just a little farther."

"Oh, can't we remove the blight tomorrow?" he asked.

I kept walking. He muttered anew.

It wasn't five minutes later that we came upon the blight of these woods: a pair of robbers. One was a man, unkempt and unarmed. He was not entirely unattractive in a disheveled, wild sort of way. The most handsome man I'd ever seen, but I'd only seen three others. And this was only if one counted my father, who had been a blackened silhouette in the bright light of the cellar door.

The second robber was a troll. The first I'd ever seen, but he looked as I'd been taught. He was short, barely as high as my shoulder, but nearly as wide as his height. His body was thin, but his limbs were thick, ending in hands and feet made for a creature twice his size. His head was a flattened oval with two large, yellow eyes, a small crooked nose, and a broad mouth capable of swallowing a hog in one bite. There were giant, pointed ears. Light fuzz ran down his mottled gray skin across the arms to his shoulders and down his spine. He was naked, save for a belt whose sole purpose was to hold a leather pouch, and he wore a ring on one of his fingers.

An interesting fact about trolls is that they are not held together by joints of flesh. Their bodies are modular. An innate magical cohesion keeps them from falling apart. The benefits to this are several. It makes them hard to kill. Only a fatal stab to the heart or head can reliably destroy one. Even then, if another troll happens upon the corpse, he can always salvage the remains as their parts are interchangeable. The lack of joints also allows them to move in ways that are impossible for other creatures. They can strike from all sorts of unpredictable angles. They're also strong as two ogres.

Fortunately, a troll left to his own devices is rarely a danger. They aren't violent by nature. A more ambitious troll might occasionally claim a bridge and extort a toll. But for the most part, they would rather be left alone.

This troll seemed possessed of a quiet sadness. I could see it in his eyes and the slump of his shoulders. As troll shoulders were usually slumped to begin with, this was a subtle difference.

The robbers didn't even bother to hide as I limped to them on a stiff leg.

"Your valuables or your life, crone."

I allowed myself a moment of pride. It was nice to know my act was working.

The bandit prodded me with a knuckle. "Can't you hear, old woman?"

"I heard you."

I raised my head enough to see the troll. He was standing back, seemingly disinterested in the robbery.

"Then give us what you have. Otherwise, I'll have to have Gwurm tear you apart. I don't like that. Leaves a terrible mess."

The troll spoke up. "He'll have me kill you anyway, miss. You're better off running for it."

"Shut up, Gwurm." The robber folded his arms across his chest. "Well, hag. What's it going to be?"

Newt fidgeted in my arms. "Let me kill him."

"I'll handle it," I replied.

The bandit stepped back. "Your duck talks."

"Quite a lot actually. Too much perhaps."

"Oh, please let me kill him. I'll be quick about it."

I boxed his snapping bill. "I said I'll handle it."

"Yes, mistress."

"A talking duck," the bandit said. "It must be magic."

"It certainly must," I agreed. "I know of no ordinary talking ducks."

"It's worth a fortune. Give it to me, crone."

"I think perhaps you overestimate his value."

"Enough of this." The bandit twisted a ring on his finger. "Kill her, Gwurm."

"Oh, hell, Pik, can't you kill this one yourself." Despite his reservations, the troll moved toward me mechanically.

I could have killed him quite easily, but I was reluctant to do so. His body was clearly not his own. Any harm he might inflict on me wouldn't be of his own doing. He was merely the weapon, and it seemed a terrible shame to break a fine sword just because it happened to be in the hands of a bandit at the moment. More importantly, Gwurm was not a sword. He was a victim of magic, and it was my duty as a good witch to correct this. Not just my duty, but my pleasure. Helping this troll would be my first true act as my own witch, and eager magic tingled in my toes, ready to do its work.

It came to me to do something dramatic like commanding the roots to rise from the ground and drag Pik screaming into the earth. But it seemed too showy for this situation and a waste of magic too, since no one was here to witness the gruesome demise other than Gwurm, Newt, and myself. And Gwurm would be impressed enough simply by being unburdened.

"I must apologize, ma'am. I don't like killing old women.

But Pik is such a lazy bastard, and he wears the ring of command to my ring of servitude."

"Oh, just shut up and kill her already, Gwurm."

The troll's reluctance showed in slow, ponderous steps. "I'd really rather not do this, ma'am. You understand."

"Quite all right, Gwurm."

I tossed my broom over the troll's head.

Another interesting fact about trolls is the magic that holds them together can be disrupted when the proper blow is struck with just the right force in just the right spot. This is not widely known among men, but a fact every witch learns. My broom rose in the air and took aim at that exact point between the troll's shoulders.

Gwurm wrapped his hands around my throat. "I'll make this quick."

The broom struck true. It bounced off the troll's thick skin, not even leaving a bruise. He gaped as if he might vomit, belched once, and fell to pieces. His fingers popped off, knuckle by knuckle. Then his hands jumped from his wrists. His forearms slipped from his elbows. His arms fell from his shoulders. And so on until he was a collection of unassembled troll parts before me. It took but a few seconds. His head was the last thing to topple from his shoulders and come to a rolling stop at my feet. His face crinkled, he sneezed, and his eyes, nose, and ears fell off.

Pik's eyes widened. "Sorcery!"

"Witchery actually."

"You're a witch?"

"The hat. The broom. The cloak. The talking duck. I expect it would be obvious. Well, perhaps not the duck."

"Can I kill him now?" Newt asked.

"Hush."

Pik, being unarmed and clearly overmatched, wasted not another moment. He ran away.

"Go get him, Newt. But don't kill him."

The duck was disappointed but jumped from my arms and dashed after the bandit.

"Wud nu mine steppun uf mee node," Gwurm requested.

"Oh. Terribly sorry." I picked up the nose and dusted it off. I found one eye. It resembled a rotten, yellow grape. I wiped it clean with my cloak and stuck it and his nose back on his face. He wiggled the nose and blinked the eye.

I found the section of finger with the ring of servitude.

"It can't be removed until I'm dead."

The enchantment on the ring was potent but sloppy. It had all the marks of shoddy commercial magic. A competent apprentice might crank out a dozen in under an hour to pay for his education. But such a flawed magic always has a loose thread, and I yanked on this one as an afterthought. The enchantment unraveled. The now ordinary ring slipped off the finger.

"Thank you. I can't tell you what a relief it is to be free of that. If I could trouble you for one last favor, might you help me locate my other eye. I can pull myself together eventually, but my eye is delicate. I'd hate to accidentally sit on it."

By the time I'd returned the second eye to its socket, Newt reappeared. He was alone, head bowed. Blood dripped from his bill.

"Well?" I asked, already knowing the explanation.

"I . . . uh . . . sort of killed him."

I shook my head and fixed him with a disappointed look.

"It wasn't my fault," he protested. "I was chasing after him, and I grabbed at him. Just so I could bring him back as you commanded. And his spine just sort of . . . came out."

"They'll do that," Gwurm said.

"See? It's almost like they were designed that way. He'll back me up, won't you?"

"It's very true. Men are rather fragile. Their heads practically fall off on their own, and their bones snap under any pressure at all."

Newt kicked the dust. "Sorry, mistress."

"It's all right," I replied, "but you must be more careful. There will be more people in the future, and I would like some assurance that you won't kill them all."

"I'll work on it."

"You'll get the hang of it," Gwurm reassured. "I find it best to treat them as if they're made of dry straw."

"I'll keep that in mind."

The sun was below the treetops. Early dusk settled on the forest.

"Newt, fetch some firewood and something to eat. We're stopping for the night."

He was so embarrassed by his spine-ripping blunder that he did so without uttering a single complaint.

I began the task of reassembling the troll. Given enough time, Gwurm could put himself back together, but that would take hours. I saw no reason he should suffer the indignity.

"You're too kind," he said as I returned his head to his shoulders. "I must say, you're being a very good sport about this."

"It wasn't your fault."

"Still, I did almost kill you."

"I don't die that easily. No harm done."

The hands were a difficult task. So many knuckles. I could have just thrown them together, but I wanted to do it right. The real trick was remembering that a troll's pinkie was longer than his ring finger.

After I'd finished his left arm, Gwurm was able to complete the rest on his own. Newt found enough wood for a small fire and a pair of rabbits for dinner. I spat on the wood, and it burned with a soft yellow flame. Then I sat by the fire and cleaned the rabbits. Another gift of my curse is that while my fingers are not clawed, I have a special knack for ripping flesh. I tossed Newt some intestines. He wolfed them down greedily.

"Your duck eats meat," Gwurm observed.

I nibbled on a raw leg. "As do I, but I think we have enough to share. Would you care for one?"

Newt perked up his head. "Mistress?"

Gwurm held up his hands. "I couldn't possibly . . ."

"Nonsense." I tossed him the second rabbit. "I insist."

"If you insist."

He chucked the entire rabbit into his mouth, chewed once, and swallowed. One of the mysteries of troll biology is how their food gets from their mouth to their unconnected stomachs. Even witches didn't know that.

Gwurm sat on the opposite side of the fire.

"So how did you come to such a fate?" I asked.

"Simple story really. Pik and I were friends. He found the rings, talked me into putting one on, and the next thing I know, I'm robbing and terrorizing the countryside."

"What were you doing before that?"

"Robbing and terrorizing mostly. I'd always done most of the terrorizing as I have a talent for it, but he handled the robbery end of things. Then came the rings, and he revealed himself for the shiftless sod he was. I'll miss him. He was my only friend."

"Not much of one," I remarked.

"True, but the best friend a troll could expect."

We sat around the campfire and didn't speak much the rest of the night. Silence didn't bother me. I'd lived in isolation all my life, and Ghastly Edna had often gone weeks without saying hardly a word. We listened to the owls and the crickets, and I counted the stars while Gwurm stared into the flames.

Logically, the undead in me should have wanted to travel after dark, but I was more content to sit back and enjoy it. It always seemed to slip away faster when I walked. When I stood still, I could imagine it might last forever.

Gwurm stretched. The gaps in his joints showed just a bit. "Falling apart always tires me out. Think I'll get some sleep. Good night."

The troll hunched over in a tight ball of crossed limbs and stooped head. It looked uncomfortable, but he was already asleep. He snored softly.

"Why'd you feed him?" Newt said.

"He looked hungry, and it was the polite thing to do."

"But the mistress warned you not to. Now we'll never get rid of him."

"Who says I want to be rid of him?"

Newt's feathers ruffled. "What?"

"He looked in need of a friend. Especially since you killed his last one."

"You can't be serious."

"Why not?"

"Are you blind? He's a troll."

"And I'm a witch. And you're a duck."

"Yes, yes, but . . ."

"Newt, are you jealous?"

He ruffled again.

I stroked the brown feathers down his back. "You've nothing to worry about."

"I'm not worried. And I'm not jealous."

"No, no. Certainly not."

Newt curled up on the spot and rested his head on my leg. "Jealous. The entire notion is absurd. Although I don't see what you could possibly want with a troll when you've already been blessed with an accomplished familiar."

He fell asleep, but I wasn't tired. The fire died, and I sat in the cool dark with Newt snuggled beside me and my new troll dozing across from me.

5

I'd helped a forest and gained a troll. Small deeds, but not bad for my first day as my own witch. The world, what little I had seen of it, was not so frightening a place, and when the dawn finally came, I found myself looking forward to the second.

Gwurm didn't speak much, but I'd never actually had someone to talk to before. I'd always been Ghastly Edna's listener. Now that I finally had a listener of my own, I discovered I had much to say. It didn't take long to tell him the details of my life. I spoke of Nasty Larry's curse, my parents' cellar, my schooling with Ghastly Edna, and her murder at the hands of men who had not been men. The tale spilled from my lips in a steady flow, and though I sensed a lack of interest on Gwurm's part, he was a polite listener.

The troll plucked off his ear and cleaned out some wax. "If I understand correctly, you're ageless, practically invulnerable, and forever beautiful. But you must eat raw meat and don't like the sun." He blew in the ear and dug some crust from the lobe. "I don't mean to belittle your situation, but it doesn't seem like much of a curse."

"I don't want to be beautiful."

"And I don't want to be reviled and feared."

Newt chimed in. "And I'd rather not have been a duck."

"Exactly. We are all given lots we would rather not have. Not that I'm complaining. There are many things I like about being a troll."

"There's nothing good about being a duck."

"It must be nice to fly."

Newt grumbled. "I can't fly."

"Oh. Swimming?"

"I don't like deep water."

"Sorry to hear that." The troll plugged the ear back in place. "In any case, none of us are true masters of our fate. Not the beginning of it anyway, and it seems to me that I was born under a worse curse than you."

"Perhaps," I agreed.

Not long after coming under Ghastly Edna's charge, I'd made the same observation. My mistress had quickly corrected me on that.

"Always remember, girl, that magic is aware. All things are in some fashion. Even those things we cannot touch like the wind, and the seasons, and gravity. But nothing is quite as aware as the magic. It plays with wizards and witches and magi, and make no mistake. It is we who serve the magic, not the other way around. And it will brook no disrespect. Always remember that your curse, while not terrible, is still a curse. Should you ever come to think of it as a gift, the magic will waste no time correcting you on this notion."

I couldn't claim to understand exactly what she'd meant by this, but I heeded the advice. I did not despise my curse, but I never considered it a blessing.

"Are you certain this road is the way to your destiny?" Gwurm asked.

"Your destiny is always wherever you go," I replied. "Usually a day or two ahead of you," I added because it seemed a witchly turn of phrase.

He shrugged. "If we keep going this way, we'll reach a settlement of men by late afternoon. Pik and I didn't go near it. It's a garrison town."

A nagging desire to see this town came to me. We are all separated from everything else by mere dollops of space and teaspoons of happenstance. This town was but a day-and-a-half journey from my woods, but I hadn't ever considered it might be.

Ghastly Edna had described several towns for she had been to many, though all long before I'd known her. They seemed fantastic places full of the virtues and blunders of men. I knew the ways of nature and magic well, but I really understood nothing of civilization. It was terrifying, in a way I was unaccustomed, to not know what to expect, but exciting as well. It could be easy, even for witches, to become too comfortable with their place in the world. But being a good witch meant exploring not just the realms of magic, but of strange civilization.

Whether it was witchliness or simple curiosity that spurred me onward, I couldn't clearly say. But there was no denying my anticipation, though I hid it from my companions. I wanted to see this town. More importantly, I needed to see it.

It proved a disappointment. It was not a town, but rather a town-to-be. The half-finished fort sat in a grassy plain. A host of tents and temporary dwellings encircled it. A great many people milled about. They set off a touch of fear in me. Though I knew that there were real towns and cities where thousands upon thousands lived, this was the most I'd ever seen. I wanted to slink away and return under cover of darkness, perhaps to steal a dog or a plump child for my supper.

"Oh, dear," I remarked.

"What?" Newt asked.

"I have an appetite for human flesh."

"And you're just discovering this now?"

I had spent much my life in isolation, but I'd never wanted to eat any of the people I'd met yet. There was something about this settlement and all its people. They triggered a long dormant predator in me, a desire to thin the herd.

"That certainly is a curse," Gwurm said. "Humans taste awful. I've only eaten one. Just a leg. I couldn't even finish it. Poor meat. Stringy and very dry. Then again, that might have just been my mother's fault. She never was a very good cook."

I was not very hungry, and my unholy appetite was easy to push away. I decided to keep myself well fed while among people to minimize the temptation.

"Is this going to be a problem?" Newt said.

"I haven't killed anyone yet," I replied.

Newt sighed. "I told you. That last one was an accident."

Before venturing any closer, I extracted a promise from my familiar that there would be no further accidents. While I was not as confident about it as I would have liked, I took him at his word. In any case, he wasn't going to get better without practice, and I could think of no better place for him to get some. It also was a good way to test the strength of my own newly discovered hunger.

Just before we reached the fort, two men came out to greet us. One was fat and sweaty. He looked a poor meal. I'd never eaten anyone, but an instinct told me he'd be all chewing and very little worthwhile meat. The second was thin and even sweatier. He was more of a midday snack. Neither tempted me much. Though they were shirtless and out of uniform, their rigid posture and exact way of walking put me in the mind of military men.

Neither seemed surprised or intimidated by Gwurm. Perhaps trolls were common in the region. Or perhaps these men just didn't care.

The fat man held up a hand. "Halt! What's your business here?"

Newt ruffled. I stamped my broom to remind him of his promise.

"I have no business. I only wish to have a look around."

"You're not a prostitute, are you?"

I shook my head slowly.

"Are you sure?" The thin one wiped his face. "Because we've already got too many prostitutes as it is. Two for every man here."

"Yes," the fat man said. "And the captain has said we aren't to allow any more. Strains the local economy, such as it is."

"Leaves us broke too."

"So don't bother lying about it, because this market is saturated, and I sincerely doubt you'd be able to earn a living."

"Ralf might pay her for a roll," the thin man observed.

"Yes, certainly, Ralf might. And Wilts. He's got strange tastes too."

"And Biggs."

"Zur."

"Oh, Zur would hand over a month's pay just to have her kick him in the crotch. But he's not all there."

"And if she uses the duck, I can think of a dozen men who would chip in to see that."

The fat man sneered. "Twisted fiends."

"Twisted," the thin man agreed.

"So, do you use the duck?"

They leaned forward, eyeing Newt with slight smiles.

Newt flapped his wings and leaped to attack. Gwurm caught him midpounce and saved the soldiers' lives. The troll walked away. Newt squirmed in his grasp.

"I'm not a prostitute," I restated.

The men straightened. "Are you quite certain?"

I nodded.

Their grins vanished, and they cleared their throats. "Good. Because this is certainly no place for such depravity."

"No place," the thin one agreed.

"You're not another desperate woman looking for a husband, are you? Because I can assure you, all the men who haven't brought their families with them aren't aching for any more womanly attention. Even if it is free."

I needed to refine my act. Perhaps a bigger, more pointed hat. Or an exaggerated, withered limb. Something was missing because no one had yet to guess my trade without me telling them.

"I'm a witch."

"A witch, eh? Captain didn't say anything about witches, did he?"

"Not that I recall."

"Anything about trolls?"

"Nothing. I would have remembered. Just prostitutes."

"I guess it's all right then. So what do you do, witch?"

I leaned heavily on my broom and raised my head that one eye might glare up at them. "I commune with forbidden spirits. I speak to beasts and plants. I cast bones. I heal. I curse." I cracked a wide smile. "And I raise the dead."

"So you don't do anything with the troll then either?"

"No. Nothing with the troll."

"Pity. Zur will be disappointed." They wandered back to the fort.

Gwurm returned to my side. He let go of Newt. The duck paced about in an angry circle, muttering.

"I was only going to maim them. Tear off a limb or two."

"No maiming either, Newt."

"As you command, mistress, but they were asking for it."

Gwurm chuckled. "It's easy not to kill people who don't deserve it. It's keeping from killing the people who irritate you that is the task."

I suggested that Newt had gotten enough practice not killing today. He and Gwurm waited at the field's edge while I dared venture amid the bustling tents and rickety wooden constructions. The soldiers' barracks were a collection of uniform canvas tents to the east. The families camped to the north. The prostitutes sat at the south. And the merchants and tradesmen had set up a makeshift marketplace to the west. It seemed a fine seed of a village, perhaps even a respectable city one day, but right now, it was just many people gathered beneath the shadow of a half-built fort.

The stench impressed me the most. Most animals have enough sense to keep a tidy home. Men were apparently an exception. Few creatures could create such filth in such short time. Disposing of it properly would have been a trade in itself. Judging by the countless mounds of dung, rotting vegetables, and decaying meat, there weren't any such tradesmen in residence. The people didn't seem to mind, but they reeked of sweat and toil themselves, so why would they? As for myself, I found some comfort in the stench through my curse.

Walking between the tents, I sized up everyone I saw as a potential meal. I discovered I was a very particular eater.

Most everyone was either too fat or too lean or too oily or too tough. There were precious few of any appeal, although there were a dozen or so that I'd have considered nibbling on under the right circumstances.

I found the most interest in the south end of town. The prostitutes came in countless varieties. Some were short and plump. Others were tall and lean. Short and lean. Tall and plump. Ugly. Pretty. Old. Young. Dark. Light. Underneath all my clothes, I was more beautiful than any. I could have made a fine living as a woman of easy virtue. Of course, as I'd never actually lain with a man, I had to wonder what might happen should I lose myself in even a brief carnal moment. As the mere thought made my mouth water, I suspected I wouldn't have much return business. My musings were interrupted by a coarse grunt.

"You there! You're new, aren't you?"

A short man emerged from one of the tents. He pulled up his pants with a scowl. He was mildly attractive with a face too chubby for his thin body and slightly crooked teeth.

My dark desires whispered, "Not bad. Suck out the eyes and save the tongue for later."

"I told the men we don't need any more prostitutes," the man grunted.

I was about to correct him on his mistake when another voice came from the same tent.

"She's not one of us. She's a witch." A woman wrapped in a blanket stepped out. She had long blond hair and a body that couldn't be hidden away so easily. She was slender without being bony, every bit as beautiful as I except for a tiredness in her round face.

My inner ghoul murmured, "Very good. A morsel to be savored."

"I'm right, aren't I?" the prostitute asked.

I nodded.

"Witch? So what do you do, witch?" the soldier asked.

"I commune with forbidden spirits. I speak to the beasts and plants. I cast bones. I heal. I curse. And I raise the dead."

"Can you get rid of warts?"

"Yes. I also know of ways to treat all the minor ailments your men might catch in their off-duty hours."

He nodded. "Very good. You can stay then." He marched back into the tent, unbuckling his pants. The woman started to follow him.

"How did you know I was a witch?"

"The hat. The broom." She shrugged. "Seems obvious."

The soldier grunted from the darkened tent. "Sunrise!"

"You'll have to excuse me."

She disappeared into the tent. I was left alone, among the throng, amid the grunts and moans and laughter of prostitutes at work.

I'd only come for a look around. I hadn't planned on staying, but here was a place in need of a witch and after living so long by myself, it was time for a change. I decided to linger for a few days at least. Perhaps more. Providing I could keep Newt from killing anyone and my own accursed cravings in check.

"No one will miss one succulent little child," the dark voice whispered.

I pretended not to hear it.

6

I told Gwurm and Newt we were staying. Gwurm was indifferent to the decision, as I expected. Newt was filled with objections, as I knew he would be, and immediately voiced those objections. It was my own fault. I'd asked him for his opinion once. The precedent was set, and I couldn't undo it now. While his protests mattered little to me (not at all, in truth), I allowed him his moment.

He hopped about and flapped his wings. We were a good distance from the camp, but still within easy view. If anyone should notice me arguing with the duck, I wouldn't have minded. It could only enhance my peculiarity and credibility as a good witch.

"But we're on the road to vengeance!" he cried. "Have you forgotten your dead mistress?"

"I haven't forgotten anything, but vengeance can wait. Or perhaps my vengeance is already here, waiting for me?"

He danced around in an angry circle. "No, it isn't!"

I smiled despite my best efforts. "I was unaware you had a sense of these things."

"Well, I do! And I can tell you that there's nothing here but people and tents and garbage. By everything festering in the bowels of Hades, it's not even a real village!" He turned to Gwurm for help. "Tell her I'm right."

"About what?"

"About this! What we're talking about."

"Sorry. Wasn't paying attention."

Newt uttered an exasperated quack. He paused long enough to collect his thoughts.

"I'm sure that wherever your vengeance waits is farther away."

I nodded slowly as if I understood his reasoning, and he continued, sounding almost calm.

"It just makes sense. No worthwhile vengeance is just a day-and-a-half 's walk away."

"I see," I said. "And how far away is one's vengeance generally? In your experience."

His head bobbed while he considered the question. "It isn't an exact science, but I figure it has to be farther than a journey of self-discovery, but shorter than an epic quest. Hundreds, even thousands, of miles."

"That seems very far," Gwurm chimed in.

Newt threw him a nasty glare. "It can be considerably less if the journey is especially perilous. A terrible monster here or a raging river of death there can trim off a few hundred."

"What do you guess a dragon to be worth?" Gwurm asked.

"Oh, I don't know." Newt sighed. "At least two or three hundred."

"And a sphinx?"

"Who knows? A lot, I guess, as that's mostly what sphinxes are for."

"What about a gnome?"

"A what?"

"A gnome."

"A what?"

I stifled a chuckle. Gwurm, very impressively, kept a perfectly straight face.

Newt rolled his eyes. "A gnome wouldn't be worth anything."

"I'm speaking of a very unpleasant gnome. A vicious, terribly irritated gnome. Perhaps with a very pointed pebble in his shoes. Digging right into the soft spot of his heel."

"What are you . . ."

"I knew a gnome like that once. Horribly rude little bugger. Mean too. Not truly dangerous, but an annoyance nonetheless. An encounter with him on the road to vengeance would have to cut at least ten or twenty miles, I would imagine."

Newt gaped.

Gwurm remained quite sincere-looking.

"Fine, fine," Newt consented. "I guess if the gnome were an especially foul-tempered little bastard he'd be worth ten or twenty."

"Not thirty?" Gwurm said.

"No. Not thirty. Even the rottenest, most vile, most terribly furious gnome in this world wouldn't be worth more than twenty miles."

"I guess not."

Gwurm hesitated long enough that Newt might think this portion of the conversation ended.

"What about a vast wasteland filled with packs of blood-thirsty mollusks?"

Something in Newt's enchanted mind popped. He lowered his head and wandered away, trying to remember what this had originally been about.

"Big ones!" Gwurm called after the duck. "Carnivorous snails the size of hounds!"

I finally allowed myself a polite chuckle. "Thank you."

His wide mouth turned up in a toothy grin. "You're very welcome."

I would never admit such to Newt, but I felt he was correct. Roads to vengeance are never that short, but my quest for revenge was measured in more than miles. It was also a journey of time, and that journey could be a very long one. Decades or centuries. Possibly even millennia. As I was ageless and very difficult to kill, I could afford patience. I didn't share this observation with Newt because though his enchanted nature granted him a long life, he still suffered the passage of time and would eventually die of old age someday. A day that might come long before my chances for revenge. This speculation would only upset him, and Newt was upset enough as it was.

In any case, I was the witch and he, only the familiar. He had no choice.

IT DIDN'T TAKE LONG to adjust to our new way of life. By the Captain's order, I was given a spare tent, torn and shoddily patched. I put it up away from the camp but close enough that I wouldn't be forgotten. It was a witchly tradition to live apart from men and all those other menlike creatures that so enjoy clustering in crushing herds. As the herd instinct in most men is so strong, they cannot help but think one who chooses solitude to be a little off. An image of strangeness is part of the witch's trade. It also made my charade of ugliness easier to maintain, and I didn't trust myself among the camp. The smells and sounds of mortals called to my curse, and I didn't want to eat anyone. Rather, I found myself very much wanting to at times, and having a place to retreat was a wise precaution.

The people were wary of Gwurm at first, but his strength and willingness to work made him a welcome addition. The soldiers were only too happy for his assistance in constructing the fort. Eventually, the camp's suspicion of the troll ebbed into acceptance and even a cautious affection. The children adored him. He'd spend hours rearranging himself for their amusement, juggling his toes, and standing on his head. The mothers would always watch him with a touch of nervousness. As if he might suddenly transform into some terrible fiend and glut himself on their offspring in a moment of hunger.

Newt did not adjust so well. He spent most of his time sulking in my tent. On those few occasions he followed me on my daily rounds, he never spoke a word among the camp. The children, sensing things the way young minds can, avoided him. The mothers were too busy watching Gwurm to pay Newt much mind. I kept a close eye on my familiar though, and there were no incidents of waterfowl blood rages.

Another interesting turn came when my broom took on a life of its own. Magic, especially witch magic, doesn't just come when called and then go away quietly. It is constantly about, curdling milk, stopping clocks, and cracking mirrors on occasion. My broom was always by my side, and it soaked up enough to gain will and animation. There were ways to cleanse this residue, but as long as it behaved itself, I saw no reason. It was nice having someone to do the sweeping.

I quickly settled into a routine. I'd wake late in the afternoon and tour the camp, treating the ailing. Blisters, aching muscles, and minor infections were the bulk of my duties. All were easily treated with herbs and simple magic. Those rare maladies of greater severity weren't much more difficult.

After tending to the sick, I'd report to the Captain, detailing the general health of the camp. Then I'd return to my tent and mix medicines. The Captain was so happy with my service that I was offered a new tent within a week. I declined the offer as the tattered one better fit my image.

At nights, I'd sit and watch the camp. I could do so for hours on end. Even after everyone but the night watch had gone to sleep. Though I was born of a mortal woman, I was not mortal. I couldn't be one of them. I didn't want to be one of them. Yet they were fascinating creatures, and I'd often think of what my life might have been like had I not been accursed.

And sometimes, I'd indulge my darker half in flights of fantasy. Daydreams in the early morning hours where I'd slide through the camp and snatch away a vulnerable morsel for my dinner. Such thoughts were part of me and to deny them would only grant them greater strength. But my appetite was easy to hold back, like a sweet tooth I never gratified.

And so a few days turned into weeks. Weeks became months. The soldiers finished their fort, and the civilians' tents transformed into more permanent constructions. And the camp became a respectable settlement.

I kept my tent and told myself (and Newt) that we would start back on our road to vengeance soon. But we lingered, living as part, yet apart, from the mortals. And the days came and went.

I KNEW OF SUNRISE the prostitute. Everyone did. She was the most beautiful woman in the settlement, the Captain's favorite whore. She'd been the only one to know I was a witch without being told, and she'd discovered my secret very quickly.

She first visited me soon after my arrival to request treatment for a rash of the Captain's. He didn't want to be seen coming to me himself. I mixed together a salve while she waited.

"Why do you hide it?" she'd finally asked on her third visit.

"I beg your pardon."

"Your beauty. Why do you hide it?"

I checked myself, but I looked as lumpy and dirty as I always did.

"You can't really disguise it," Sunrise said. "You can rub that grime on your face and hobble about and bury yourself beneath a mountain of soiled gowns and tattered frocks, but it's still there to see. Not that many would. Most only see what they expect."

"You won't tell, will you?"

"Why would I? I do very well as the prettiest here."

"I'm a witch, not a prostitute."

"And believe me, I'm grateful. I'm not used to competition."

I finished mixing the salve and sent her on her way. Newt, who sat sullenly in the corner, spoke.

"You should kill her."

My broom disagreed and stopped sweeping the dirt long enough to twirl, its equivalent to an enthusiastic shake of the head.

"She promised not to tell," I replied.

"You can't trust people. Safer to just kill her. I can make it look like an accident, if that's what you're worried about."

My broom smacked him on the bottom. He snapped at it. They whirled about. Newt muttered curses. The broom shook and hopped.

"Enough of that."

He grumbled. "He started it."

The broom jumped in a minor tantrum. It had decided early into its animation that it was a "she." I grabbed her by her handle and began to sweep. It always calmed her and after a few seconds, she kept at it all by herself.

"You should kill her, mistress."

"Perhaps, but I don't think I will."

Newt went back to the corner to sulk. My broom swept with jaunty joy.

Thus began my friendship with Sunrise the prostitute. She would come by my tent every three days or so. At first, to collect the Captain's salve, then simply to chat. She reminded me of Ghastly Edna in many ways. She was observant, quietly wise, gifted with a view of the world neither sanguine nor cynical but somewhere between. I liked her very much. As did my broom. And Gwurm. And Newt as well, though he would never cease moping long enough to admit it. He even started speaking in front of her, and one crisp evening, he found himself in a familiar argument.

"And how many miles do you reckon an active volcano to be worth?" she posed.

"It's not a technical subject. It's not as if Fate itself is keeping a tally. Not an exact one anyway."

"Of course not. But you must have a general figure in mind."

"That's not my point."

"Seventy miles?"

Newt threw up his wings. "Why do I even bother?"

"Why indeed," I replied, taking a seat on the bench beside Sunrise.

He strolled back into the tent. I handed Sunrise a cup of

hot tea brewed especially for her. I didn't drink tea. It disagreed with my digestion.

"You shouldn't tease him like that," I said.

"Why shouldn't I? Gwurm gets to. You get to. Even your broom gets to. It's only fair I take my turn."

"True."

She sipped her tea. "Have you given any thought to your name?"

"Yes. I've decided I don't need one."

We'd had this disagreement several times. My parents had neglected to name their accursed daughter, and to Ghastly Edna, I had always been "dear," or "child," or "girl." The people of Fort Stalwart managed "hag" or "crone." There never was any confusion, and I rather liked not having a proper name. It seemed very witchful.

"Everyone needs a name."

"Not everyone."

"Your duck has a name. Your troll has a name."

"My broom doesn't."

"Yes, she does. Isn't that right, Penelope?" My broom floated over and leaned against Sunrise's shoulder. "I know it isn't a very good name for a witch's broom, but she picked it."

I had no objection to naming my broom as this too seemed very witchful.

Two soldiers approached my tent. I knew from the sheepish glint in the younger one's eyes why they were here. My inner ghoul found little appetizing about the old man, but of the youth it whispered, "Not quite ripe yet, but in another year or two, a savory feast."

The older soldier pushed his charge toward Sunrise. The boy couldn't look her in the eyes. He stared at his boots and stammered.

Sunrise smiled in that patient, knowing way of hers. The way Ghastly Edna would have smiled had she been a prostitute.

The older soldier chuckled. "Vertis was wondering if maybe he might have the pleasure of your company, miss."

"Is that so, Vertis?"

The youth nodded.

"He's been saving for two months, miss. All the other men said he should find a cheaper woman, but he's got his mind set."

"Such a compliment from a fine, strapping lad. I'm flattered."

Sunrise willed a soft blush. She could will herself to glow too in a way that I might duplicate with magic. Only hers was nothing so mundane as magic, but natural talent and practice.

Vertis giggled like a child.

She took his money and told him to meet her in her cabin in ten minutes. The older soldier thanked her, and they left.

Sunrise jangled the coins in her hands.

"What is it like?" I asked, surprising even myself. I'd been pondering the question for some time.

"That all depends. When it's done right, it's difficult to describe. You could always find out for yourself. Any man in that camp would hack off a limb to lay with you if you took off that outfit."

"I can't do that."

"Why not?"

I began, "A good witch . . ."

"Not that again. I don't believe it. I would think carnal impulses were allowed under your code."

"I'm afraid of what I might do," I admitted.

"The curse? I suppose that's justified. Although I think you could find a man willing to take the risk for a moment of your passion. No, your curse is just a convenient excuse. Because, curse aside, you are very much a normal person. And like most normal people, you want your first time to be something special."

"Was yours?"

She laughed. "Heavens no. Most aren't, but that doesn't mean you should give up on the hope. Who knows? Perhaps one day you'll find the right man. And you'll know him because he'll be the one you'll desire enough to risk devouring. But no need to rush. You're ageless. Take your time.

"In the meanwhile, you're not missing much. It can be a beautiful thing, but usually it's just a few minutes of bumping, grunting, and sweating. Not altogether unpleasant even then, but nothing to fret about."

She stood. "Good evening, Penelope. Good evening, witch."

Penelope tilted in a bow, and Sunrise went off to work.

Her words comforted me. A witch has little use for love, but I wanted to know a man once, if only for the experience. My stomach growled. The scent of flesh drifting from the settlement playing on my nose. I ran my forked tongue across my lips. I pushed such thoughts from my mind and limped into my tent for something to eat.

7

wurm held up a handful of berries.

I popped one in my mouth and spat it on the ground. "No. They're only blueberries."

"Isn't that what we're looking for?" Newt asked.

"We're looking for berries that are blue. Not blueberries. I'm not baking a pie."

Gwurm shoved his handful into his mouth. He spoke while chewing. Juice dribbled down his chin. "I think I saw some over this way."

"You think?" Newt said.

"Well, they're blue."

"If you're going to be snippy, Newt," I said, "you can just go home."

My familiar grumbled. He'd always grumbled, even in Ghastly Edna's service, but the tendency had grown worse of late. When he wasn't complaining, he was muttering. Or glowering with unspoken irritation. There wasn't much for a ferocious, part demon duck to do in this village. There hadn't been much in Ghastly Edna's isolated cabin either, but that was before he'd gotten his taste for blood.

He'd tried applying his killing lust to more productive ends by hunting game for the village. It just wasn't the same. I gave him credit for trying and allowed him his muttering.

Gwurm led us to the blue berries that yet again proved to be blueberries. I did find some scraps of moss though that would help treat infections.

"What do you need these for anyway?" Newt asked.

"I'm mixing a poison."

"Really?"

"Yes."

"You're going to kill someone?"

"Perhaps."

"Who? Don't tell me. Let me guess. That fat man, the smithy! No, not him. I know. That snooty woman with the six children. The one who said I had a silly walk." His eyes shone with enthusiasm for the first time in months.

"I haven't decided yet."

Gwurm brought some more berries. "How about these?"

"Those are just blueberries," Newt said. "Can't you tell the difference? I think there's some this way." He dashed into some bushes. "Over here! I think I've found them."

The berries were the exact ones I needed. He watched me collect them with a sinister glee.

"What's next?"

"I need some black crickets for a potion of itching boils. I'm thinking of pouring it into the village well. Just for amusement."

Newt practically squealed with delight and began his bug hunt.

"You aren't going to kill anyone," said Gwurm.

"Hush. Don't ruin it for him."

After Newt had brought the crickets, I sent him after some tree sap to sicken the beasts. Then pinecones to bring nightmares to the children and roots to send the soldiers into murderous rage. Once he realized they were all ingredients for salves, tonics, and ointments, he'd be very disappointed and return to his grumbling. But he was happy for the moment.

"Now this is more like it, mistress. Nothing against the healing, but it's only proper you finally inflict some woe on these people. Just to keep in practice for when you really need it."

We walked back to the village. I entertained Newt with tales of curses and afflictions I intended to send down on Fort Stalwart. Plagues of projectile vomiting and exploding skulls, and other maladies. He skipped along, offering suggestions of his own. Gwurm put forth a few as well, and Penelope twitched in my hand at approval of the truly dreadful ones.

"Rot all the food," Gwurm proposed.

"No," Newt said. "Don't just rot it. Fill it with maggots. But not so anyone can see by looking. That way, they'll bite into an apple and get a mouthful of worms."

"Poisonous worms," Gwurm added.

"Poisonous, screaming worms. Big gooey white ones full of veins that shriek when you bite into them."

"Excellent suggestion," I said. "I shall have to remember that one." And I would, as it was a very good idea, should I ever desire to inflict a true plague.

Newt and Gwurm played their game and came up with several other worthwhile possibilities. Newt was the most excited I'd ever seen him, including our years with Ghastly Edna. The demon in him delighted in thoughts of cruel mischief, and I was truly sorry that this trick would only work once.

Gwurm pointed down the road. "Somebody's coming."

We stopped and observed a horse and a rider coming our

way at a brisk trot. His appearance surprised me. No one ever came from the west. No one but me. It was unsettled land, the kind of country where a witch and her charge might live unmolested.

"Are we going to kill him?" Newt asked.

"We'll see."

"If we kill him before he gets to the village, no one will ever know."

"I said, we'll see."

A powerful aura of magic covered the rider and his horse. It was not witch magic, but there were many varieties. I had only a passing familiarity with all but the witching kind, but I couldn't perceive its exact purpose.

Despite the enchantment upon him, I didn't think him a disciple of the arcane. He didn't look like a wizard or sorcerer. He was tall and lean, adorned in a chain mail vest and casual garb. A sword hung on his hip. This too possessed some unfamiliar enchantment. He was a very dark man. I didn't know men came in such a dark shade. His hair, cropped short, was black as coal. His eyes were even darker if such a thing were possible. His horse should have been black, or at least a deep, rich brown. But it was gray and a very light gray at that, almost white.

An invisible sign marked his forehead. I could see it through a witch's vision. The brand was the source of his enchanted aura.

Newt winced and belched softly. "I don't feel so good." The rider drew closer, and Newt gurgled. "I think I'm going to be ill." When the man was but a few feet away, the duck mumbled a curse and ran, retching, into the deeper forest.

The man wasn't handsome in a traditional sense. At least, I didn't think so. Yet he was pleasing to look upon, and I could not get myself to look away. Especially from those eyes. Finally, I gathered enough sense to lower my head and hide most of him behind my brim.

Distantly, the heaves of a vomiting duck reached my ears. It was an odd sound, beginning as a quack and ending in a hoarse gasp.

The man brought his horse to a halt. "Ho there, my good woman. Is this troll bothering you?" He loosely gripped his sword hilt.

"Actually, he's with me." I raised my head enough that everything below his nose fell below my brim. He had a strong, round jaw.

Newt stumbled to the road, smacking his bill and moaning. He glimpsed the man and gagged. My familiar dashed back into the bushes and commenced vomiting anew.

"Is that your duck as well?" the rider asked.

"He is."

"Is he ill?"

"Apparently so. Nothing serious, I suspect."

I raised my hat to glimpse the man's eyes. He met my gaze without blinking. I was unaccustomed to that. Most people turned from my sight. Either because they thought I was a madwoman, not to risk antagonizing, or knew I was a witch, and feared the evil I might inflict through my stare. But he didn't, and neither did I.

I couldn't sort through all the dark whisperings of my curse. I wanted to devour this man as I had none before. I didn't know why. He was a healthy specimen, but there were many healthy specimens at the settlement. Yet, even as I imagined sinking my teeth into his flesh, an inexplicable nausea seized me. Nothing so serious as the sickness Newt was suffering. In fact, it was not an entirely displeasing sensation.

We stared into each other's eyes for what seemed a very long time. He turned away finally and broke whatever strange spell held me. I quickly lowered my gaze away from those hypnotic eyes.

He cleared his throat and avoided looking directly at me. "Is this the way to Fort Stalwart?"

"Yes. Just keep to the road, and you'll be upon it in another mile."

"Thank you. Good day, good woman, troll. I hope your duck feels better."

He spurred his horse to a gallop. I watched him go. I had no choice. Something, perhaps his magic aura, made me. I noticed the fullness of his shoulders and wondered what it might be to nibble at the flesh with soft, gentle nips. Then to tear it away to savory mouthfuls. Then I would turn him over and split his chest, scooping out the delicacies within. I'd lap up the blood for dessert.

I wouldn't eat his eyes. Those, for reasons not entirely clear to me, I wanted to save.

As if sensing my thoughts, the man glanced back with a severe frown across his face. I wanted to look away, but I didn't. I stared without bothering to hide it until he disappeared around a bend in the forest.

Newt dragged himself from the bushes.

"Dark gods, such purity of heart. The demon in me was unprepared for it."

"You've never met a White Knight before then," Gwurm explained. "They're famous for their virtue."

"He seemed very dark for a White Knight," I said.

"They enjoy a small but diverse membership."

I bent down on one knee and wiped Newt's bill with the hem of my dress. "Feeling better now?"

"Now that he's gone, I'll be okay."

"Come along then. We have much to do."

"Oh, right. The boils. I'd nearly forgotten."

"Yes," I agreed. "The boils and the rotting food."

We started back to the fort, and I dallied, preserving Newt's happiness as long as I could.

The settlement buzzed by early evening at the arrival of a genuine White Knight. While performing my daily rounds, I listened and learned. Everyone knew of the White Knights though none had ever seen one in the flesh. They were an order of heroes dedicated to vanquishing evil in all its forms. They slew unruly monsters, deposed mad kings, put down illegitimate rebellions, and labored to make the world a better place. They were most famous for their virtue that rendered them invulnerable so long as they kept themselves pure.

I suspected this might be true to a degree. But his invincibility was as much due to the invisible brand on his forehead as his pure heart, and true invulnerability is beyond magic. Any enchantment, however well aided by a virtuous soul, has a flaw somewhere.

Everyone was interested in this White Knight. Even Sunrise, which surprised me. I didn't think her the type to swoon over a man she hadn't even seen. She'd been working on his arrival and hadn't gotten a glimpse before he'd disappeared into the fort.

She threw question after question at me while sitting in my tent.

"What did he look like? Was he handsome? He must have been handsome." She didn't squeal, but she came very close.

"He was attractive," I replied, "but handsome, I think not. His ears were too large. Not in an arresting way, but note-worthy."

"And tall? Was he tall?"

"He seemed tall, but he was sitting on a horse. It was hard to tell."

"But he must have been fair skinned with shimmering locks of gold."

"He was darker than any man I've ever seen."

"So, he is a not quite handsome, possibly tall or not, dark man."

I nodded.

"I won't say I'm not disappointed. Although there is a certain romance to the darkness."

"Legends are always better from afar," I said. "He was truly pure of heart. He made Newt sick. And he had the most handsome, deep black eyes."

Sunrise tapped her teacup. "You're smitten."

"Am I?"

"Very much so."

I believed her. On matters of love and lust, I trusted Sunrise as I had Ghastly Edna on witchly subjects. To be sure, she tested me.

"When you speak of him, you smile, and you are very spare with your smiles."

I felt the slight grin on my lips. "Is that all there is to it?"

"Not all. When you think of him, do you feel a flutter inside?"

I paid attention to my body and found, if not a flutter, then a flittering in my stomach.

"Flittering is even worse," she said. "Do you find yourself wanting to be near him, to kiss him?"

"I want to eat his face."

"And if, while eating his face, your lips should happen to touch his . . ."

The flittering in my stomach moved lower and tingled softly in places that had never tingled before. I smiled, and realizing my smiling, I blushed.

"Most definitely smitten." Sunrise patted my hand to comfort me in much the same way Ghastly Edna had on occasion. "It's nothing to be embarrassed by. It's perfectly natural."

Newt chuckled. "Didn't you hear her? She wants to eat his face. There's nothing natural about that."

"Oh, be quiet. This is a good thing. You should be happy for her."

"Have you ever devoured a man?" I asked.

"No. But I'm a mortal woman. You're a witch, and cursed, and undead. So I think the ghoulish impulses are perfectly healthy."

This was logical, and I pushed aside my embarrassment. "Do you really think this is a good thing?"

"I see nothing wrong with it. It just shows that you're more human than you thought."

"Can I really love him?"

Sunrise laughed sweetly. "I said nothing about love. I said smitten. It can lead to love, but more often than not, it is merely a temporary infatuation."

"How do I know which it is?"

"You'll find out in due course."

Newt scowled. "She can't be smitten. He's a White Knight."

"Which only makes him more dashing and romantic."

"But she's a witch. Witches and White Knights don't mix."

"Who's to say?"

"You didn't sense his virtue. It's an abomination. Unnatural, I tell you. Not a speck of sin at all."

"Not even a speck?" Sunrise asked.

"Perhaps a speck. He is a mortal man, after all. But not nearly as much as would be healthy. I suspect he's never known a woman. Nor can such desire dwell in his heart."

Silently, I agreed. The White Knight was a poor choice, and I felt foolish. But Sunrise explained that no one chooses to be smitten. It just happens, and I felt better.

"You could have picked an easier man, but with my help and your considerable unwitchly assets, he might be yours."

"No. I can't."

"Why not?"

"Because it isn't right. I can't kill a good man."

"Perhaps if you had a large dinner before . . ."

"You heard her," Newt barked. "She isn't interested. Although if she did consume him in her passion . . ." He grinned in demonic fashion.

"I'm doing nothing of the sort. These feelings will go away, won't they?"

"Eventually," she said. "It's your choice, but should you change your mind, feel free to come to me with any questions you might have."

I thanked her for the offer, but on this, I was inflexible. Ghastly Edna had warned me of my curse. Now I understood what she'd meant. To desire a man was to hunger for his flesh. This might not have been a problem except that as I was a very picky eater, I was also a very picky lover. I couldn't eat a good man, and I didn't want a bad one. I resigned myself to eternal virginity.

"I wonder why he's come?" Sunrise pondered.

"Gwurm says the White Knights wander the world, trusting fate to take them to wrongs needing righting. Most likely, he's just passing through. I can't think of any wrong righting required here."

"If he were just passing through, I don't think he would have stopped and talked to the soldiers."

"If you'd really like to know, I can find out." There was more to the offer than a friendly favor. I wanted to see the dark White Knight, even if seeing him was all I could ever do.

"Newt, I need your body."

My familiar balked. "I'm using it right now."

"Only for moping."

I threw him a disapproving glare, and he walked to my side. I bent down and kissed his bill. Switching bodies with my familiar was a small magic. I thrust my mind into him. His jumped from his body and fell into mine for easy storage. My skin could have been an immobile prison for him, but I allowed him to move in it as a polite gesture.

I looked into my emerald green eyes. All the grime on my face did little to hide my beauty. Fortunate for me so few looked below the surface.

Newt glowered with my mouth. He set me down on the table where I mixed medicines.

He spoke with my voice. "Egad, what a form." He felt my lips and the teeth. He pulled at the ears and ran his hands up and down my body. He squeezed my left breast and patted my bottom. Then ran fingers down my stomach to my thigh and back to . . .

"Would you please stop fondling my flesh?"

"Sorry." He stood, but my body swayed almost off its feet. He flapped my arms to regain his balance. They weren't wings, and it didn't help. Sunrise caught him before he could topple over. "The weight distribution is a little tricky." He sat. "All in all not a bad form. I'm not sure I care for all the bare skin or the feet. But I've always wanted teeth and what fine teeth they are. Sharp and deadly. I bet you could crack bones with these." He chomped the air and gnashed my teeth.

"You can crack bones with your bill," I reminded.

"It's not the same."

"There's some fresh pheasants over there. Crack their bones all you like while I'm away."

He picked one bird from the small collection and ground my teeth enthusiastically.

I hopped off the table. I'd borrowed animal forms before as part of my education. Ghastly Edna had taught me to listen to the body. "Tell it where you want to go, dear, and it will tell you how to get there." Newt's body moved easily. His odd walk, programmed into the flesh by his years of uninterrupted use, remained part of it.

Sunrise parted the tent flap for me, and we stepped outside.

Gwurm, who made a habit of sitting outside my tent should I need him, raised his head. He was short an eye and rolling something from cheek to cheek. "Leaving so soon?"

I explained my switch with Newt and how I was off to the fort to check on the White Knight.

He spit out his missing eye and licked it to a lustrous, saliva-coated shine before popping it back into its socket. "How does being a duck who can't fly help?"

"Newt can fly. He's just forgotten, but my mistress taught me so I could take full advantage of a bird's body. It's very basic. Jump in the air, flap your wings, and mind the ground."

I stretched out my wings to loosen them. Sunrise and Gwurm wished me luck, and I was off. It took a few hops, but soon I was flying. It was a lurching, ungraceful spectacle, but better than any flight Newt had taken. I soared over the settlement in wide circles until I'd gotten the hang of it.

I banked to a flying pattern over the fort proper. I'd never seen it from this angle. It was a square of stone walls with only one gate. Smaller buildings of wood and stone had been built within. Lanterns and moonlight lit the large open areas. There weren't many soldiers. Most were in the barracks, attending the financial needs of prostitutes, or spending time with their families. One duck slipped past the night guard with very little trouble.

Finding the Knight was also easy. Half of Newt's demon essence belonged to his mind, but the other half rested in his body. I walked a few minutes, and let my uneasy stomach guide me to the Captain's office, which was a logical place to go anyway. The window was too high for me to look through. I hid in the shadows and listened.

"This is terrible!" moaned the Captain. "Horrible! This is supposed to be a quiet region. Nothing ever happens here."

"Exactly why I believe they are coming this way," the Knight replied. Even just his voice put a smile on my bill even as my nausea increased. "They intend to push their way up into the kingdom, past an unguarded border. You were fortunate to put this fort up when you did."

"Fortunate." The Captain grunted the word as one might a curse. "Yes, fortunate."

Then came silence. Not true silence, but whispered mutterings I assumed to be coming from the Captain.

I spotted a crawling beetle nearby.

"You, come here." I spoke softly in the language of insects.

Controlling insects is very basic magic. All one has to do is speak, providing a talent for talking to bugs, and they'll respond to any suggestion without hesitation. They're too simple to know their own wishes from another's.

"I need your eyes." I would have been polite, but politeness would only confuse the beetle. I cast a minor spell attuning my vision to the bug's. "Fly to the window, and see what's going on."

The beetle did so in due haste. I learned that a bug's eyes are made for a bug's world, and in a bug's world, everything fits into three categories: Things you can eat, Things that can eat you, and Everything else. The Captain and the Knight were monstrous blurs. I couldn't tell one from the other or the furniture. Another spell rectified the problem, and the world became clear.

The dark White Knight was better-looking than I remembered. His ears did stick out, even more than I'd first noticed, but it just made them easier to nibble on. He was taller than I remembered too. Glimpsing him through a bug's eyes was probably the reason for that. I watched him a minute, studying the lines of his body without hearing the conversation. Then the Captain finally said something that caught my attention.

"I've heard tales but didn't think them true."

"It's true. I've seen it with my own eyes."

"But goblings don't amass in hordes. It's unheard of." The Captain leaned over the table to pour himself a glass of wine. "Exactly how many goblings are in a horde?"

"I didn't perform an exact count. Just take the largest number you can imagine and double it. Then double that for good measure."

The Captain frowned, gulped down his wine, performed the mental calculations, and frowned deeper. "I'll organize an evacuation immediately."

"Very good. And I've already formulated some battle strategies that should help. I'll begin drilling your men in the morning."

The Captain squinted. "Perhaps you misunderstand. I'm talking about a complete evacuation. Soldiers included."

"The soldiers will be staying." The White Knight spoke with quiet authority. It was not a command so much as a fact shared with the unenlightened Captain.

"Surely, you can see that this is a small fort. We aren't a match for such a force. I've got only five companies."

"Five hundred will have to suffice." Again, he said it as an indisputable truth.

"Not these five hundred. These are the five hundred worst soldiers in the kingdom. Most of them haven't seen a battle. Those that have are alive only because the death maidens weren't paying close enough attention. That's why Fort Stalwart was commissioned in the first place. It's not a fort. It's a dumping ground for all those soldiers barely competent enough to avoid dishonorable discharges. It was deliberately put here because this is where nothing ever happens."

The Knight said nothing. He stood tall. His face betrayed not a hint of despair or fear.

"You see my point?" the Captain asked.

The Knight still said nothing.

"This is a horde. A gobling horde. This requires the best men available. Or at least not the very worst."

"Those men are not here," the White Knight observed.

"We'll send for them."

"By then, it will be too late. The goblings will have pushed deeper into the realm, and once the horde is entrenched, it will be nearly impossible to get rid of. I fear the damage they'd inflict in the meantime."

"I fear the damage these men might inflict on themselves with their own swords."

"Five hundred men will be enough," the White Knight said. "I've seen the destruction this horde has wrought on the ravaged countryside. I've been tracking it for months, always too late to mount a defense. Now that I finally have the opportunity, I won't throw it away. I have pledged my honor that the rampage ends here."

The mark on the Knight's forehead shimmered. A wisp of magic glowed around the Captain's heart, where a man's courage is found. The fear fell from his face though it didn't disappear entirely.

"I'll talk to the men in the morning. There won't be a soldier within twenty miles by the afternoon, I can assure you."

"I shall speak with them. They'll see the importance of standing up to this threat." The White Knight smiled. "I can assure you. Good evening, Captain."

Looking very tired, the Captain slumped into a chair. "Good evening."

The Knight exited the office. I wanted the beetle to follow him, but an insect's mind can only hold a thought so long. It flew from the window before I could whisper another command. I ended my spell and returned to looking through my own eyes. Or Newt's own eyes, but they were mine for the moment.

The White Knight stood not ten feet away, and he had quite obviously glimpsed me even hidden away in the shadows.

I'd been caught, and I panicked. I turned and ran right into a wall that I'd forgotten. I lost my balance and my sense of my duck's body and fell over.

Gentle hands righted me. The touch burned the demon in Newt's flesh. They released me to my unsteady webbed feet.

"Easy there, duck. Watch where you're going."

I glanced up at the Knight. He smiled, and I nearly forgot myself and smiled back. Normal ducks couldn't smile, and I caught myself. It helped that I was throwing up.

I felt terrible. My stomach convulsed. My eyes watered. This was only half of what Newt had suffered. I didn't truly puke. I just spit up a mouthful of foul dribble that rolled up my throat and out my bill.

"Still feeling poorly, I see."

I raised my head and glanced into those dark eyes and ears made for nibbling. My nausea grew. I suspected this was quite normal, the kind of nervous stomach one feels when smitten.

"I think we should get you home, duck."

He swept me up in his arms. I felt ill, but not quite as ill as before. Newt's body was developing a tolerance, even if my nervous stomach was still swirling. He held me close, despite the risk of fowl vomit. He was very warm, made to seem even warmer by the chill in the air.

I was a creature made to dwell in darkness. Darkness is cold, and cold is how I preferred to be. A good chill is subtle, comforting without being obnoxious. Heat is rudely invasive, but in the Knight's arms, I discovered the first good warmth I'd known. Even through the flesh of Newt's duck body, it filled my mind with carnal tingles. This could only lead to trouble. Even seeing him, I realized, had been a mistake. I should have jumped from his arms and flown away. I snuggled closer, resting my head against his chest. Wrong or not, I couldn't leave his warmth. I told myself this was a small indulgence, that as long as I was using Newt's body, there couldn't be any lasting harm. I almost believed it too.

The Knight inquired as to my ownership from two passing soldiers.

"That's the witch's duck, sir," the first replied.

"I thought the witch's duck had fangs," said the second.

"Ducks don't have fangs."

"Not normal ducks, but I would think a witch's duck would. And eyes that glow in the night. And claws on the feet."

"Hers doesn't have any of that. I've seen it up close a dozen times. It's just a duck. Snooty little beast, but very normal otherwise."

"How can a bird be snooty?"

"If a bird can have fangs, I have no problem believing it can be haughty."

"So it does have fangs."

"No, it doesn't. Although, thinking about it, I see your argument. A witch has no business associating with a snobbish, normal duck."

The White Knight interrupted to ask where the witch lived. Then he left the soldiers to their discussion of what sort of ducks a witch should associate with.

"At the very least, it should be black," the first observed before we fell out of earshot.

The Knight carried me through the settlement. He stroked my neck and spine. An urge to burrow into his chest and curl up in the damp heat inside his heart came to me. Should I ever actually touch him while I was an accursed woman, I couldn't imagine what I might do.

We arrived at my tent far too soon and not soon enough. The White Knight bowed to Sunrise. Then, much to my pleasant surprise, he bowed to Gwurm. He didn't bow to Penelope, but I think we would have had he known her alive in her fashion.

"Is this the witch's tent?"

Sunrise nodded. "There you are, Newt. We've been look-ing everywhere for you."

"Is the witch in?"

She hesitated, although she hid this behind a pleasant smile. "One moment. I'll fetch her."

I was too distracted by the Knight's firm, yet soft, embrace to realize this for the mistake it was. Sunrise went into my tent. Whispers were exchanged within. After a very loud grunt from Sunrise that I couldn't quite decipher, they emerged.

Newt scowled. I don't think I'd ever used my face to scowl before, and I made a note to never let it scowl again. It was a shade too hideous. Even a witch should take care to not overdo her ghastliness. It was a horrid expression that cast shadows over my eyes and made my teeth seem terribly pointy and threatening. There were feathers and a spot of blood on my chin.

This didn't upset me. Much. It was best to look dreadful before the Knight, given my feelings toward him. Newt had forgotten my hat, and my hair, long and silky and shining even in the faint light, was draped over my shoulder as if on display. It was a lapse I never would have made, but Newt was new to the art of looking witchly.

Newt spit flecks of bone. "I'd wondered where he'd got-ten to."

The Knight handed me over. I missed his touch the mo-ment it was taken away. Out of his arms, I had no reason to remain in Newt's feathers. I undid the magic, and our minds returned to their proper bodies. The demon in Newt's mind united with the essence in his flesh, and he instantly threw up. He was kind enough to turn his head away.

"Are you certain he's well?" the Knight asked with genuine concern.

"He's part demon," I said.

"Possessed?"

"No, not possessed. But there is a dab of demon in him. Enough to make him sick in the presence of true virtue." I gave Newt to Gwurm. He strolled away, carrying Newt a comfortable distance from the White Knight's vomit-inducing virtue.

There was no way to gracefully retreat. I disregarded politeness without excusing myself and ducked into my tent. The conversation carried on, but I was too busy tending to my appearance to listen. I tucked my hair under my hat and pulled the brim low as it would go. Then I rubbed dirt over my grimy face. I should've hid until the Knight went away, but I didn't have that much sense. I stepped out, keeping my head down and eyes on the ground.

"My sincerest apologies for your duck, good woman," said the Knight. "I thought I was helping the poor creature."

"It's the thought that counts," Sunrise said. "Might we know your name, good sir?"

"How impolite of me." He took her hand and bowed. "I am Wyst of the West, Defender of the Weak, Destroyer of the Foul, Sworn Champion of Decency, Avowed Foe of Evil." He bent lower to touch his forehead to her hand. "And I am honored to make your acquaintance, miss . . . ?"

"Sunrise. And you've met Newt. The troll is Gwurm."

My broom tapped Sunrise's shoulder.

"Oh, yes. This is Penelope."

I could only see the Knight's boots. They turned in my direction, and the heels clicked together. "And you are?"

"She has no name," Sunrise replied.

I called upon my best mysterious whisper. "Does the wind need a name? Do the stones or the stars or the trees? To name these things is both foolish and unneeded. Putting a name to them doesn't make them be any more than they already are."

I allowed myself a small smile. I sounded very much like Ghastly Edna at that moment.

"How very true." He bowed, but I didn't offer my hand. "And very witchly."

The compliment reddened my cheeks. I turned my back and felt those tingles that seemed only to be growing stronger despite my best efforts.

"Could we reward you with something to eat?" Sunrise asked.

"I eat only bread."

"Some tea then?"

"I drink only water, and I really must get back to the fort. There are grave matters I must attend to."

"Of course."

Wyst of the West, Defender of the Weak, Destroyer of the Foul, Sworn Champion of Decency, Avowed Foe of Evil, bid us a pleasant evening, bowed once more, and started back to the settlement proper at a brisk walk.

"You were right," Sunrise observed. "He isn't exactly handsome. Not in an obvious manner. But the features of his face combine subtly in a very pleasing fashion. It's better than handsome because handsome can fool you. Most anyone can be handsome in the right circumstance, but a pleasing face only gets better the more you look at it."

Penelope twirled and somersaulted through the air in agreement. I was glad to know that this was not merely my imagination.

"Why were you trying to get him to stay?" I said.

"Just trying to help. You may be a very fine witch, but when it comes to romance, you have less experience than most children."

I started to protest, but she had none of that.

"I won't argue the point. You may be privy to forbidden secrets, but I know a few secrets myself. This is greater than both of you. Any notions you entertain otherwise are merely wishful thinking. Now what did you learn?"

I told of the approaching gobling horde and how the White Knight had come here to lead the men of Fort Stalwart against it. My thoughts were elsewhere though. Not on the Knight, but on Sunrise's words. It took a half hour of contemplation before I grasped their true meaning. By then, she'd finished her last cup of tea and was setting off to work.

"Did you say, greater than both of us?" I asked.

"Yes. Couldn't you tell?"

"Tell what?"

"Oh, dear nameless witch, you didn't notice, did you?"

"Notice what?" I felt vaguely annoyed.

She laughed. My embarrassment caused me to blush, something I seemed to be doing often lately.

"Why Wyst of the West, dear. He's smitten with you as well."

I didn't sleep that night. Another of my undead gifts was a talent for borrowing vigor against future rest. The longest I'd ever gone without sleep had been a week. I could have easily gone longer, but Ghastly Edna had ordered me into bed. I'd slept for two weeks, so soundly not even magic could wake me. She'd warned me then to watch myself. It would be easy to slip into a habit of staying awake for years, then slumbering away decades. As with all her warnings, I took it seriously, but I just couldn't make myself go to bed. I stared at the fort and thought of Wyst of the West in lustful, unwitchly ways.

I thought of the gobling horde too. It was a contradiction in logic. Goblings did not amass in hordes. They were a voraciously carnivorous species. Anything a gobling catches—including other goblings—it eats. There had to be some magic involved in this, and as the witch of Fort Stalwart, it was my duty to get to the bottom of it.

Mostly though, I thought of the White Knight, his warm, lean body intertwined with mine, how his dark flesh would taste, his eyes, and those oh-so-delectable ears that so needed a good, long nibbling.

In the morning, I went to the fort to see Wyst address the soldiers. Gwurm and Newt accompanied me. We were early, and while we waited for the men to wake and assemble, I explained the contradiction inherent in a gobling horde.

"Hold a moment," Newt asked. "If goblings eat everything, including other goblings, how do they reproduce?"

"They're asexual," Gwurm replied. "Every week or so a gobling squats and lays a gooey blob that grows into another gobling. Providing the original doesn't eat the glob, which they often do."

Newt puckered his bill. "Disgusting."

"They're foul little creatures. Far be it for me to slander an entire species, gods know we trolls have suffered from that practice, but I've yet to run across one that didn't need killing.

"I visited a city in the Wastes once. They had gobling fights. They'd throw a pair in a large cage and take bets which would consume the other. Gruesome spectacle. I only watched once. That was enough. The two fiendish little beasts twirled about in a slavering, hissing, blood-spurting blur. A few seconds and it was over. That match was a draw. There was nothing left of either but a scrap of wing and puddles of yellow blood."

Newt narrowed an eye. "You're making that up."

"I am not. I was told it was not uncommon, given their insatiable appetites."

Gwurm liked to tease Newt, but in this, he sounded sincere. I certainly believed it possible, which only made the prospect of a horde of the beasts all the more terrible.

The soldiers assembled, and we watched from the fort gate. The Captain introduced Wyst of the West, and the White Knight began a speech that was no doubt sincere in its passion. I couldn't hear much of what was said, but I saw the Knight's inspiration enchantment work its magic on the assembly.

Most were moved. Their hearts filled with a soft glow that

gave them courage. Enough to keep them from deserting for a while at least.

Those easily enchanted or truly brave shone bright in the crowd. There weren't many of these. Perhaps twenty-five of the five hundred. This was more than I expected, and I knew that these men would lay down their lives as long as they fought by the White Knight's side.

Finally, there were the craven few without an ounce of valor in their hearts for the magic to play upon. These men would vanish by dusk, if not sooner. I guessed their number at fifty, less than I'd expected.

Wyst did not speak long, trusting in his magic to reach the men. The Captain issued orders. Some soldiers were to notify the civilians of the hasty evacuation. Most were to prepare for tactical drills with the White Knight. I gathered the horde was only three or four days away, leaving us not much time to prepare.

When the Captain retired to his office, I told him of my intention to stay. Both the Captain and Newt fixed me with peculiar glances.

"Are you mad?" the Captain asked. "Do you have an inkling of what we're in for?"

"A good witch walks beside death."

"I've yet to see magic be much use on a battlefield. Still, some armies do swear by it. The Tyrle Kingdoms reportedly employ several regiments of zombies with some effectiveness, and every man in Hurgle's Marauders is enchanted to explode when killed, which is very distracting in the middle of a fight, I can personally attest. Not to mention horribly messy." He rubbed his eyes, full of worry and weariness. "You can stay, but please don't enchant my men without consulting with me first."

"Thank you. I think I know of something to sour the taste of your soldiers."

"Would that stop the goblings from eating them?"

"Nothing overcomes a gobling's appetite," I replied, "but it would lessen their zeal."

"That's something at least, I suppose."

I promised to deliver the tonic by tomorrow morning, and the Captain dismissed me with a noteworthy lack of enthusiasm.

Outside, Gwurm was speaking with Wyst of the West. I stayed back and waited for them to finish. Newt, who could no longer stay quiet, spoke low enough that only I could hear.

"Why are we staying?"

"Because this is my job," I said in an equally low whisper.

"Your job is vengeance. Remember your dead mistress."

I swatted him hard across the backside with my broom. He jumped, forgot his oath of silence among men, and swore.

"Why did you do that?"

I smacked him again, harder this time. Newt shouted out, "Damn it! That hurt!"

"Good. Now listen, and listen well. I welcome your opinion. Feel free to offer it whenever you like. But make no mistake about it, I make the final decisions on what we will do, where we will go, and who we will kill. Is that understood?"

"Yes, yes, mistress. Whatever you say," he grunted without much enthusiasm.

I let go of Penelope. She struck him softly across his tender seat and jumped back to my hand.

"Of course, mistress. I meant no disrespect."

"Yes, you did, and I'll have no more of it. If you're unhappy, take your leave. Otherwise, shut up and stop second-guessing everything I do."

He grumbled. The demon in him so hated being dressed down, but an unreliable familiar would do me little good. Penelope trembled in my grasp, eager for another swat.

"I'm sorry, mistress. You're right, of course. I overstepped my bounds, and I humbly beg your forgiveness."

He wasn't truly sorry. Nor was he the type to humbly beg for anything. Expecting sincerity from a duck with a pinch of demon was asking too much. It was enough that he maintained a false, yet respectable, humility.

Penelope shook, begging for another shot. I squeezed her tight, and she relented.

"Very good. I'm pleased we understand each other."

One thin soldier no more than sixteen years old had been close enough to catch our conversation. He measured Newt with a vaguely shocked expression. He was not so much frightened as surprised.

My familiar hissed in a decidedly unducky manner. "That's right. I talk. I also devour souls, and what a tasty little soul I'll bet you have."

He took a single step toward the soldier. The boy turned and tripped over his own feet. Newt chuckled while the young man scurried away.

Gwurm and Wyst of the West parted. I worried the Knight might want to speak with me, but he went to preparing the soldiers for their drills. Gwurm returned to my side.

"Nice chap," Gwurm remarked. "He just wanted to apologize for judging my character based solely on my species. Says there's even a troll in his order who's distinguished himself as an exemplary champion."

Gwurm had not given the slightest hint of insult after their first meeting, but just because he accepted such inconveniences as a troll's burden didn't make them right. Wyst's apology showed his good character, and his good character only made me hunger for him more in ways both carnal and carnivorous.

I kept my eyes low and buried such desires beneath more immediate concerns. But it wasn't easy, and it was proving more difficult each time.

IN THE SAFETY OF my tent, I borrowed Newt's body again. He didn't complain about the switch. He liked wearing my body. My green eyes gleamed with sinister delights. He had no doubt dreamed up all manner of twisted, demon-born fantasies of what he might do with it given free rein. I warned him he only enjoyed its full use by my good graces. Should he behave in any inappropriate way, the privilege would be revoked.

He acted as if he didn't need to be told this. I made a point of telling him anyway. Then I dispatched him and Gwurm to gather the ingredients I'd need for the Captain's tonic. They set off on their task, and I set off on mine.

I stepped out of my tent, found a bare spot, and stomped my web foot four times. Then I shouted because one must be loud to attract the slumbering earth's attention.

"Hello there, good earth. Any goblings down there?"

The earth replied with a vaguely feminine voice, yet deep and slow as the earth should have. "No. No goblings down here."

"Could you point the way to the nearest batch?"

It took a minute for the earth to take in the question, but she knew the answer. The earth was hardly aware of anything happening atop her but knew all that went on below the surface. An arrow drew itself in the dirt. I thanked the earth for her help, but by then she had gone back to sleep.

I took to the air, circling the fort once to stretch my wings. I kept from looking down for fear of glimpsing Wyst of the West. There were more important matters at hand.

I soared over the forest, stopping every fifteen minutes to check with the earth, whose directions, while reliable, were always in need of some adjusting. After a few hours, I found the horde.

There was no need to consult the earth because the forest below grew deathly quiet. Not a chirp or a chitter or a squeal rose from the trees. All the birds and beasts that hadn't been eaten had fled the area. I landed without worry. Goblings were nocturnal. They spent their days sleeping in burrows. I spotted dozens of entrances in the soil. No efforts had been made to hide them. And why should there have been? The creatures were dug deep into the earth, and any attempt to flush them out would only drive them deeper. A legion equipped with the finest shovels and sharpest swords could've spent weeks trying with nothing to show but blistered palms and a handful of gobling corpses out of thousands.

I glanced down into a dark hole. Goblings were about duck-size, and I would have to squeeze down into the depths if I were to learn anything more. Newt's body was a match for a gobling or two, but there was still a danger. If I should get his borrowed body killed, my soul would simply snap back into my own flesh, push out Newt, and he'd expire. Familiars were made to serve, but I had gotten attached to my demon duck, disrespectful as he might be. Sentimentality aside, a good witch takes care with her familiar.

I deemed it worth the risk and stepped into the darkened

burrow. Though my own eyes would have worked better, Newt's could see reasonably well. I moved slowly, carefully, and soon came across a slumbering gobling. It was a noisy little creature. Its body twitched as it snored, grumbled, and snorted in a fitful sleep.

I didn't get too close as I studied it. It looked as I'd been taught goblings should. Two arms. Two legs. A square head with a large mouth, small eyes, and giant ears. Small leather wings grew from its shoulders, but goblings were notoriously bad fliers. Worse even than Newt. I sensed no magic in this creature, but just because I didn't see enchantment didn't rule out the involvement of magic. Magic can be concealed even from a witch's eye. It usually wasn't considered worth the effort.

If I was to learn any more, I'd have to take this gobling back for more in-depth inspection. It wouldn't be much trouble to kill it in its sleep, drag it to the surface, and fly it back to the fort. Getting it back alive would have been preferable but unfeasible.

The gobling sniffed and stirred. A shiny, orange pinpoint lit the tunnel. By the time I'd realized it was one of the gobling's eyes, it had already scrambled to its feet and came at me, screeching.

The demon in Newt's flesh reacted without a thought from me. It thrust my bill into the creature's throat. Blood spurted from the gash. It splattered on my face and bill. I swallowed some of it and discovered gobling blood tasted not bad at all, the tang of rabbit with the sweetness of deer, though I disliked the aftertaste. The gobling writhed a minute, hissing and spitting, before expiring.

I took a solid bite of an ear (not easy without teeth) and I began hauling it from the burrow. Newt's body was strong, especially for a duck, and the gobling would be easy enough to carry back in flight with a rest here and there.

I was so pleased with my catch that I almost didn't notice the grunts coming from deeper in the tunnel. From the depths, shapes were rising. Each of them sported two pinpoints of orange eyes. They growled in ravenous fashion.

I counted five of the creatures. There were probably even more waiting, crowding forward. They were cautious, which was fortunate. I couldn't fight them all. I dragged my prize toward the surface, and they followed along, getting ever closer. I'd gotten halfway out the burrow when one finally latched on to the corpse's foot and, with a growl, yanked it from my bill.

Hands would have made this easier. I guess Newt was used to his lack of them, but they truly were practical tools. I lunged at the gobling and nipped off a bit of finger. The creature let go and retreated. I hastily swallowed the finger, gripped the corpse by its arm, and hauled it out of the dark and into the light, where the goblings would not follow.

Then I sat and caught my breath. Goblings tasted very good. It was no mystery why they devoured each other. I was tempted to go back and grab another for a snack. Instead, I bit off the big toe of the one I had and chewed it slowly. I wondered how humans tasted in comparison. An instinct told me they were even better. And Wyst of the West would surely have a flavor beyond lesser men, but this was perhaps an assumption of my growing affection.

A voice interrupted my musings. "A duck eating a gobling. There's a sight I'd never thought to see."

A gray fox sat on a flat stone. She smiled. Foxes usually did.

"I have demon in my flesh," I replied.

"Yes, and a witch in your mind."

I didn't know I looked surprised, but I must have.

She smiled wider. "Oh, I've seen one or two witches in borrowed bodies before. One even borrowed mine once."

"You're very observant, I can see."

"Well, I am a fox. A very clever fox at that, if I say so myself."

I sat on my gobling. "Not that I doubt you, but what would a very clever fox be doing around here when every other living thing has the good sense to be elsewhere?"

"I never said I had good sense. I merely claimed to be clever, but the problem with being clever is that I get bored easily. So when the goblings came along, I began a game. Every night, they rise from their burrows and scour the woods for every morsel, and I do my best to avoid finding myself in their stomachs."

"A dangerous game."

"As all the very best games are. And why, I must ask, should a witch's mind in a demon duck's body dare risk herself for a gobling corpse. Surely, they aren't that delicious."

"You're very curious," I replied.

The fox smiled again. Rather, she smiled differently than before. "A hazard of being too clever, I'm afraid."

I explained how I needed a specimen to study that I might discover if magic was indeed involved in this horde of goblings.

She stopped smiling and playfully swished her tail. "I am no witch, merely a fox, and I can tell there is magic in this." She walked over and sniffed the corpse. "For one, this is not a true gobling. None of them are."

"How so?"

"I couldn't say. I'm not that clever, but they are not genuine flesh and blood. Can't you tell?"

"No, but I'm no fox, just a witch." I kicked the corpse. It felt solid. Yet it was already stiffening and stone cold but minutes after its death. These were surely signs something was amiss.

I remembered the wolf's remark on Ghastly Edna's killers. They had been men who were not men. Was there a connection, or were creatures of false flesh more common than my sheltered existence had led me to believe? I didn't know, but it was certainly noteworthy. Perhaps my vengeance was not so far away as Newt suspected.

I thanked the fox for her help. She wandered off to get some sleep before the evening games began, and I flew back to the fort, my dead gobling clamped in my bill.

10

After returning Newt and myself to our proper bodies, I examined my dead gobling inside my tent. A cursory inspection showed something unnatural at work. The corpse was decaying remarkably quickly only hours after death, and my sensitive nose detected none of the stench of rot the undead in me so relished. In fact, the corpse smelled hardly at all. I leaned close and sniffed it up and down. There was an odor of dirt, moss, and a dozen faint aromas this gobling would have collected from the forest. Of the gobling itself, there was nothing. Though it looked real and felt real and tasted real enough, it didn't seem to exist at all in smell. Such an anomaly could only be magic.

Newt watched but had other interests. "What's it like to fly?"

"It's nice," I answered while running my fingers across the gobling's square face.

"Nice?"

"As a form of travel, it is very convenient. Although I think I prefer walking."

"You're not just saying that, are you? Just to make me not feel bad about not being able to."

"Not at all."

"Because I've always been led to believe that flying is wonderful."

I flipped the gobling on its stomach and prodded it along its spine. "Flying is like most talents. Everyone who can't do it assumes it must be greater than it is, and everyone who can knows it for what it is."

"You're talking in circles," he said.

"I know."

"I wish you wouldn't. It's confusing sometimes."

"It's meant to be."

"So is flying good or not?"

"It's good, but I prefer having hands to wings."

"They're very practical, I grant you."

I flipped the gobling back over and tore open its belly. I stuck my hands wrist deep into the cold innards. They were already dried and shriveled.

Newt hopped on the table and watched as I yanked the gobling's insides out. Again, there was no odor and barely any fluids. I catalogued the various organs as I spread them before me. Everything seemed in order.

I dipped a finger in the brackish slime leaking from the gobling and licked it. I offered Newt a lick for a second opinion.

"Not bad. Kind of bland."

"Exactly. But when it was fresh, it tasted delicious. So unless gobling meat turns in a matter of hours, this fellow is gradually fading away, one sense at a time."

"Yes, so?"

"That means something. Something important."

"What?"

"I don't know."

I hunched over the gobling and stared at it. Its one half-opened, orange eye stared back, defying me to glean its secrets.

Newt abruptly brought up a new subject. "I made some

observations about your body while I was in it. Would you like to hear them?"

I didn't reply, engrossed in contemplation of the gutted corpse.

Newt took this as a sign to keep talking. "For one thing, you're much stronger than you let on. I bet you could break a man's neck."

Only half listening, I replied, "At the proper angle, most easily, but a good witch doesn't resort to brute tactics."

"And another thing, I was studying your naked body earlier."

I frowned.

"Don't worry. I was inside. No one could see me."

I was too intent on the gobling to bother with a lecture.

"And I started thinking," Newt said. "If this is a curse, why should you be so beautiful? At first, I thought a mistake had been made. Then I remembered our mistress saying once or twice that magic doesn't make mistakes."

As did I, and my attention shifted more to my familiar than the corpse.

"That is right, isn't it?" asked Newt.

"Yes. Magic lacks only the will to act on its own," I said. "That's where witches and wizards and the like come in. Through us, it finds purpose."

"You offer suggestions, and the magic acts upon those suggestions. Usually exactly as requested of it, since it isn't very creative on its own. But sometimes, just sometimes, it does come up with an idea it likes better."

"You're saying my curse made me beautiful on purpose."

His head bobbed up and down. "If mistakes are impossible, then I'd have to believe so. And if you were intentionally made as beautiful as you are, then I asked myself to what end?"

"I trust you came up with a theory."

"You're not a horrible beast meant to be skulking around in graveyards. You're a seductive predator, a ghoul wrapped in soft flesh that might draw men into your arms where they might find death in your loving embrace."

My carnal desires were closely linked to my appetite. Almost inseparable. In my undead mind, a good man and a good meal were one and the same. This bothered me. I didn't know why. I'd already resigned myself to never indulge in those twin pleasures of the flesh. But having Newt link them so closely and so logically made me realize how cursed I was.

Newt meant it as a compliment. He looked at me differently now. It was a quiet awe, a newfound respect. I was a perfectly designed predator, even if I didn't want to be.

Rather than dwell upon it, I returned to my study of the gobling. I hastily stuffed the guts back inside, ran my fingers along the split torso, searing the flesh closed with magic. I held up the little, green body. Its vacant orange eyes rolled back in its head. Its black tongue hung from open lips.

"Well, my little friend, you seem dead, but I'm guessing you were never truly alive. Let's find out, shall we?"

I channeled my power for raising the dead into the gobling. There was no soul in the meat. There shouldn't have been, but I suspected the creature had never possessed one. If that was so, then any semblance of life or death was questionable at best. I ignored the absent soul and willed the gobling animate.

The creature jerked to life. As it was badly damaged and decayed, there wasn't much energy. It flailed its arms and legs limply. It flapped its wings. It gnashed its teeth and hissed barely audibly.

Newt hopped back.

I held the gobling down on the table. Even if the little beast wasn't real, I didn't want it to suffer. I picked up a dagger and put it to my forehead. I took a moment to put some magic in the blade and drove it into the gobling's back. It popped like a soap bubble. Nothing was left behind.

"How did you do that?" Newt asked.

"Quite easily." I laid the dagger aside and smiled. "I unbelieved it."

I didn't bother with further explanations. I saved that for the Captain and Wyst of the West. This discovery could be of great use to the soldiers of Fort Stalwart, providing they could understand it.

The tent flapped open. I reached for my hat.

"It's just me." Sunrise stepped inside. Penelope, who had been guarding the tent, hovered in beside her. "I wanted to say good-bye before leaving. I assume you'll be staying."

"It is my duty to aid to the defense of these people from this sort of threat."

"Yes. Your duty."

She smiled wryly, and I guessed her thoughts. They were my own as well. It was an inevitable speculation that this gobling horde was merely a convenient excuse. That my true reason for staying stemmed from my growing affection for Wyst of the West. I denied the notion, but even I couldn't comfortably dismiss it. Even if it was true, I would still be of help against this menace.

"I trust the evacuation is going smoothly," I said.

"As smooth as could be expected. No one is happy about it, but none want to be here when the goblings arrive. The Captain has issued instructions that we should travel north and keep traveling unless we hear otherwise."

"A sound suggestion."

An awkward quiet filled the tent. I liked Sunrise very much. She was my friend and my mentor on the strange ways of the living. Now we were parting, and good sense told me this might be the very last time I ever saw her. I thought perhaps I wanted to hug her. But my upbringing left me uncomfortable with such close contact. I couldn't even remember ever touching my parents, and I'd only hugged Ghastly Edna once. And that was only after she'd been killed and surely a permissible exception.

I decided this was not and trusted she would understand. "Safe journey to you, Sunrise."

"Good fortune to you, witch. And to you, Newt, Penelope."

My broom dipped in a bow, and Newt nodded to Sunrise. She left my tent, and I began sorting through the various ingredients for the Captain's tonic.

I KNEW THE CAPTAIN would have difficulty understanding what I had to tell, but understand he must if the men of Fort Stalwart were to stand a chance against the horde. I spent an hour tuning my presentation before finally limping off to speak with him.

The town-to-be was still, nearly empty. Where there had been dozens of lights, there was a lake of dark and quiet, deserted constructions. The stragglers skulked along the settlement like shadows, piling their possessions into wagons. I'd never truly lived among the humans, yet I felt sadder for their absence.

At the fort proper, I informed a soldier that I would need to speak with the Captain and would be waiting in his office. I unlocked the door with magic and found a seat. Newt sat at my feet, and we waited. Penelope entertained herself by sweeping the dusty floor. She'd collected most of it in a corner when the Captain finally arrived. He was not alone. Wyst of the West entered after him.

Newt gurgled, but he didn't vomit. His tolerance for the White Knight's purity was growing.

I lowered my head, pressing my chin to my chest and keeping my eyes low.

Penelope kept joyfully sweeping.

"I trust this is important," the Captain said.

I raised my head and glimpsed Wyst of the West. In a brief moment of fantasy, I imagined myself pouncing upon him to nuzzle and gnaw his face. I smiled slightly, despite myself. He smiled back, and I averted my eyes to the Captain.

I reached into a loose sleeve and removed a small clay vial. "A tonic of ill-taste. Pour it into the men's stew, and they'll taste horrible for days. Horrible enough to deter even a gobling's appetite."

"Thank you. Is that it?"

"No. I've made a discovery about the horde. A discovery that could be of great help."

The Captain looked skeptical, but he almost always did.

Wyst of the West finally spoke. "Something involving magic, I presume."

"Sorcery, to be exact," I replied while very deliberately not looking at him.

Ghastly Edna had taught me as much as she could about the other schools of magic. There were many, and all had their province. Wizards practiced the art of incantation, manipulating the world through words. Thaumaturgists mastered magic through science while shamans viewed it as a primeval force to be called upon through blood offerings and fireside dances. Witches held no solid opinion of magic but were wise enough to know that this in itself was an opinion. And sorcerers pursued the art of crafting illusions. There were countless other followers of the secret ways, and they were all right in their philosophy because magic generally acts as expected.

"I've dealt with sorcerers before," said Wyst of the West. "They're not dangerous. All smoke and bluster."

"Mostly," I agreed, "but even smoke has substance."

I reached into my sleeve and removed a small lizard. I dangled the reptile by its tail. Its skin shifted from yellow to black to green to other random colors.

"I've never seen a lizard like that," the Captain said.

"That's because it does not exist save through my will and magic." I placed it on the table, where it skittered in small aimless circles.

The Captain tried to touch it, but it passed through his hand. "Incredible. It looks so real."

"It's nothing. Any sorcerer's apprentice could do better, but it took a master to create a phantasmal horde of goblings."

I allowed the Captain and Wyst of the West a moment to absorb the information.

"The goblings aren't real?" the Captain asked.

"That's impossible. I've seen the damage they've done myself. Their rampage hasn't been illusion. Just ask the good people they've terrorized. Look at the land they're ravaged."

Wyst frowned. His lower lip stuck out, and I wanted so very badly to run my forked tongue across it.

"How can something not real cause any damage?" said the Captain.

This would be the most difficult part, to teach these men that real and unreal, just as dead and undead, were merely a matter of degrees. Organizing my thoughts was difficult with Wyst of the West so close. Fortunately, I'd prepared in advance.

"I didn't say their rampage was imaginary. Merely that they are, in essence, no more real than this lizard I have made. Which I shall now unmake." I snapped my fingers, and the lizard vanished.

The Captain's eyes lit up. "You can unmake the horde?"

"This lizard was a weak illusion. The goblings are much stronger. So strong that even reality has been fooled into accepting them as true."

"So they are real."

"As real as a dream."

The Captain sighed. "I'm getting a headache."

"They are a dream," I explained, "but it is a dream shared by the world. And when every man, every beast, every tree, and every rock shares in the same illusion, then a dream can become reality. To a point."

"Well, if they're real enough to kill and ravage I fail to see how knowing any of this will help."

Wyst of the West agreed. "Yes, witch. You said this would be of help, didn't you?"

He looked into my eyes, and I didn't turn away this time. I had to smile, but I hoped it came across as vague and mysterious rather than beguiled by his dark eyes.

"Yes, the magic of the horde is potent, but there is a flaw. Even a shared dream is still just a dream. And dreams, like any illusion, can be dispelled by strong enough doubt and, in this case, a little magic. I can place just a drop of enchantment on your men's weapons. Enough that the slightest cut will unmake the dream."

Again, the Captain's eyes lit up, but he was ready to be disappointed this time. "But?"

"The men must know in their hearts, without any doubt, that what they find is but an army of phantoms to call upon the magic."

"An army of phantoms that are nonetheless real enough to devour them alive," the Captain said.

"There will be men. Those lacking enough imagination to even truly believe a shared dream. Others with too much that they suspect the whole world just a dream. Such men, properly armed, will be the horde's undoing. If there are enough of them."

"And exactly how many will be enough?" the Captain dared ask.

"More than you will have," I replied honestly, "but as the goblings are as close to real as phantoms can be, they can also be fought and killed without magic. Those few capable of unbelieving the horde will simply be more efficient. If you're fortunate, the unbelievers shall be enough to turn the tide."

"You don't sound very confident."

I could make no promises, and I let the men know it with a somber face. The Captain was not as enlightened as I'd hoped, but now was a good time to make a traditional witchly exit without saying another word, leaving my audience both a little wiser and a little more befuddled.

Wyst of the West stood between me and the door. He stepped aside as I passed close. I thought him repulsed by my mask of ugliness, but he kept looking me in the eye. Repelled people never did that. Then again, rarely did I look in someone's eyes, but I couldn't stop myself. Sunrise had been right. Those eyes, those ears, those shoulders, that dark, delicious flesh, and that pure, brave soul. Those were my reasons for being here.

Those reasons nearly spoiled my departure, but I found the will to turn from that pleasing face. I walked out the door, very proud of myself for making it with my witchly dignity intact. I paused outside to gasp and shudder free of the tingles left within me.

Only then did I realize I'd forgotten my limp and my hunch. Such mistakes were unforgivable, but they paled beside the absence of my familiar and my broom. They were supposed to follow me out of the office. Now I faced a dilemma. Either go back and retrieve them, thus destroying whatever shreds remained of my dramatic exit, or return to my tent without them. The door opened while I debated. Newt walked out. Penelope floated behind him.

"Sorry," he said. "I was so busy holding down my dinner, I didn't notice you leave."

Penelope jiggled an apology of her own. The Captain's dusty floors were certainly a terrible distraction for the poor dear. It was her broomly nature.

I forgave them. I'd suffered my own diversions in Wyst's presence. Penelope drifted into my hand, and Newt took his place at my side. I hunched deeper and dragged my leg as if raising it off the ground would cause it to snap off.

I made it only eight sluggish steps before the White Knight's voice called to me. "Hold, witch."

A desire to run seized me. I didn't know which direction. Away seemed wrong. Toward him seemed wrong too.

"Yes?" My voice crackled from a dry throat, very witchly and entirely unintentional. I kept my back to him.

"I just wanted to thank you." I thought I sensed a nervous tone in his words, but I was no master of human behavior.

I turned my head enough to glimpse his fuzzy silhouette from the corner of my eye.

He cleared his throat. "These people are fortunate to have you."

I offered no reply.

"You've given them a chance."

"They always had a chance," I said. "My contribution merely lessens the likelihood of a massacre. Victory shall be hard won still. Men will die, and they will likely die in vain."

His tone became somber. "Yes. I know."

Witches don't look at death itself as good or evil. Like any force of nature, it could be neither and both. But these people were under my charge, and I had no desire to see them throw away their lives as dinner for a horde of phantoms.

Wyst of the West said nothing. He turned and walked away. I did the same, allowing myself some small pride for maintaining a witchly demeanor.

Newt chuckled. He wanted me to ask what he found so amusing, but I wasn't interested. This didn't deter him. He chortled and snickered all the way back to the tent, and when I didn't ask why, he finally offered his opinion without solicitation.

"You should just bed and devour him and get it over with. It's going to happen sooner or later. Putting it off is just diverting your attention."

I didn't want to get into this argument. It wasn't that I dismissed his opinion. It was just something I didn't want to hear.

"It's more than infatuation," he continued. "I'm not saying normal impulses aren't involved, but I think there's more to it. Fish swim. Tigers hunt. Goblings eat. You seduce. It's your nature. It's what you're designed for."

I stared ahead and offered no comment.

"I would imagine you're very good at it. Carnal relations, I mean. And this White Knight can't have much experience. Your passion alone would probably kill him. Then you could devour him, and we'd all be spared those embarrassing scenes in the future. Not to mention your grumbling stomach."

It was true my stomach did grumble ever so slightly in Wyst of the West's presence. I'd hoped none had noticed. I hurried to my tent to get something to eat as quickly as my false limp allowed.

Newt kept his bill shut for the rest of the evening. He merely sat in the corner and chuckled in a galling manner. I would've scolded him, but I was too busy sating my appetite. I devoured three rabbits and two pheasants whole. Fur, feathers, bones, organs, everything. I ate until I could eat no more, until I felt as if another bite would surely split my belly open. Yet my hunger remained, and all the pheasants and rabbit flesh in this world would never satisfy my appetite. Only Wyst of the West could do that.

This was more than a smitten heart, more than even lustful desire. This was my curse at work. I was not made for chastity. My instincts had chosen Wyst as my prey, but if we'd never met, they would have picked another. Temptation could only be avoided by absolute isolation, but I'd developed a taste, so to speak, for people. I'd have liked to believe I could find a village of lepers or ogres or ogre lepers to live among, but the same dilemma would present itself in time. Be they men, ogres, gnomes, kobolds, or any other such creature, I would find a target to seduce and consume. It was my nature.

And, suddenly, darkened misery seemed a very welcoming place indeed.

I didn't want to bother enchanting every sword in the fort when we'd be fortunate to find ten men of the correct nature. I had better uses for my time. I devised a simple but effective test for the soldiers and began administering it the next morning. The Captain lent me the kitchen for that purpose.

Gwurm helped by managing the line, and Penelope busied herself by sweeping dust from one side of the kitchen to the other. Newt sat and watched. He found each test most amusing.

Gwurm let the two hundred and fourteenth soldier leave and let in the two hundred and fifteenth, a man of undistinguished features. They were all beginning to look alike. He stood before me. I held up a stone and spoke without looking at him.

"This rock is not real. It has only the substance your perceptions give it. Do you understand?"

There was a pause when I imagined he was nodding, but I couldn't say as I wasn't looking at him.

"Yes. I believe so," he said.

"Good." I tossed the stone between my hands. "Now I will throw this imaginary rock at you, and as you understand it is not real, it will not hurt you."

I cocked my arm and hurled the rock. He didn't flinch. It struck him in the stomach, and he doubled over, gasping. This was expected as the rock was quite real.

Newt fell over in a fit of quacking hysterics. "Oh, that's great." He panted breathlessly. "That never gets old."

The soldier straightened. His face reddened and scowled. I understood his anger, but he'd passed the test. The first to not recoil from my "imaginary" stone. It was perhaps cruel to pelt a man with a real rock but conjuring a phantom stone was a waste of magic when the genuine item worked as well.

"Your name, soldier?"

"Pyutr, ma'am."

I wrote it on my list of potential unbelievers. The list consisted solely of his name at the moment.

"You may go now."

Newt chuckled. "That was almost as good as the one you tagged in the groin." He collected the stone and returned it to me. "But my favorite was the soldier you hit in the shin who did all the swearing and the little dance." He hopped about in a reenactment, remarkably accurate given the differences between a man and a duck.

The next soldier appeared, and Newt sat eagerly.

"This rock is not real . . ." I began once again.

My familiar stifled a chortle. Tears ran down his watering eyes.

So it went the remainder of the morning. Soldiers came in. I gave my speech. I threw my rock. Newt heaved with laughter. The Captain was my last test. He failed. He sat and rubbed his bruised knee while checking the list.

He couldn't read it. My parents had neglected such education, and Ghastly Edna had never learned herself. The lore of witches is taught through doing, not reading. But writing was a useful skill, so I'd developed my own script of squiggles and symbols I found both lovely and practical. Though it always seemed to be evolving, growing more sophisticated over the years, I never had any trouble reading it. I think there was magic involved. I wasn't so much creating a new script as discovering an old one that never was.

The Captain handed over the list. "Will there be enough to do the job?"

"Thirteen," I said. "You'll be lucky if six are possessed of the skepticism required."

"And will six be enough?"

"I couldn't say."

"Damn it! I thought witches knew the future."

"Knowing what will be is not the same as knowing how it will come to pass."

The Captain sighed. He was a man very near the breaking point, and I pitied him. I was tempted to give him an answer and tell him I knew the future. Somewhere in my tomorrows lies either vengeance or death or both. But, of the brave men of Fort Stalwart, Ghastly Edna hadn't made mention.

"No one can catch tomorrow."

The Captain grinned. "Very true. And almost wise. Tell me, did they teach you such nearly enlightened yet vaguely mysterious phrases in witch's school or do you make them up as you go?"

"I little of both," I admitted.

"It must be tiring, speaking in riddles and circles."

"Sometimes."

Newt quacked, warning to be wary of sharing too much with the Captain. Part of the witchly ways is to maintain a veil of mystery. Witches should never be thought of as human, even if they usually are. Once I'd asked Ghastly Edna the reason for this tradition. "Because that is the way it has always been" had been her answer.

I'd admitted too much to the Captain already, but I couldn't see the harm. He'd likely be dead in a few days. This saddened me. He was a good man. Not handsome or dashing or especially competent, but good. I had no desire to see a good man wasted.

My mouth watered. He wouldn't have triggered such a response normally, but I was under tremendous stress. It made holding to a strict diet all the more difficult.

If the Captain noticed my grumbling stomach, he was polite enough not to mention it. I excused myself to begin my enchanting. Thirteen swords would require a few hours of work.

Newt once again spoke up without prompting. "If you're not going to eat the White Knight, you should pick someone else. One soldier won't be missed, and even if it didn't solve the problem, it should tide you over until the goblings get here."

My familiar made sense as he so often did. The demon in him knew how to make evil seem practical and necessary. It was true that one soldier would not be missed, that if his sacrifice served to give me strength to concentrate on more important matters, then it could be worth it.

This was assuming that consuming a man I didn't truly desire would satisfy me. It seemed just as conceivable that it would only serve as an appetizer. Once I gave in to the impulse, I might find myself incapable of eating just one.

Wyst of the West could probably satisfy me for a long time. The Captain might appease my stomach for a month or two. I doubted an ordinary man could keep me full for three days. The only way to find out was to actually devour a man.

Regardless of any moral dilemmas, now was not the time to study my cannibalistic urges.

On our way to the armory, Newt whispered temptations. "Oh, there's a nice, fat one. Bet he'd fill you up. Or how about that handsome, young specimen. Lots of lean muscle."

He shut up while I asked the weaponmaster for his thirteen finest swords. While he retrieved them, Newt murmured, "A tasty morsel, don't you think?"

I waved my broom in small circles over him while mumbling.

"What are you doing?"

I touched him lightly on the head, and all his feathers fell off in one instant molt. He was still gaping at the pile of white fluff when the weaponmaster returned. Gwurm took the bundled swords from the weaponmaster, who ogled bald Newt but didn't say anything.

Other soldiers lacked his control. They pointed and laughed at the featherless fowl. Gwurm merely smiled while Newt threw annoyed glances. It was a hard lesson for a duck that wanted to be terrifying, but it kept him quiet.

Gwurm dropped the bundle on the bench outside my tent. "If you won't be needing me for anything, I should be drilling with the men."

I wished him well and granted him leave. He cast one last amused smile in Newt's direction.

"That's a good look for you," said Gwurm. "Nothing scarier than an angry plucked duck. If you cut off your head, you'd be every cook's worst nightmare."

Rage flashed in Newt's eyes. He looked about to pounce upon the troll. I didn't know who would kill who in a fight, and I had no desire to find out just now.

"Newt, inside."

Muttering, he did as told.

Gwurm left for drills, and Penelope decided to go with him, merely looking for an excuse to visit the fort's dusty floors again. I had no objections. She just wanted to be helpful. I doubted the soldiers would appreciate their dust-free fort, but in times of trouble, we all must contribute what we can.

Newt poked his head out of the tent. "This isn't permanent, is it?"

The spell would only last until dusk, but I didn't tell him. I even suggested that perhaps Gwurm had a good point, and I was thinking of magically removing his head. Not only would it make him a more proper witch's duck, but his cast aside skull sounded like a tasty snack. He disappeared back inside with a disgruntled quack.

I laid out the swords on the ground before me. Thirteen was a nice witchly number. It was a quirk of magic that enchanting thirteen swords was easier than one or twelve or fourteen. Only the magic knew why this was, and it kept these reasons to itself. But magic, by its very nature, defies true understanding. It follows its own rules, and often ignores those rules when it feels like it.

I arranged the swords in a circle, blades outward. Then I sat in the ring's center and spent the next four hours with my head down, mumbling, and enchanting. Technically, witches do not enchant. We curse. It's a slight difference. I endowed the swords with the power to dispel illusions in the right hands, but as they were cursed, any man who called upon the magic would age a day for every phantom destroyed.

Cursing is tedious, uninteresting work. Most witch magic is not particularly flashy. It gets the job done without making a big show. Wizards love throwing up their hands, bellowing, and shooting sparks in the air. Or so Ghastly Edna had taught. It was their stock and trade. But witchly showmanship was mostly in the feigned madness, pointed hat, unflattering frocks, and raspy crackles.

Several hours of uninterrupted cursing later, I took a break. I opened my eyes. The swords shimmered with half-finished magic. It was coming along nicely, and I stood with a slight smile.

I turned and saw Wyst of the West sitting on the bench beside my tent. I had no idea how long he'd been there. It could've been hours. It was an old witch's trick to pay him no mind and act as if I'd known he was there all along and merely had yet to address him. I hobbled into the tent, right past him, and poured myself a bowl of boar's blood, kept warm and salty by magic. Newt glared but wasn't speaking to me. I didn't ask if he'd noticed how long the White Knight had been waiting.

I took a sip of blood, wiped my mouth, thought better of it, and took another drink without wiping it away. I let the red cover my upper lip and dribble down my chin. Just enough I reckoned to be unappealing without overdoing it. Then I stepped out of the tent, walked past Wyst of the West once again, and paced a slow circle around the thirteen half-cursed swords.

He had yet to say anything or even make a noise. I decided I'd been witchly enough.

"Do you plan on sitting there all day?" I tried to sound as if I didn't care, but truth be told, his presence unnerved me. Only Ghastly Edna's superior schooling prevented me from showing it.

"I've come for the test," he replied.

"There's no need."

He stood, looking very insulted. "You tested every man in the fort. I see no reason I should be an exception."

I chuckled. "I saw no reason to bother with a test that I'd already know you'd fail."

"What makes you think I'd fail? I understand well what you've told me about these goblings."

"Understand perhaps. But to understand is not always enough."

"Are you going to test me or not?" It was the first time I'd heard him sound even remotely cross.

Rather than argue the point, I agreed. I found a flat stone, explained its "imaginary" nature, and threw it right at his face. He didn't flinch. The stone stopped an inch from his nose. It hung there a moment, held by his protective aura, before falling to the ground.

"Now do you see? There's no way to know if you held your ground because you believed me or because you knew your magic would protect you."

He nudged the stone with his boot. "I see, but I also know that I believed you."

"Yes, I think you did, but sometimes understanding and belief aren't enough. You've spent too long hunting this horde. No matter how much you think you understand, no matter what your strength of will, some part of you will always think the goblings real."

He looked as if he might argue but thought better of it.

I asked, "And what do you need an enchanted sword for when you already possess a fine magic sword yourself?"

He adjusted the weapon on his hip. "The enchantments on my weapon only serve to give courage to the men who fight by my side and keep the blade ever sharp and rust-free. But for phantom goblings, it has no special powers."

"I'm certain it will serve you well enough when the time comes."

Wyst drew his enchanted weapon. Sensitive as I was to light and capable of perceiving the powerful magic blazing on the blade, I winced. Such potent enchantments were the stuff of legend, the product of years of master enchanters. Anyone who looked upon the unsheathed weapon would feel either invincible by the White Knight's side or stricken with sickly fear if standing against him. My eyes adjusted to the brightness just as he returned the weapon to its scabbard.

"That is a great power you carry," I remarked.

"A great power for great good."

"Or great tragedy," I whispered.

He heard anyway. "What do you mean by that?"

"Nothing."

There was no hiding the anger in his voice this time. "Stop talking riddles, and speak plainly!"

I allowed myself a long glance at his pleasing face. His eyebrows were furrowed, and he glared. I should have thrown a half-wise, half-mad chuckle at him and gone back to my sword cursing. It would have been the witchly thing to do. As I so often did in the White Knight's presence, I fumbled my witchfulness.

I limped close to him, keeping my head stooped and one squinted eye aimed at his chin. "Without your magic, you couldn't convince a handful of men to stand against the gobling horde. When the time comes, many will die."

"They are soldiers. It is their duty."

I allowed myself a chuckle. He was trying to convince himself more than me.

"True, that is," I agreed. "But that does not change the fact that most would have abandoned their duty without your influence."

"Those without honor."

"True, that is too, but the common man would trade his honor for his life any day. And precious few would throw it away on a lost cause."

"This is not a lost cause."

I hobbled away and whirled my hands in a peculiar way. "Perhaps not. Perhaps it is merely a nearly lost cause, an almost fool's crusade. But these soldiers would care little for such distinctions."

Wyst of the West stood rigid. He gripped the hilt of his sword with white knuckles. "These men fight, and yes, some will die, to prevent greater disaster."

"Again, this is true. But in the end, no matter how right the fight, no matter how necessary the sacrifice, you will ultimately be responsible for whatever happens." I lowered into a deep crouch and spoke with a rasp. "That is a burden I wouldn't care for myself."

His form went slack, and I glimpsed a terrible weariness in his eyes, if only for a moment. I knew then I'd struck a nerve. It was the witch's way to help men face such hard truths, but Wyst of the West needed no help. His was a virtuous soul, and every death must have weighed heavy on that soul.

He stood straight again. His sadness disappeared behind a mask of sobriety. "The order teaches that evil and injustice must be fought, that they cannot be ignored and wished away by good intentions. That sometimes, sacrifices must be made for the greater good."

"Yet another undeniable truth."

I sat in the circle of swords, making it seem as if getting to the ground was a great effort for weak knees. I lowered my head and waited for him to go away.

He didn't.

I sat there with my eyes closed and thought distracting thoughts. I mentally recited remedies and secret witchly lore and anything else to keep me from thinking of him. Underneath all that strength and virtue, Wyst of the West was still a man. As vulnerable to guilt and regret and the pain gathered simply through living. I wanted to comfort him, to clutch him to me and push away his pain if only for a little while. Such compassion was forbidden by my trade. And my curse.

"One last thing, witch," he said.

I kept my head down and my eyes closed. "Yes?"

"How is your duck?"

I called for Newt. He emerged from the tent in all his embarrassed baldness.

"Oh, my. That isn't my fault, is it?" Wyst asked.

"It's his own doing," I replied. "Nothing serious. He'll be fine in a day or two."

"Glad to hear it."

The White Knight and I exchanged brief glances. I couldn't offer him a comforting hug, but his burdened soul was lightened by my plucked familiar. Wyst of the West smiled, and I smiled back. Then he bid us good day and left. I didn't watch him go.

Newt waddled to my side. "If you're not going to eat him, can I at least kill him?"

"I very much doubt you could."

He shrugged. "Just the same, I'd be willing to give it a go."

He strolled back into the tent, and I went back to work.

he days before the gobling horde's arrival were busy. The soldiers drilled relentlessly with the aid of the White Knight's inspirational presence. The goblings were certain to rely on sheer crushing numbers. The men of Fort Stalwart, in turn, would have to rely on superior teamwork. They were arranged in groups of three who were to stand back-to-back-to-back. In theory, this allowed every man to concentrate on the dangers at his face. In practice, I suspected it would not go so smoothly. Men would surely break when confronted with dozens of gnashing teeth despite the Knight's presence. Once a soldier of a trio fell, the other two were presumably close to follow. But there was no denying the transformation of clumsy, inept soldiers into a determined, if not especially skilled, fighting force.

I was very busy myself. Each day, I borrowed Newt's body and checked the goblings' advance. They progressed directly for the fort. This was no coincidence. Just as the phantasmal men had been sent to kill Ghastly Edna, so this horde had been made to destroy this outpost. I was certain of that. For what larger purpose, I couldn't say. My mistress and this fort had nothing in common, save their isolated and harmless nature. Yet they weren't random targets.

I thought much on this conclusion. Ghastly Edna had never

mentioned any sorcerers with grudges against her, and this imaginary horde was powerful magic for such an insignificant fort. I couldn't see the reason for either attack, but there was time enough for such mysteries after the gobling horde was destroyed.

Newt's spirits rose as the horde neared. Giddiness replaced his sour disposition. Every day meant his chance to kill drew closer. The demon in him looked forward to bloodshed. Any bloodshed. The trees near my tent bore deep gashes and slices from hours of his own restless practice. Opportunities for outright slaughter were rare, and he wanted to be in top form when the time came. Sometimes I'd watch him rehearse. During an especially zealous session, he felled a pair of trees with a single swipe of each wing. He hacked them into kindling amid satisfied quacks.

Gwurm and Wyst became good friends. My troll developed a great respect for the White Knight. It was not exactly hero worship, but it came close. I saw no harm in it. There were worse men to admire, and Wyst of the West clearly came to value Gwurm's friendship. He saw Gwurm as more than merely a valuable addition to the fort's barely competent fighting ranks. More than once, I glimpsed the troll and the Knight conversing on breaks between drilling. Gwurm, being of good humor, could even bring a smile to Wyst's perpetually somber face on occasion.

Such smiles were all too brief. Wyst was an attractive man, but he was undeniably handsome when he smiled. It was a crooked grin, and a dimple showed on his left cheek. Every time I glimpsed it, I couldn't help but smile myself. And fantasize about things unwitchly.

As for my broom, she grew more anxious every passing day. She started sweeping everything in sight with a nervous fever. Getting her to sit still was next to impossible. I had to hold her tight on those times I needed her at my side. Penelope twitched even then. Had I not been strong as I was, I wouldn't have been able to keep hold. But at least it looked properly witchly to see me wrestle and scold my broom on occasion.

I myself was so busy that my cannibalistic urges fell to the wayside where I easily ignored them. After cursing the swords, I spent a day recruiting beasts to the cause. I spent another mixing medicines for after the battle, assuming there would be survivors. A dubious assumption, but it was always best to be prepared. Another two days went in the pursuit of collecting and bottling various spirits found deeper in the forest. I found some rot nymphs nesting in a dead log, and a slumbering earth lord in an apple seed. Nothing that would be of much help in the conflict, but some wonderful finds still.

Finally, I performed a ritual of good fortune on Fort Stalwart and its men. I walked through the fort mumbling, occasionally screeching, sometimes merely shouting, dipping my fingers in a bowl of water, and sprinkling it about to ward away evil spirits. None of it was true magic, but made the men feel better knowing their witch was hard at work, and they'd need every last scrap of confidence when the time came. Ghastly Edna had always said that in most cases, false magic was just as good as the real thing. Sometimes even better.

Then came the day when I met with the Captain and told him that this would be the night. He took me at my word and didn't even bother to send out scouts to double-check. I was pleased to have earned his trust. He took the news well, but he'd had time to prepare himself.

"Can I ask you something, witch?"

I nodded.

"Why are you still here?"

I'd already asked myself that question sometime during those days. The answer was an easy one. I cared about this town-to-be, these people. My vengeance motivated me as well. The defeated horde would lead me to its creator, but revenge was not my true purpose. I wanted to destroy this threat and restore Fort Stalwart to all her bustling status. She was but a ghost now, a memory of what she'd been. I missed her, what she was and what she might become provided she wasn't devoured by goblings.

Part of me wanted to share this with the Captain, but another part knew better. I'd already become too familiar with him. He regarded me too much as a person and not nearly enough as a witch. So instead of answering the question, I did what any good witch would do and offered a cryptic reply that could mean as much or as little as he wanted to make of it.

"Everyone must be somewhere, and this is as good as anyplace else."

He laughed. "One day, you'll give me a straight answer."

"One day." I pulled my hat low. "Perhaps."

THE EVENING BEFORE THE battle, I borrowed Newt's body for one last scouting flight. I drifted low over the trees, not really thinking much on the goblings. At this point, the horde occupied little of my thoughts. While the men of the fort clearly grew more preoccupied at the prospect of this fight, I hadn't been taught to think like that.

"Worrying is a fine thing, dear," Ghastly Edna had said.

"To worry is to acknowledge that the world is unpredictable, and there is power in understanding one's own powerlessness at times. But too often, worry takes on a life of its own. Men are quite prone to this. They'll plague themselves with so many 'what if's and 'if only's that they soon forget to ponder the true possibilities before them. Which inevitably leads to poor decisions. Whatever happens will happen. Sometimes we have say over the future. Sometimes we do not. Either way, worrying alone never accomplishes anything."

So I didn't. I'd done all I could, and when the time came, I would do more. For now, it was all just waiting.

The sun had nearly surrendered all its light to dusk as I settled in the middle of the gobling horde burrows. The creatures stirred restlessly in their holes, readying for the night.

The gray fox stepped from the bushes to greet me. "Good eve to you, witch."

"Good eve to you, fox. Still alive, I see."

"Yes." She grinned slyly. "I'm afraid these goblings haven't proven nearly the challenge I'd hoped. I'm just far too clever."

"There are worse faults," I said.

"Very true."

"Your game may well end tonight."

The fox nibbled at her fluffy tail. "I was growing bored with it anyway."

Braver goblings crept from their burrows. They kept to the shadows. Their eyes glittered all around us.

I spread my wings. "I must be off then. Good game to you, fox."

"Good battle to you, witch."

I took flight as the goblings closed in on the gray fox from every direction. She scratched lazily behind her ear.

Several more ambitious goblings scampered up a tree and tried to fly after me. Three immediately tumbled from the sky. Imaginary goblings flew no better than the genuine beasts. Two others managed to reach me though one kept spinning around with each flap of its wings. That one, I simply dodged without bother. The other tried to bite off my foot. I crushed its skull with a single demon-infused kick and kept on my way, leaving the chattering shrieks of the horde behind. As expected, they were going the same direction as I, toward Fort Stalwart.

The fight wouldn't take place in the fort proper but in a clearing to the south. It was here that the goblings would emerge from the denser woods at their present course. The soldiers would meet them there within sight of Fort Stalwart.

I'd summoned a touch of magic to push away the clouds and coax the moon full and bright. It was nearly as clear as day. The battle would be dangerous enough without men stumbling about in the dark. The soldiers were most impressed with this feat of magic that in truth was the easiest task I'd done of late. But men think of the heavens as vast and uncontrollable along with anything else they cannot touch.

Word had spread that tonight was the night. Every man had known it was coming, and a grim anticipation had been hovering over Fort Stalwart. It ceased hovering and pounced upon the soldiers' hearts. Wyst of the West's magical aura of gallantry kept outright terror from claiming most, but even the White Knight's impressive enchantments could only dull the fear, diminishing it to a grim trepidation, a quiet frightfulness.

There had yet to be any last-minute deserters, proving how powerful Wyst's magic was. Even without it, he was a presence of heroic determination. Everyone knew the White Knights capable of great deeds. Legends of such circulated through the fort as the men clung to their fading courage. It helped calm the fear because none realized that for every valiant, impossible triumph against impossible odds, there were thousands of forgotten foolhardy slaughters. But Wyst of the West was so certain of victory, even I couldn't deny it as an almost forgone conclusion at times. Glorious feats might be accomplished when men gathered their will together, and Wyst had enough will for all the fort's soldiers. And then some.

Wyst of the West stood at the forefront. The Captain and Gwurm took their places at his side. I landed before the Knight and called upon a small magic to speak in my own voice and not Newt's.

"They'll be here within the hour."

The Captain sighed heavily. Gwurm kept to sharpening his sword with a stone. Wyst of the West kept staring sullenly into the woods. Though I knew worry lay in his heart, he kept it from his face.

There was one small preparation left me. I flew to the back of the battlefield where Newt waited in my body along with a small assembly of thirty-nine bats and thirteen owls. They stirred as restlessly as the men. I returned Newt and my souls to their proper flesh and held up a bowl of thick, dark red liquid.

"You must drink this."

The first bat crawled forward and lapped at the contents. He twisted his already twisted face. "This blood has gone bad."

"It has always been bad. It is the blood of the undead, my blood. I sprinkled in some spices to make it more palatable."

The beasts each took their sip, complaining in turn.

Time fell away while we waited. It didn't stop. Nor did it drag or pass very quickly. It just ceased to be. One moment claimed the field. A moment of waiting that saw soldiers milling about both anxiously and fearfully. Some wanted to get it over with. Others wanted it to last as long as possible. And finally, mercifully, the waiting ended.

Orange pinpoints shimmered at the forest's edge. First dozens. Then hundreds. Then thousands. Countless pairs of beady, shining gobling eyes gazed upon the army they'd come to slaughter. The shadowy creatures kept in the darkness, and it was easy to imagine the horde as a single, enormous beast with ten thousand eyes and slavering jaws.

As it turned out, there was a bit more waiting to do as the horde took silent measure of the army. I found it hard to believe the horde knew fear, but there was no mistaking its hesitation. It had come expecting the element of surprise, to devour half the soldiers before they were even awake. Now it faced a prepared foe.

"What are they waiting for?" Newt asked, his voice dry with bloodlust.

"Death comes in its own time," I replied.

He threw a glare. He wasn't in the mood for one of my witchly phrases.

Pair by pair, the orange eyes slipped back into the darkness of the wood. The army murmured in confusion. Some no doubt even entertained the notion that the horde had retreated. I knew better.

The earsplitting shriek of ten thousand gobling voices shattered the air. Goblings poured from the forest in a great cloud. Truly, more of a hopping tide as most goblings in the air crashed to earth within seconds. There were so many. So many more than even I'd conceived of. And they just kept coming.

The army took several steps backward. The men were seconds from breaking into chaos when Wyst of the West drew his enchanted sword. Its gleaming power washed over the soldiers and gave them the courage they needed. He shouted the charge. I don't think anyone could have heard over all the horde's shrieking, but the White Knight dashed forward, sword held high, and the men followed him into battle.

Newt ruffled. The demon rose up in his flesh. The only sign of this was a bloodthirsty burn in his eyes.

"Not yet," I said.

The army and the horde collided. Despite all the rigorous training and my own contributions, I half expected the goblings to gush over the soldiers, reducing them to a field of bloodred grass and gnawed bones. This was how most of the men in the front of the charge fared. An avalanche of goblings buried many. Others ran about with the beasts clamped to their throats and limbs. There were screams, certainly, but nothing could be heard save the hungry shrieks of the horde. It looked as if the army would only serve as the horde's next meal. Then the miraculous happened. The soldiers started fighting back. Even more miraculously, they actually did so with some effect.

Of course, a soldier couldn't swing a sword in this battle without striking a gobling or three. Yet the horde mingled with the army without overwhelming it. It was impossible to see much in the chaos. Goblings died in the groves. Men fell. It was too early to guess as to who would be the victor, but as nearly all the army remained unconsumed, I could only take this as a good omen. And reading omens is a witch's trade.

Goblings spread from the orderly jumble of the battlefield

and, naturally, many scrambled my way. I let them approach close enough that I might glimpse the wrinkles under their shining orange eyes.

I threw up my arm, thrusting my broom high. A needlessly dramatic gesture, more worthy of a wizard than a witch, but even witches are allowed to indulge themselves on occasion.

Newt bellowed with all his demonic might. His ferocious quack was the first sound I'd heard over the goblings' cries. He bound forward, wings spread, head low, drooling just a bit. The bats and owls flew after and over him. The beasts had drank my blood, taken on my will, and were instruments of my own unbelief. The contingency of goblings disintegrated with every slashing claw and biting fang. Some popped like bubbles. Others deflated into empty skins. Others only partially disappeared, losing limb, wing, or even head to glancing slices. My flying beasts kept on. There weren't enough to face the true horde, but they could circle the battle, striking down any goblings trying to slip from the field.

As for Newt, his job was to keep the goblings from pestering me. He was a gobling-slaying whirlwind. His fervor manifested in an artful variety of slaughter. Disemboweling. Beheading. Dismembering. Chopping. Mincing. De-boning. No two goblings died exactly the same way. Truly, Newt was an artist, and I felt bad he didn't get to exercise his talent more often.

While the men, bats, owls, troll, and demon duck fought in the defense of the realm, I found a stump to sit on and watch. There was nothing else to do. I could pick up a sword and slay goblings, but this would've been unwitchly and wouldn't make much difference. One more sword wouldn't turn the battle. Until some difficulty of a more sorcerous kind appeared, my part was done.

Newt took his place at my side. Yellow gobling ichor covered him bill to webbed toe. He grinned widely. "Well, that's that. Seems none of the little beasts want anything more to do with us anymore."

The piles of goblings slain by Newt's razor-sharp bill and serrated feathers lay close by, and the rest decided that was enough. I expected Newt to ask permission to rejoin the battle, but he hopped on the stump. He curled up beside me, looking happier than I'd ever seen. If nothing else, at least he'd gained something from this. I stroked along his slime-drenched neck.

"They're doing better than I expected," he remarked. "The men, I mean."

I reckoned the volume of gobling shrieks to have lessened by half, but I also guessed half the army to have fallen. The army and the horde were too evenly matched. Wyst of the West's training and my contributions had prevented a slaughter. But if the army stopped the horde at the cost of every man's life, then victory would belong to the goblings. Sorcerous illusions could be remade. Dead soldiers stayed dead.

I searched the madness of the battle for familiar faces. Wyst of the West, Gwurm at his side, appeared among the throng. The Captain wasn't with them. Wyst and Gwurm struck down dozens of goblings before being swallowed into the chaos. I glimpsed soldiers carrying my enchanted swords and found them to be every bit as effective as I'd hoped. Goblings dissolved beneath the cursed blades, but for every one slain, ten rose to take its place. It was a contest of tactics against numbers. After a while, I stopped watching and studied the stars, only barely hearing the cries of goblings, the wet slice of blades cutting into flesh, and the ripping of teeth and claws. It was a lovely night, and the undead in me enjoyed the stench of sweat, blood, and ugly death rising from the field.

Wisely, I'd eaten a big meal before the fight to keep my curse from distracting me. Dark thoughts still whispered. I was so busy ignoring them that when my opportunity finally came, I almost didn't notice.

It started as a ripple in the ether, the ambient magic in the air. Powers were being invoked. The horde's shrieks lowered in pitch. Goblings stopped fighting and burrowed, kicking up clouds of dust. They disappeared into the earth, leaving a field of confused soldiers and gobling corpses.

"Are they giving up?" Newt asked.

I knelt down and put a palm to the ground. The world below throbbed with raw magic. Whatever, whoever, was behind the horde was changing the rules. Victory through defeat wasn't enough.

Slimy flesh bubbled from the holes. What had once been ten thousand goblings was now one hideous amalgamation, a creature of nightmares that could only exist through darkest sorcery. The soldiers didn't know what to do with this new foe. They stood confounded as mounds of eyes, mouths, limbs, and wings grew in the field. The countless little faces growled.

Finally, Wyst of the West attacked. His enchanted sword sank into the mass of gobling flesh up to his wrist. Wyst struggled as the blob sucked him up to his shoulder. Then, with a satisfied bellow, the horde swallowed the White Knight whole.

My heart stopped. Its beating wasn't strictly necessary, but this was the first time it had ever just ceased its reliable rhythms.

The field exploded, and the beast revealed itself in all its terrifying power. The horde towered one hundred feet high. Tendrils shot out and dragged men to gruesome deaths. The air filled with screams and crunching bones.

Wyst had been the army's courage. Faced with this horrible foe, the men broke. They scrambled for their lives. It was the wisest course of action. The horde could no longer be defeated by enchanted blades or heroic determination.

"Stay here, Newt. You too, Penelope."

"What are you—"

I strode forward through the rush of fleeing soldiers. They were too panicked to notice my lack of limp. When my hat fell off, I doubted anyone gave it much thought. The horde swept forward, a ravenous tower of phantom flesh. Too powerful for an army, but wholly vulnerable to one witch willing to do what she must.

What once had been ten thousand illusions was now one. Tremendous in size. Awesome in might. Terrifying in its endless devouring hunger. But while I couldn't destroy ten thousand phantoms, one—even one of such sorcerous might—was far more vulnerable.

Perhaps I was walking into the horrible death Ghastly Edna had prophesied. Even stranger, perhaps this was my vengeance. Not for my mistress, but for Wyst of the West. Even if I couldn't love him, I could avenge him. He'd given his life to stop the horde. I could do no less.

The horde paused before me. Its countless eyes studied this morsel standing before them. For a moment, I thought it might have sensed my trap, but I was too tempting a snack. With a hungry snarl, the horde rushed forward and engulfed me.

It was dark and hot inside the beast. I couldn't see. I could barely breathe. The horde's insides smelled of rotting meat and pungent decay. Things brushed against me. Tortured screams reached my ears. There was death in the darkness, a death terrible enough to repulse even my own accursed nature. Dozens of sharp fangs tore away bloody chunks of my tempting alabaster flesh. Acrid saliva burned my nostrils and my skin. I ignored the agony as best I could. I thought of Wyst and how his lips might have tasted had I ever gotten the chance.

How long I remained in the belly of the beast I couldn't say, but suddenly the horde stopped eating me. It uttered a low, queasy grumble, and I found myself vomited into the cool night air. I hit the ground a bloody mess. Had I truly been alive, I most surely would have been dead. My curse wasn't bothered by such trivialities as being half devoured. My right leg was tattered, red flesh ending at the knee. The skin and muscle of my hands and fingers were stripped to the bone. When I drew in deep breaths, air slipped away through gashes in my throat.

The mountain of goblings quivered. Its thousands of mouths grimaced. It swayed to and fro and came crashing down in a groaning mound of slime. The illusion had eaten my flesh, and in my flesh was the power of my unbelief. And unbelief, along with witchly magic, was a most virulent poison to a phantom.

The horde convulsed as it dissolved. It blackened and shriveled. It whined and hissed. Within minutes, it was nothing more than a pool of greenish goo. Eyes and teeth and soldiers' corpses were strewn about, covered in yellow muck. In the middle of it all lay Wyst of the West.

He stirred and groaned. He was covered in slime. Un-eaten. Alive.

And my heart started beating again.

13

My *curse restored me* with such potent efficiency that I was whole by the dawn. Even my stump of a leg grew back as strong and whole as if it'd never been lost. For a while at least, I looked witchly without having to work at it. It made tending the wounded easier.

And there were a great many wounded and remarkably few dead. Men had fallen, but their teamwork had kept the goblings from finishing the job in most cases. Of Fort Stalwart's five hundred soldiers, only a hundred numbered among the dead. Over three hundred were injured. Some had only been nibbled on, able to patch themselves up without my help. Many more had been devoured to various extents. There was an epidemic of missing parts. Men were made of so many bite-sized pieces: ears, fingers, lips, noses, hands, feet. Though men preferred having all their parts, their loss wasn't truly life-threatening with some rudimentary treatment.

There were far fewer men needing more from me. Those more seriously wounded were usually dead. Though men were delicate creatures, they might survive grievous harm that surprised even me. Perhaps survive was too strong a word. Rather, they managed to put off their death for a few hours.

I did what I could for those fading heroes, but even a witch's magic can't stave off death when it must come. I accepted this with the wisdom that all men must perish eventually.

Just an hour after dawn, after I'd treated the rest of the men, I reported to the Captain's quarters. Like most of the soldiers, he hadn't survived the battle unscathed. He'd lost his right hand down a gobling's snapping jaws. Strangely, this didn't bother him in the least. He was too glad to be alive and considered himself fortunate. Justly so. Other men had lost much more.

Newt shuffled in behind me, covered in dried gobling goo. The Captain and Wyst of the West looked me up and down.

"You're looking better, witch," the Captain remarked.

"That which does not kill me rarely bothers me for very long. It is my curse."

He glanced at his bandaged stump. "Doesn't seem like much of a curse to me."

I smiled. "As all good curses should seem."

Of all the men, only Wyst of the West remained unharmed. His enchantment had prevented a single gobling bite, even after he'd been swallowed whole. This wasn't to say he was invincible. I was certain if I hadn't unbelieved the horde, he would have suffocated in its gruesome folds.

"How are the men faring?" Wyst asked.

"Well enough. Most will live, but many will never fight again."

Wyst nodded solemnly. "Their brave sacrifice will be remembered."

The Captain chuckled. "I don't think so. When people speak of this battle, they won't talk of the soldiers. They never do. No, they'll remember the courageous White Knight who led the fight." He nodded my way. "Perhaps the witch who finished the horde. History remembers its heroes and villains. Everything else is lost to time.

"It's as it should be. To fight and die is expected of every good soldier. And honestly, without your help, we'd have been slaughtered. The victory is yours, not ours."

This was only half true. Certainly the men would have perished alone against the horde, but neither Wyst nor I could have defeated the goblings without the army's support. But heroes are carried on the backs of a thousand forgotten faces.

Wyst of the West almost argued the point. Right or wrong, that was the way of the world's memory.

"It doesn't matter," the Captain said. "Right here, right now, we're alive. The horde is beaten. The realm is saved. That's why I called you here, witch. To offer you a taste of my favorite wine." He held up an hourglass-shaped bottle. "I save it for special occasions. I think this qualifies."

He poured three glasses. The deep red liquid looked like blood but smelled of sweet grapes that had grown in a patch near Ghastly Edna's cabin.

Wyst politely refused his glass. "I don't drink wine."

The Captain grinned. "Very well. More for the witch and I then."

"I don't drink wine either," I replied, "but I will take a glass."

I held it under my nose. The scent reminded me of home.

"I could use a drink," said Newt. His quiet act had finally lost its appeal.

Neither man seemed surprised by Newt's sudden speech. He was a witch's duck after all. If he wasn't going to be midnight black or fanged, then talking seemed only appropriate. He hopped on the table, and the Captain cheerfully poured my familiar a drink.

"To victory," the Captain toasted. He tapped his glass on my own and Newt's. He gulped down his drink while Newt lapped at his and I inhaled pleasant remembrances. I allowed the Captain his moment, all too brief alas. Then I ended it.

"The horde has been defeated, but its shadow remains."

The Captain set his wine aside, a quizzical expression on his face, but Wyst of the West knew what I meant.

"The goblings are dead, aren't they?" the Captain asked.

"As they were never truly alive," I replied, "they could never truly be killed. But they are as dead as phantoms can ever be. No, the horde is finished, but it was never the true threat."

The Captain drew in a deep breath. "More riddles, witch?"

"No riddle." Wyst clasped his hands behind his back. He looked me in the eye, and I didn't look away. "The goblings were a product of sorcery. Whatever power created them sent the horde here for a purpose. Just because the horde was defeated, doesn't mean they won't try again."

The Captain paled. "Another horde?"

"A possibility," I said, "but I think not. The horde was beaten. Whatever comes next, and something will come, will not be so easily defeated."

The Captain lowered his head. This was news he didn't want to hear. "Easily? Are you saying we could be facing something worse?"

"I'm not. Because I will find the sorcerer responsible. And I will kill him."

Newt quacked for more wine, which the Captain poured. "How?"

"His own magic shall lead me to him. I leave tomorrow."

"And I'll go with you," said Wyst.

I looked deep into his eyes and he into mine. "As you wish."

I'd already known he would be coming along. As a White Knight, it was his obligation. I welcomed the company. Not only because he was an able champion, a worthy ally on a dangerous journey. But because after thinking him dead, I'd realized just how much he'd come to mean to me. My limited experience told me I was no longer smitten. This was something more. And I sensed it, or perhaps merely hoped it, within Wyst of the West as well. I couldn't deny it any longer.

I tapped my broom twice on the floor. "Come, Newt. We must prepare for our journey."

Newt slurped down the last of his wine and followed me out the door. I cast one last glance over my shoulder at Wyst. He smiled, but it was a slight smile. I tried not to make it more than it was. What could a handsome, chaste White Knight want with a hideous, undead witch?

Not two steps out the door, Newt had to contribute his opinion. "Why are we taking him along? He'll just distract you."

He expected me to argue, but he was quite correct. Even now, my mind was a splintered fragment of properly witchly thoughts and fleshly desires. Such diversions could only hinder me on my destiny, perhaps even lead me to my horrible death.

And honestly, I didn't care a whit.

GWURM ADDED A FEW more imaginary, dead goblings to the small pile outside my tent. "Is that enough?"

I nodded, standing before the mound.

"They're already starting to turn," Gwurm observed. "I don't think they'll last more than a few hours."

"I don't need the corpses. Only the raw magic within them."

I grabbed a gobling from the pile and held it over a bowl. I stared into its crossed eyes and mumbled. The green corpse dissolved, melting between my fingers. Most of it evaporated into the true nothing that it was, but a few silver drops fell into the bowl. Newt and Gwurm leaned closer to watch the shimmering fluid slide like a living thing up one side of the bowl and down the other. I quickly snatched another gobling and repeated the procedure. My companions watched for a while, but the distillation of phantoms quickly grew boring.

"What happened to your nose?" Newt asked.

The troll felt the hooked, red protrusion on his face. "You don't like it?"

"The old one looked better. This one's the wrong color. And it's far too big for your face."

Gwurm sighed. "I know. Unfortunately, my old one was eaten by a gobling." He sniffed and snorted and flared his nostrils. "I was hoping it might look distinguished."

"No. Just big. But the purple eye looks good. Old one get eaten too?"

"Sucked right out of the socket by one of the little bastards."

"Where'd you get the parts?"

Gwurm patted the pouch on his belt. "It pays to be prepared."

"What else have you got in there?"

Gwurm opened the pouch and glanced inside. "A tongue, some teeth, a terrific big toe I save for special occasions." He tied it closed. "And of course, my unmentionables."

"What unmentionables?"

"Well, if I could mention them, they wouldn't be unmentionables, would they?"

"Oh. So that's where you keep them."

"Certainly," Gwurm replied. "Where else would you expect? Wouldn't be polite to walk about with them dangling for all the world to see, would it? Not to mention I prefer them wrapped up nice and warm. Promotes reliability when I need them."

"I guess." Newt grinned. "But it seems an awful small pouch to be carrying all that."

Gwurm twisted his new red nose with a displeased frown. "I'll have you know it's not the size of your unmentionables, it's how you use them." He popped off the nose, snarled at it, and snapped it back on, upside down.

"That looks better, but you might drown if it rains."

The troll spun it into its proper position and shrugged.

"You know what you should have done. You should have put on the bad nose before the battle. That way, you'd still have your old one."

"That's a very good idea. I'll have to remember that next time." He crossed his one yellow eye and one purple eye to glare at the nose. "Are you certain it doesn't look even a little bit distinguished."

"No. Just big and red."

Gwurm growled.

Newt chuckled.

It took but an hour to distill the goblings into their raw magic. The tall mound was reduced to a small bowl of fluid silver. It throbbed, ebbing and expanding as if breathing. Newt and Gwurm watched as I coughed up a wad of phlegm and spat it into the pure sorcery. The yellow and red lump lay atop the liquid. I waved a hand, grunted, and the spittle sank slowly into the silver with a bubbling hiss. The ooze darkened and gurgled.

"What are you doing?" Newt asked.

It was a pointless question. I couldn't explain it to him. In many ways, I didn't know myself. Witch magic is not an exact craft, and Ghastly Edna's tutelage had never been rote study. Rather, it was more of an art, an intuition. My mistress couldn't have taught me magic for every situation. Life was far too unpredictable. But I knew this would work. I knew without knowing.

I poured the bowl's contents onto the dirt. The dull gray liquid swirled, broke apart into a dozen tiny puddles, and rejoined. I bent down and broke the surface with two fingers. It rippled, and in its depth, images formed. The art of divining is nothing more than clearing your mind and trusting the magic to show you what it wished. So I watched, and I learned.

Newt stared into the depths by my side. He didn't see anything beyond the slipping gray and black patterns. Certainly they looked pretty to his eyes, but he couldn't glimpse the shapes within shapes. There were fields of grass, a forgotten road, a bridge, bothersome half faeries, a river, and a place of memories forgotten. A land that didn't exist waited at the end. It wasn't an exact map but a journey of images that would make sense in its own time.

The silver pool burned away in a slow yellow flame. The scent of seared moss and wet wolf hair was left behind. A patch of grass spontaneously sprouted, uprooted itself, and scampered away as a random aftereffect of the universe reabsorbing the raw magic.

"Did it work?" Newt asked.

"Yes."

"You saw the way to our vengeance?"

It was technically my vengeance, not his. But demons have a great passion for revenge, and I was willing to share. I was less concerned with avenging my mistress. Preventing Fort Stalwart any more woe was more my true goal. Motive was irrelevant, and if by doing one I accomplished the other, then this would be a stroke of good fortune.

"When do we leave?" Newt asked with a grin.

"Soon."

"How far is it?"

"As far as it is."

"Will there be perils?"

"Most certainly."

"What sort of perils?"

"Oh, the usual sort, I expect," I replied.

The grin faded from his bill. "You don't have to talk in circles with me. I'm your familiar."

"Yes, but it's good to keep in practice. Now, go clean yourself up."

Newt was far too excited to get upset. He dashed into the tent to wash the gobling slime from his feathers. He stuck his head outside the flap. "Are you certain we have to take the White Knight along?"

"Quite certain."

He was far too zealous to be bothered by this either.

Gwurm was still fussing with his red nose. He'd twist it one way, then another. Nothing looked right, especially since I sensed a streak of vanity in the troll. Men might find it strange that such an unsightly creature cared so much about one misshapen nose. Though Gwurm was the only troll I'd known, I felt positive he was quite handsome by trollish standards. Even if I was wrong, one didn't have to be beautiful to be vain.

I held out a hand. "Can I see it a moment?"

He plucked off the offensive crescent and gave it to me. I clasped it in both hands, pressed my palms together, and rolled them in four small circles. Then I held up a new nose. It was his exact shade of gray and rounded, less hookish.

He twisted it onto his face. "Eye dink yu furgud sumdin."

I took back the nose long enough to poke out two nostrils. He held it between fingers and thumb and studied it with one squinted eye. "Not bad. Strong without being overbearing. Excellent symmetry. And I think it will add some character to my profile." He plugged it into place and pretended to gaze thoughtfully in the distance. "What do you think?"

"Quite handsome," I replied. "Perhaps even a touch distinguished."

"Do you really think so?"

"Certainly."

I started toward my tent.

"I couldn't help notice you're whole again," Gwurm said.

I held up a hand that only hours ago was a few threads of bloody flesh clinging to bone. Now there wasn't even a scar. I wiggled the fingers and didn't feel a stitch of pain. My new leg was as strong and reliable as the old. I'd known myself practically immortal, but I'd never been hurt so badly before. I'd hoped the damage would at least last the day.

"I didn't want to make you feel self-conscious," Gwurm said. "I just wanted to tell you that when I first saw you dragging yourself across the field, just after you'd defeated the horde, that I thought to myself that you were the most dreadfully appalling sight I had ever laid eyes upon, a corpse mocking death and all the natural world." He adjusted his nose a little to the left and smiled. "Just something I thought you'd like to know."

I kept my back to him to hide the blush upon my cheek. As men and trolls, even witches had their vanity.

14

*I**t had been a** tiring day, and both my familiar and my troll
fell asleep soon after dusk. My undead nature denied me
sleep once again. Penelope didn't ever sleep, though such
things were difficult to discern with a broom. I passed the
long night staring into the sky and reading the stars.

A voice interrupted my stargazing sometime in the early
morning hours. "Looking for something?"

I didn't glance down at the gray fox standing by my feet.
"Still alive, I see."

"Yes. Those goblings were a tremendous disappointment.
Although I did enjoy the battle. Very colorful. Very unpredictable."

"You were watching."

"Curiosity is an affliction I bear proudly as a fox. So you'll
understand that I must ask, what do you hope to see up
there?"

I stopped gazing long enough to glimpse the fox's grinning
face. "Nothing. And everything. Isn't it enough to just look at
the stars?"

"I wouldn't know." Her tail flicked side to side. "I've never
found them very interesting. But we beasts aren't of the
mind to see them as men do. They're too distant. Just something to fill the part of the sky not occupied by the moon."

"That's how most men perceive them," I said.

"Well, men aren't as far removed from animals as they might pretend. Their hands are their gifts, not their minds." She lay in the grass and rolled on her back. "Tell me, what does a witch see in the sky?"

"Omens."

She squinted and scanned the heavens from one horizon to the other. "What does an omen look like?"

"Everything. And nothing."

The fox chuckled lightly. Whereas Newt found my witchly way with words annoying, she appreciated the twisted and turning phrases. "Can we beasts see omens?"

"I don't know. If any beast can, I would imagine a clever and curious fox could."

She rubbed her nose with her forepaws in a show of humility. "Then I think I'll watch with you."

The fox joined me in my omen-searching, and being both clever and curious, she soon spotted a sign in the twinkling heavens.

"Is that one?" she asked of a pair of shooting stars.

"Yes. You have a good eye."

"What's it mean?"

I help up my hand as if to touch the sky. "It portends the birth of a monster in the southlands, who shall one day threaten a kingdom."

"My, that is a good one."

"Very good. You've got a knack."

She looked a short while before picking out a row of five twinkling stars.

"Ah, another excellent find. Those stars speak of a love that is doomed to be swallowed by the sea."

"Really?"

I nodded.

Beside being clever and curious, the fox was also skeptical. She asked about a patch of clouds she expected to have no significance. A notion I corrected.

"Somewhere, a curious fox is asking questions."

She squinted at the moon. "Is everything an omen?"

"When one knows how to see them, the universe shares its secrets easily. Perhaps too easily. In the hooting of the owls I hear of a fort's soldier suffering a terrible nightmare. In the fluid waves of the grass, I see a termite mound waging war against a neighboring anthill. Those falling leaves, their swirling flights speak of a priest's indigestion and a serving girl's stubbed toe at the same time."

"Must be terribly distracting."

"It is. But only at first. Then one learns to ignore the vast, trivial majority. That is the real talent. Not in seeing omens, but in not seeing them."

"So I gathered. But I must say I am glad to be a fox and not a witch. I wouldn't want to learn something to unlearn it."

"There's a great deal of unlearning in the witch's trade," I admitted. "There is a limit to how many forbidden secrets a mind can safely carry."

We resumed omen-watching. As I was in an oracle's frame of mind, I still glimpsed the occasional portent. Nothing too important. Just the stomach flu of a king I'd never know whispered by a gossiping breeze and the pure joy of a new mother somewhere to the north shown in dancing shadows. A flight of birds told of a continent that would be sunk by a careless wizard's apprentice. That one could be prevented, but as I didn't see which continent or when, I gave it little thought.

A stag dashed from the wood, chased by a wolf. The wolf

caught the stag, sinking her teeth into its flank, but he kicked free. By the time the stunned wolf had regained his senses, the stag had escaped. The disappointed wolf skulked away. Spontaneously, two plump, dead geese fell from the sky. They landed but thirty feet from the wolf, who didn't notice and walked away hungry.

"That must be a terrific omen," said the fox.

"Actually, that is just a very unlucky wolf."

Then I finally saw my omen in the face of the moon. It spoke of a dangerous journey being undertaken. It was a vague sign, and without a doubt, it spoke of a hundred such journeys across the world. But I relied on my witchly judgment and decided it applied to my quest as well. Even if it didn't, I was tired of waiting.

"You'll excuse me, fox, but I must seek out my vengeance."

"Early hour for vengeance-seeking," she said.

The first hints of dawn were tracing the edge of the horizon. "All things come in their own time."

"Might I ask one last question?" Her curiosity compelled her to ask without waiting permission. "This quest of vengeance you're about to begin, did you see danger in it?"

"It would be a poor quest otherwise."

"How much?"

"More than enough, my good sense tells me."

"Do you mind if I come along then?"

"You're very welcome to."

She started toward the woods. "Very good. I'll see you along then."

"Where are you going?"

The fox turned and grinned. "I said I'd see you along. You won't see me. Good vengeance to you, witch."

"Good following to you, fox."

She disappeared into the darker shadows of the forest.

Gwurm slumbered beside my tent in his usual slumped posture. In this light, he looked very much like a snoring rock. I smacked him across the back with my broom. What would have been a bruising crack to a man was barely a tap to the thick-skinned troll. He raised his head and untangled his limbs. Trolls were either awake or asleep, and he stood instantly alert.

"Is it time?"

"Yes."

"Should I fetch the White Knight?"

"No need."

I stirred the air with my fingers, and a morning mist descended from my hand. It gathered at my feet in a soft blue cloud. The mist rose as playful air spirits danced within, visible as glimpses of dancing shapes. The cloud zipped around my head and beneath Gwurm's legs.

"That's enough now. Off you go."

The mist giggled and floated off toward Fort Stalwart.

I went into my tent and found Newt. He proved harder to wake than Gwurm. Though he had a passion for vengeance, he was also prone to moments of laziness. Such contradictions were part of his demon nature.

"It's not even dawn yet."

I began filling a sack with witchly odds and ends I might need on this journey. I grabbed up mixing bowls, bottled spirits, healing herbs, and my moldy squirrel hide. It was strange how such a little thing could mean so much. It reminded me of Ghastly Edna, my home with her, and my new home here. Just rubbing the thinning fur between my fingers made me feel better. Not all magic lay in death curses, hungry phantoms, demon waterfowl, and animate brooms. Most magic wasn't even magic. It just was. Smiling, I placed the hide against my cheek.

Newt sighed sleepily and opened one eye halfway. "That's a very big sack to be carrying."

"Gwurm can manage it."

He jerked awake. "We're not taking him along, are we? Bad enough we have to bring the White Knight. This whole journey is going to be a long, queasy stomach for me."

For a duck, he groused very well.

"You'll get used to it."

"Don't you think it would be a good idea to leave someone behind to watch the tent."

"Are you volunteering?"

He sputtered.

"Perhaps you're right," I said. "Wouldn't do to have mere mortals nosing about, discovering forbidden secrets only witches are supposed to know."

"Well, that's true, but what is a witch without her familiar at her side?"

"Yes, but I can think of none I trust more with my secrets."

Newt flapped and hopped. "There's Gwurm. What about Gwurm?"

I dropped my squirrel hide into the sack. "I didn't think you liked him."

"Of course, I don't." He shook his head and puckered his bill. "He's too smart for a troll. And he gets along too well with the White Knight if you ask me. Especially for a witch's companion. But he's loyal. I have to give him that."

"And trustworthy?" I posed.

"Very trustworthy!" Newt shouted enthusiastically.

"And good to have around when danger is about?"

"Yes! I mean, he's strong and a good fighter." He swore

under his breath. "An adequate fighter, but his trollish nature more than makes up for his lack of talent."

"I see. So he's loyal and trustworthy, strong, perhaps a little too intelligent but good to have at your back when facing peril. All in all, he seems a very good companion for a dangerous quest of vengeance."

Newt's bill dropped open. "I didn't . . ."

"Yes, you make an excellent point. It seems foolish to not take him along." I smiled. "Thank you, Newt."

He glared when he thought I couldn't see, but I glimpsed it from the corner of my eye. It was his own fault for engaging a witch in a duel of words. Ghastly Edna had taught me the way of twisting dialogue.

"As for my secrecy . . ." I held up a crooked stick decorated with tatters of cloth, black and red feathers, and beaded strings. A grim badger skull sat at the top. The charm had no real power other than invoking superstitious fear in mortal minds, but it was protection enough. All my secrets would be traveling with me. The totem was a witchly touch, something to remind Fort Stalwart who lived in this tent and who would one day be returning to it, fate willing. I also thought it was rather pretty for a hideous, fear-invoking fetish.

Gwurm poked his head in the tent. "The Knight is here."

Newt belched wetly. "I know." He smacked his bill and stuck out his tongue.

I stepped outside. Wyst of the West and his gray horse stood beside Gwurm. I cast each a fleeting glance and stabbed my stick into the earth. I adjusted it to a crooked angle and took a moment to admire it.

"You summoned me, witch?" Wyst asked.

I traced three fingers on the badger's skull. It turned a

shade of dark red as if covered in blood. I tapped it again, and it shifted to a deep black.

"The spirits have spoken. It's time to begin."

Wyst of the West offered me a horse for the journey, but Gwurm proved suited for the job. His shoulders were wide and comfortable, and there was enough room for me and Newt on one side and my sack on the other. The troll's short legs were still able to keep up with the horse's brisk trot.

Newt wasn't happy. Wyst's virtue put the duck in ill temper, and he disliked Gwurm. He wasn't very fond of Penelope either. At least he didn't harbor any disfavor toward Wyst's horse although I suspected this too would come in time.

15

Wyst trusted me to guide him on the right path. Or perhaps he expected to not understand a witch's guidance. Either way, questions would have been pointless. All the answers I possessed made little sense to me at the moment, and I wouldn't have given them to him in any form he might have understood.

We passed the morning in silence. Sometimes Wyst rode slightly ahead. Sometimes, a little behind. Never alongside. Occasionally, he'd glance over his shoulder, or I'd glance over mine, and we'd look briefly into each other's eyes. And I would have no idea what he was thinking.

Wyst could be thoroughly inscrutable. It was part of his trade. White Knights were paragons of unflappable heroism. Underneath that stoic nature and righteous enchantments, I knew he was very much a mortal man. Perhaps this was merely wishful thinking on my part. Perhaps years of unspoiled virtue had killed any fleshly desires. Yet, in those glances, I felt certain I saw something, but did I see something because it was there or because I wanted it to be there? And did I really want it to be there?

Of course, I did.

Which begged the actual question, were these the desires

of a smitten heart or accursed appetite? I suspected a little of each. Desire was often a many-headed beast.

My thoughts on the subject were interrupted by Newt. "You do realize that we're traveling northeast?"

I tried to ignore him, but this was merely wishful thinking.

"And that the horde came from the south?"

"Quite aware."

Newt took a moment to groom his wing.

"Just making sure you knew."

He groomed the other wing.

"Because, it just seems to me, that if we were to follow the horde to its origin, south would be a better direction."

"I can see why you might think that. That's why you are the familiar and I am the witch."

Newt frowned, and Gwurm chuckled.

Newt couldn't argue, but the demon in him couldn't drop the point entirely. "So how far north is this sorcerer?"

My vision was making more sense with every passing hour. I shared what I knew, well aware it wouldn't satisfy him.

"Four trials. Trial by peril. Trial by strength. Trial by combat. And trial by magic."

"Trials? Didn't the vision mention perhaps something along the lines of miles or days?"

I merely smiled.

"I was hoping for something more practical," Newt said.

"Visions are rarely practical. Useful, sometimes. Insightful, often. Practical, hardly ever."

"It's a poor arrangement, if you ask me."

"I don't know about that," Gwurm said. "Always seems to me that knowing too much takes the fun out of it. It's the not knowing that makes life worth living. Who can forget the lesson of Doomed Bill?"

"Who?"

I was glad Newt asked because I was curious too. Asking would have gone against my witchly training. Gwurm was only too happy to share the tale.

"It happened that one day a prince was born in a small kingdom. Now a great many people are born any given day, and enough of those people are princes that Bill's arrival into this world wasn't all that special an event. The king already had four sons, so more heirs weren't really needed. In fact, an overabundance of heirs has been the undoing of as many kingdoms as a deficiency. But this isn't the story of a political back-stabbing and courtly intrigue it well might have been under different circumstances because Bill was born under the shadow of death.

"Now accounts differ exactly how it happened. I've heard it told a dozen different ways. Some say the palace midwife glimpsed a terrible portent in Bill's afterbirth which she proclaimed before expiring from fright. Others whisper that he was born with the date tattooed on his forehead. But the way I've heard most, the way I like best, is that as the newborn prince was being placed in his crib for the first time, the nursery doors flew open and in stepped the withered, gray figure of Death himself.

"'Bill,' the specter pronounced in an appropriately terrible and frightening voice, 'I have come for you.'"

Gwurm stretched out a hand, index finger extended.

"Naturally, this sent most everyone scurrying in fear. Only the prince's nursemaid had the bravery to stand before Death and plead for the child's life.

"Death of course would have none of that. But out of respect for the nursemaid's courage, he showed her his Black Scroll upon which the names and dates of every death that was, is, or ever will be is written. Just to quiet any further arguments.

"The nursemaid took one look at the scroll and observed that while Bill's name was on it, it was the wrong date. That the prince was fated to perish ninety-three years from this night."

Gwurm was an excellent storyteller, and Newt couldn't stop from asking, "What happened?"

Gwurm shrugged. "Death double-checked his list, discovered the maid to be right, apologized to everyone involved, and went on his way.

"But that wasn't the end of it. For Bill was cursed with the knowledge that no man should ever carry. He knew his day of death. In fact, because the nursemaid couldn't keep a secret, soon everyone did. And Prince Bill became quickly known as Doomed Bill.

"And from that moment on, poor Doomed Bill spent his life, all ninety-three years of it, waiting for death. Just waiting and waiting and waiting. Accomplishing nothing. Enjoying nothing. While others lived and loved and went about discovering the pleasures and pains of being, Bill just sat in his castle and moped. And when the fateful day arrived, Death came for him again."

Newt shifted on my lap. "So he wasted his life? That's the moral of the story? Some ridiculous prince throws away his life because he's stupid, and this is supposed to enlighten us?"

I hadn't noticed Wyst had slowed to ride closer. He kept looking ahead. I only knew he'd been listening by his sudden remark. "That's not the end of the story."

"Oh, good." Newt glowered at the Knight and troll.

Gwurm grinned slyly. "So Death taps Doomed Bill on the shoulder with one gnarled finger, holds the Black Scroll before Bill, and apologizes for the lateness of his arrival. Naturally, this surprised Doomed Bill who knew Death to be right on time.

"But as it turned out, Death had been correct the first time. Doomed Bill had been fated to perish his first night on this world."

Newt grunted. "Wait a minute. Death made a mistake?"

"According to the story."

"Death doesn't make mistakes."

"Everyone makes mistakes. Occasionally."

Newt snorted. "But people don't not die because of misread scrolls."

"It's just a story."

"Yes, but it doesn't make sense. Fate doesn't make mistakes. If it did, it wouldn't be fate. It would be, well, I don't know what. But it wouldn't be fate."

"I'm only repeating it as I've heard it."

"Fate makes mistakes," I said. "Quite frequently, in fact. It's just rare for someone to be in a position to notice."

Gwurm chuckled. "You're missing the point. There are things better left unknown."

"No. You're missing the point. He didn't know anything. He just thought he knew."

"That's the same thing."

"No. It's not."

"It's just a story," Gwurm relented. "Take from it what you will."

It grew quiet again, and I used the time to sift through my vision. The four trials ahead could come in any order, and each would surely be more dangerous than the last. Such was the nature of all worthwhile quests. Although I didn't know what form each would take, I thought us well prepared.

Gwurm had strength and good wits. Wyst of the West was both virtuous and brave. Newt had an eagerness to slaughter whatever might need slaughtering. My own witchly powers were formidable. And Penelope could keep the clutter at bay.

Newt spoke up. "Do you know what I've learned from that story?"

"That life is not in the knowing," I replied, "but in the finding out."

"No."

"That the wasted life is not worth living," Gwurm said.

"No."

Wyst of the West turned his head in our direction. "That no one, not even Fate itself, knows exactly what tomorrow brings?"

"No." Newt puffed out his chest and glared at the world in general. "Death should take more care with his paperwork."

16

A **worthwhile quest always** involved a great deal of nothing happening. Nothing noteworthy anyway. These are
the forgotten moments of legend, twenty years of dull and
unremarkable wandering condensed into a line or two on an
epic poem. A good storyteller knows what's worth telling
and what's not and what merits mention without excessive
details.

Nothing happened, and nothing kept happening for nine
days and nine nights.

But on the tenth day, an event of note finally came to pass.
Our small band of traveling vengeance-seekers came across a
pack of disagreeable elves. It wasn't so much a trial as an
inconvenience.

My mistress had told me of elves and their sorry lot. As
bastard children of mortals and faeries, they were of two
worlds and master of neither. It was a poor mating. Faeries
were innately magical creatures, but their magic was wildly
chaotic. Mixing it with mortal flesh halved its already dubious reliability while in no way dimming its potency. Elves
were nature spirits wrapped in smothering mortality. Though
mostly harmless, they could be dangerous in the same way a
monkey carrying a torch might set a forest ablaze.

We happened upon the elves late in the morning. They'd

set themselves up as guardians of an assemblage of planks bridging a short ravine. There were six of them. The tallest was half-ogre and stood a little over four feet. The shortest was half-goblin and barely a foot and a half. The other four were half-men. Like all elves, each looked like a short, thin version of their mortal parent with pointed ears, bushy eyebrows, and silver eyes. The half-ogre held a spear twice his height. The others were unarmed, but this didn't stop them from standing in our way.

"Halt!" the tallest elf growled. "None shall pass without paying the toll."

As a troll, Gwurm knew something about bridge-tolling. He appointed himself our negotiator and stepped forward. From my perch atop his shoulders, the elves seemed very, very small.

"How much?"

The spear-carrying leader smiled. "All your money."

"All of it, you say?"

The elf squinted. "Yes, all of it."

"Everything we have?"

"Yes! Every piece of gold, every scrap of silver, every worthless copper coin in your pockets."

"A little expensive, isn't it?"

The elf smacked the blunted end of his spear into the ground. "If you're thinking you can cross without paying, I wouldn't try it. We've got powers you couldn't possibly dream of."

"Is that so?" Gwurm glanced about our party from undead witch to animate broom to demon duck to invincible White Knight.

"You doubt our magic?"

"I say we make them pay double," the half-goblin shouted.

"Yes, double!" another seconded.

"Very well." The half-ogre raised his spear in proclamation. "Double the toll for you!"

"Double all the money we have?" Gwurm asked.

The flaw in such a toll seemed lost on the elves.

"I can see you're a force to be reckoned with. It seems a reasonable price. We'll pay it."

The elves murmured excitedly. The half-ogre quieted them down with a hard glare and pointed his spear at his feet. "Deposit your riches at our feet, and you may pass unmolested."

"Very well." Gwurm waved his hand at the spot. "Done."

The elves looked to their leader questioningly. He glanced to the bare earth as if to see something that wasn't there. "What's this?"

"You said all our riches, every piece of gold, every scrap of silver, and worthless copper coin. Well, that's all of it."

This was true. None of our party carried money. Witches, ducks, and brooms had no need for it. And Wyst of the West, as a White Knight, had taken an oath of poverty. Trolls might carry a coin or two on occasion, but not this day.

The elves muttered among themselves, sorting through the flaw in their demands. Finally, the half-ogre pointed his finger at Gwurm and said, "Ah, but we said double!"

"Double of nothing is nothing," Gwurm explained. "But if you'd like, we can give you thrice of nothing."

"Oh, why not quadruple it," said Newt. "We can afford it."

"Why not?" Gwurm agreed.

Most of the elves were thrilled with the offer until their leader smacked a cohort with his spear. "You idiots." He raised his spear again, a gesture he seemed very fond of. "If you won't pay our toll, you'll face our wrath. You fools have no idea what you're facing."

"Pray tell, what might that be?" Gwurm inquired.

The half-ogre puffed out his chest that, by elf standards, was quite full but hardly threatening. He lowered his spear only to raise it again. "First, there is Yog. He can spit fire. Then there is Rof who can summon rocks from the sky when he sneezes. And Gok, able to change his shape at will into terrifying creatures you couldn't even comprehend. And Vop, well, Vop can talk to worms."

The half-goblin added, "And snails. Worms and snails!"

"Yes, Vop, yes. And snails." He switched his spear to his other hand without lowering the weapon. "And I, Doz the Mighty, can bring life to the inanimate."

"Don't forget, Sof," an elf remarked.

"Hell's bowels, Gok. I was trying to keep him a secret."

"Sorry."

"Well, the damage is done. Sof, foolish full mortals, is our greatest weapon. He's invisible and can strike from anywhere, anytime. One by one, he can strike you down as your companions watch helplessly." He laughed. Unfortunately, elf voices are terrible for sinister cackling.

"Can I kill him?" Newt asked.

"Not yet." I patted his head. "Maybe later."

I glanced to Wyst. There was a trace of a smile on his lips.

"Strike now, my brothers!" Doz the Mighty shouted. "Show them what happens to those who defy us!"

The elves milled about their leader in a show of confusion.

Doz lowered his spear and ground his teeth. "What are you waiting for?"

"Uh . . . well, we've never struck before, Doz. We aren't sure how."

"Fine. I'll show you. You first, Rof."

Rof, who could summon rocks from the sky when he sneezed,

stepped forward. He drew in a few quick breaths. His nose twitched. His head drew back. And nothing happened.

"Well?" Doz asked.

"I can't." His nostrils flared. "Maybe if my allergies were acting up."

"Fine, fine. Yog, roast them."

Rof stepped back dejectedly as Yog prepared to spit fire. He puckered up and spat. Flame dribbled from his lips and sizzled away at his feet. He hunched over, clenched his fists, and spat again. A gout of flame erupted from his mouth and blackened his face.

"Damn it, Yog. I thought you were practicing."

Yog was too busy beating out his smoking eyebrows to apologize.

Next came Gok the shape-changer. His attempt went smoother than his companions. In a flash, he transformed into a vicious wild boar. It had wicked tusks and crimson eyes and sharp hooves. Unfortunately, it was barely the size of a large rat. While Doz the Mighty berated Gok, Gok grunted in an effort to grow larger. He expanded to twice his size, belched, then shrank to half his previous volume.

"My turn," Vop the worm-talker announced. He stepped forward with bold determination.

"Step back, Vop."

The snail-talking elf backed away. Gok the shape-changer, who seemed trapped in his tiny boar form, retreated to the back of the group.

"I guess it's up to me." Doz the Mighty released his spear. It floated forward and hovered before Gwurm. "Now you'll know fear, fools. How will you fight a weapon that has no wielder?"

The spear danced about, jabbing at the troll without actually attempting to stab him.

"Now grovel before me, and I may spare your lives."

Gwurm grabbed the spear in one thick hand. The weapon twisted and trembled in his unbreakable grip.

"That's not fair! You can't do that! Let it go!"

Gwurm released it. The spear hopped back and shook angrily. It traced intricate patterns in the air with its point.

Penelope jumped from my hand and faced the spear. The broom caressed the spear up and down with her bristles. Doz's spear shivered, bowed to Penelope, and floated aside. She returned to my side.

"Stupid spear." Doz the Mighty folded his arms across his chest. "But there is one left. The last and most deadly of our band. That's right, Sof. Strike! Strike now!"

No strike came.

"Sof! What are you waiting for?"

Still, no strike came.

"Damn it, where's Sof?"

The elves offered a collective shrug.

"Who saw him last?"

They exchanged whispers.

Vop the worm-speaker said, "Uh, thinking on it, I've never seen Sof."

"Me neither," Rof the rock-sneezer said.

"Me either," Yog the fire-spitter added.

Gok the shape-changer, still a boar, snorted his agreement.

Doz the Mighty shook his head slowly. "Well, this is just embarrassing."

A sneeze came from the back.

"I did it! I did it!" Rof squealed with his elf voice.

The sky darkened. A shrill screech filled the air, and a monstrous red bird swooped from the sky.

"Aha!" Doz the Mighty thrust his hands high. "Now you shall see the grave errors of your ways!"

The roc swept from the sky, snatched up the band of elves, and soared away, quickly disappearing into the horizon. Only Doz's spear was left behind.

"Can we pass?" Gwurm asked.

A disembodied voice spoke. "Sure. Go ahead."

We bid Sof the Invisible and the spear a good morning and went on our way.

17

Though Wyst and I could go days without saying much of anything, we did exchange a few words over the course of our quest. Nothing of much importance from a questing perspective, merely polite salutations of "Good morning" and "Good night" with the occasional observation about the weather or scenery or some such other trifle. Though words were a wondrous invention, both tremendously practical and inexhaustible in supply, there was no need to waste them. The silence was contagious, afflicting both Newt and Gwurm. My broom and Wyst's horse were the only ones not noticeably affected.

The truth was, I wasn't at all comfortable speaking to Wyst for very long. I didn't trust my discipline. One unwitchly slip of the tongue could reveal too much of my growing affection for him, which was difficult enough to hide without saying anything. Too often I caught myself smiling at him or staring at the graceful sway of his full shoulders. Fantasies, both carnal and cannibal, fell into my mind without warning, and each seemed harder to dispel than the last. None of these symptoms truly surprised me, but I was startled by the suddenness of their severity.

I couldn't read Wyst's mind, but I caught him smiling at me as often as he caught me. I suspected, like my own smiles, there were many more times when I didn't catch him. Often his eyes seemed to wander, however briefly, up and down my body. Almost as if he could see the shapely form beneath my wrinkled gowns. Each passing day, I was less and less willing to dismiss these signs as products of my own desires. This led to an odd dilemma.

Did Wyst see through my witchly disguise, or did he prefer his women plump and haggish? The latter notion meant that my curse might deny me the very man I desired. Such irony as repulsive beauty was not beyond possibility where a potent death curse was at play. And somewhere in the hell where long-dead, mad wizards might dwell, Nasty Larry was probably enjoying a good chuckle between tortured shrieks.

Such dilemmas aside, it was inevitable that Wyst and I would find ourselves in deeper conversation.

Bread was all Wyst ever ate. He lived upon two thin pieces a day. One in the morning when he awoke and one in the evening before he went to sleep. The meager diet and his personal enchantments sustained him very well. Even when he retired for the evening, he never seemed truly tired. And his body was the perfect balance between lean grace and masculine strength. At least, I thought so, and I'd spent enough hours studying it despite my efforts not to.

It was one of these moments of unwitchly indulgence that began a chat I'd been laboring to avoid. I was watching Wyst partake of his evening meal, wondering at what thoughts might be dancing behind his deep, dark eyes. I lost myself in the wondering and hadn't even realized he'd noticed my staring until it was far too late to pass it away as a casual glance.

He smiled from across the campfire. "Would you like some?" He held up a piece of dry, unappealing bread that I quickly accepted to cover my staring.

Newt gaped. He no doubt found the notion of eating any-thing without blood even more repellent than I. His bill dropped, and his eyes crossed.

Ghastly Edna had subsisted mostly on bread and rabbit and wild berries, but all I'd ever eaten was meat. Even as a newborn, I'd had a good set of teeth. The kind of sharp, snapping fangs that discourage a mother from drawing her undead child to her breast.

I sniffed the bread. It had hardly any scent, and nothing that put me in mind of dinner. But I felt I must, so I took a very small bite, chewed the morsel once, and forced myself to swallow. It couldn't hurt me, but it wasn't something I wanted to do again.

Newt's tongue dangled from the side of his bill.

I gulped down some raw pheasant to keep myself from gagging.

"It's . . ." I struggled to find a word that was both truthful, yet not too harsh.

Wyst found it for me. "Bland yet edible."

I nodded.

He grinned. "I wasn't always a White Knight. I remember what food tastes like. Vaguely."

Though I knew Wyst to be a mortal man, the admittance struck me. I'd gotten the impression that White Knights were much like witches. Much of their trade involved acting odd. Not a witchly strangeness, but a chaste peculiarity. For to deny one's self the simple pleasures of the flesh was cer-tainly unusual.

Such lapses of character were unavoidable after spend-ing enough time with someone. As a professional courtesy, I should have ignored it, but I couldn't stop myself from search-ing for the mortal man.

"Do you miss it?"

Had Wyst pretended not to hear the question, I would have pretended I'd never asked it. "Not much. Although I do find myself aching for a good apple cider on rare occasion."

I set my own bread aside as if I might actually finish eating it. Newt eyed the slice and backed away a few steps.

"And what about yourself?" Wyst asked. "Do you ever find yourself aching for something?"

From anyone else, the question might have been bold, but he'd answered mine. It was only fair I answer his.

"It's difficult to miss what you've never had."

Wyst took a sip of water from his canteen. "I wouldn't know about that. It's the things we've never had that we sometimes miss the most."

"I've never had an appetite for anything but flesh, raw and red. It's my curse. So it really isn't the same as denying myself a pleasure. It's more like giving jewelry to a tortoise. Neither necessary, nor appreciated."

Wyst nodded. His eyes strayed to the evening stars as he finished the last of his meal. "I see. So there are no indulgences you deny?"

This was an important moment. A good witch would offer a reply that hid away her humanity. A dozen responses came to me, all of them appropriate in their vagueness. I didn't choose any of them.

"There are"—I lowered my hat to cover the blush reddening my cheeks—"temptations."

Newt mumbled. In many ways, he was a more demanding master than Ghastly Edna, but he wasn't my master. His opinion counted for little.

"Newt, fetch some wood for the fire."

He squinted at the healthy flames and the small yet ample

supply of fresh branches beside it. "Why don't you send Gwurm? He's bigger and has hands."

I glanced over at my troll, curled up, boulderlike, in his early evening retirement. "He's asleep."

"So wake him."

My familiar looked into my eyes and attempted to stare me down. His insolence had grown bothersome of late, and another lesson was in order. I should have given them more often, but his contrary nature sprang from his demon. I disliked having to punish him for his enchanted nature. He was, much like myself, engaged in a constant struggle with a part of himself. I only disciplined him when I felt he wasn't giving the conflict enough effort.

I removed my shawl and tossed it over him. "Now where did I put that Newt?" I asked softly. Then I lifted the shawl to reveal a single white feather left in the duck's place.

Wyst knew me well enough to know I hadn't done Newt permanent harm. "Where did you send him?"

"I misplaced him, so I suspect he's in that place where all misplaced things go: that secret locus where lost keys, loose coins, and almost-yet-not-quite-forgotten memories wait to be found. He'll turn up eventually, like all lost things. Most likely when we aren't even looking for him.

"How does one become a White Knight?" It broke witchly protocol to ask such a question and reveal that there were things I didn't know. With Newt lost, I found myself even less concerned with my witchliness. I wasn't willing to completely abandon it, but it was easier not to worry when the only witnesses were a sleeping troll, a broom, and a horse.

"It's a secret."

"Witches are very good at keeping secrets."

Wyst and I exchanged slight smiles.

"Yes, I suppose they are."

He took his third and last sip of water for the evening and returned his canteen to his pack. Then he laid down on his blanket on the cold, hard ground. It was all I could do to keep myself from pouncing upon him, running my hands down his chest, and maybe biting off his nose. Before that urge grew irresistible, he started his story, looking into the sky as he did.

"No man is truly good or evil. They may be greatly one or the other, but they always have its opposite to some degree. And sometimes, certain men, through either chance or design, find their souls in perfect balance. Both good and evil in exact equality. And when a man reaches this state, fate takes special notice of him and chooses him for greatness. I was such a man.

"The Order employs seers whose only purpose is to wander the land, find men like this, and recruit them. I was in a tavern, half-drunk, when one of these seers found me."

I tried to imagine what Wyst might look like half-drunk, but even a witch's imagination had its limits.

He closed his eyes and folded his hands across his chest. "This seer explained to me that I was at a very important moment in my life. A soul can't maintain this perfect balance for long, and one way or another, something would tip me in one direction. Then, as is the tradition, he offered a glimpse of what either choice would bring. After which, I chose to accept his offer and become a champion of right."

"You make it sound so easy."

"It was."

"But if your soul was in perfect balance, not good or evil but neither and both, how could you decide at all?"

He turned on his side, his back to me. "Usually there's a sign. Some spend months waiting for it, but I wasn't that patient. I flipped a coin."

I laughed. I'd laughed before, but never like this. It was soft and musical and very mortal. I didn't mind at all.

"So how does one become a witch?" Wyst asked.

"It's a secret."

Wyst propped himself on an elbow and turned his head in my direction. "White Knights are very good with secrets."

I gazed into those deep, dark eyes. A heat rose in my chest, and my stomach grumbled. And I savored the sensations.

"Yes, I suppose they are."

18

Another week passed without a single trial to confront us. Nor anything even as interesting as a spot of disagreeable weather or inconvenience of elves. Newt remained lost, but had he been around, he would have surely observed this journey as far too pleasant for a quest of vengeance. I could wait for as long as required, possessing the near limitless patience that came with being ageless and a good witch, but my conversations with Wyst of the West did help pass the time.

It was nice to have someone to share my secrets with. I'd shared them with Newt and Gwurm and even Sunrise, but that had been a one-sided affair. My exchanges with Wyst were fair trades.

He told me of his youth, of his mother and father, of childhood friends and enemies, and what it had been like to be a mortal boy. I spoke of dark cellars, of Ghastly Edna and Nasty Larry, of not seeing the sky until I was eighteen, and what it had been like to be an accursed girl.

We spoke of hidden desires. Small ones, not overwhelming in their importance, but things we rarely admitted to. I learned his favorite food had been turtle soup, that he loved swimming, and that he had a great fondness for dogs. He learned my favorite treat was fresh rabbit brains, that I enjoyed making crafts with bones, and that I too had a certain fondness for dogs, though of a more rapacious sort.

Wyst never judged me. Nor did he pity me. Gwurm and Sunrise hadn't either, but White Knights lived different lives than trolls and prostitutes. It seemed a rare thing that men who had taken the mantle of unspoiled virtue could remain so accepting of others, even if forced by magic and fate into more unwholesome existence. I had to wonder if Wyst was an exceptional White Knight or if all his order were such paragons of righteousness and humility. If so, then the White Knights deserved every bit of their legendary reputation.

I didn't share all my secrets. I kept my beauty and my carnal desires to myself. Certainly Wyst of the West left a few unspoken himself. Everyone should carry a secret or two, if only for mystery's sake.

By the end of the week, we were traveling side by side, close enough to reach out and touch one another. We never did.

But it was nice enough to simply enjoy the possibility.

ON THE SEVENTEENTH DAY of our quest, we came across a river. Men may, in their obsessive fashion, divide the water along imaginary lines, but every witch knows there is only one river in all the world. It winds through the land, gathering wisdom to carry to the ocean. A wise witch always pauses to collect some of this knowledge whenever she can.

Wyst watered his horse and filled his canteens while Gwurm removed his head and dunked it along the shore. I bent on my knees and consulted the shallow stream.

"Greetings, River."

"Hello, witch," the water replied. "Lovely morning, isn't it? I always enjoy a lovely morning. Almost as much as I do enjoy a lovely evening. But I must confess rainy evenings are my favorite by far. Not that I've anything against the sun. But it can dry me out so. Sometimes when it rains enough, I get to run across so much more of the land. I love to carry away the soil and imagine what a fine canyon I might carve one day. Not that I'm impatient, mind you . . ."

The River always chattered without end, and I allowed him to blather a few more moments before interrupting.

"Pardon me, River, but I'm on a quest."

"A quest of vengeance," the River said.

"So you know."

"One does hear things."

I ran my fingers along the cold stream. "I was hoping you might offer me some advice. I saw a river in a vision, and I think you're my guide to wherever I must go."

"Indeed, I am, and I must say it is a great honor to be part of your undertaking. I've been important in countless others, but this is especially satisfying. Not to casually dismiss those that came before, but . . ."

I interrupted the River again. Fortunately, he never took offense.

"What is it about my vengeance that makes it so important?"

"Something to do with the shape of things to come. Like myself, you'll carve a great passage in the record of time. Or perhaps you'll simply dry out unnoticed as I've done on occasion."

I stooped lower, placing my ear near the water. "How so?"

"Alas, I don't know. That knowledge must lay farther downstream, and your tomorrow awaits upstream, where I can only know less than I do now. But no matter. I've done my part."

"Thank you, River."

"You're quite welcome, and good luck to you, witch. I envy you in a way. I must always travel onward, never looking back, never stopping. Sometimes I think I'd like to stop, even if only for a little while. Or perhaps even go back and see the things I might have missed. Could you do me a favor, witch? There's a lemon tree upstream with dangling branches. It hardly ever drops a lemon. Just teases me, that tree. Could you perhaps take the time to pitch a lemon or two into me? Won't take you but a moment."

"Certainly."

"Thank you. I do so enjoy a fresh lemon. Not so much as I enjoy apricots. But there aren't any apricot trees where you're headed, and I wouldn't dream of asking . . ."

The River kept talking, but I stopped listening. I informed Wyst and Gwurm that we would be following this stream and waited for someone to point out that we would be going a southwesterly angle after two weeks of traveling north. Neither made the observation, and Newt was still lost. And the brook's babbling was of no great importance.

Not far upstream, the lemon tree waited. A robin, a crow, and a vulture perched in its branches.

"Keep away," said the tree. "These are my lemons and I'll give them to the brook when I wish."

"Just a few, if you don't mind." I tapped the tree thrice with my knuckles, and two lemons fell into the River.

"Thank you," said the River.

"Well, you won't get any more from me," groused the tree.

I glanced up into the branches again. The robin and the crow remained, but a falcon perched where the vulture had been. All three jumped and soared overhead in wide circles.

It was then that I was struck by a sudden premonition. This was my very first premonition. I'd read the future in omens, but that was easy when one knew how. A true premonition was to know something without aid of signs or portents. It wasn't quite the same as having the magic talk to you. It was more like catching a whispered snippet the magic didn't mind you overhearing. Of course, like most premonitions, this was vague and mysterious information.

"Those birds have been sent to kill me," I said as I climbed on Gwurm's shoulders.

Wyst raised a hand to shade his eyes and looked upon the two ravens and a sizable albatross. Birds hardly posed a threat to me. Or Gwurm or Wyst either. Perhaps the albatross might snatch up Penelope and carry her away, but even my broom was no easy target. Wyst didn't sound skeptical as he asked, "By who?"

"By the sorcerer we seek, most likely."

"More illusions of flesh?" Gwurm asked.

Wyst replied, "Not quite. They're chimera. Shape-shifting creatures, beasts of the dream planes employed by sorcerers. Dangerous as anything alive because they can become anything that has lived and a thousand things that never have."

As I watched, the albatross became a small winged lizard, and a raven transformed into a yellow pelican.

Wyst spurred his horse onward. He didn't seem afraid, but he never did. He tutored us on what to expect while the creatures, in various winged forms, trailed from the air.

"The most important thing to remember is that chimera are compulsive shape-shifters. They can't hold any particular form for long, and that unpredictability can work against as much as for them. Their minds, like their bodies, are fluid, incapable of keeping to any strategy. One moment, you'll be facing a dragon-headed lion and the next, it will be a puppy or a weasel or perhaps a bass. Strike at these vulnerable moments."

A glance showed the chimera flying lower and closer.

"They'll warn before they attack."

The chimera followed for another hour. I mostly ignored them, only occasionally allowing myself a curious glimpse. The assortment of shapes was always different. First, three owls of different colors. Then a mallard, a goose, and a hummingbird. Then a condor, a larger hummingbird, and a flying chicken. Then a bat, a winged serpent, and an eight-legged turtle treading the air with its churning legs.

The chimera swooped just over our heads and screeched with warbling voices. They landed just ahead.

Wyst drew his sword. "They're ready."

Gwurm knelt to allow me to climb off his shoulders. He set aside my sack and cracked his knuckles. An odd act for a troll, given their lack of fleshly joints.

The chimera moved closer. Each took on a different form. There was a liquid grace to their shifting. Heads and limbs sprouted and shrank away and changed. Fur became scales became skin became feathers. Yet no matter what they became, whether natural beast or strange amalgamation, they always seemed to be wearing the right form. My witchly instincts told me the chimera's shapes weren't dictated by chance. There was a pattern at work, albeit the indecipherable pattern of living dreams. Understanding what cannot be understood is a witch's trade.

The first chimera became a great, hairy bear. The head shrank into the body and grew out of its chest. Its forearms became insectlike, ending in bladed hooks. The second chimera became a very traditional ogre. The third took on a serpentine form with a moose's head and a row of deadly spikes running down its spine.

We paired off. Penelope and I faced the bear-thing. Gwurm stood before the ogre. Wyst readied himself to battle the moose-headed serpent.

I knew what I must do to defeat my chimera, but I wasn't a talented enough witch to decipher three dreams at once. I trusted Gwurm and Wyst to overcome their own.

I whispered instructions to Penelope. She twitched her understanding, and then the trial began.

The ogre chimera charged Gwurm, but trolls are twice as strong as ogres. Gwurm hefted his opponent high in the air and slammed it to the ground. The chimera shifted into a monstrous bull. Gwurm held tight to the bucking beast.

Wyst and the serpent circled each other warily. The chimera snapped and snarled. The White Knight stabbed at it. Neither had drawn blood yet.

I was able to watch all this because my own magic had reduced the earth to sucking mud beneath the bear-thing's feet. It sank into the ground, screeching and howling. One bladed arm was the last to disappear. It wasn't defeated. I was merely guiding it into a more acceptable form.

The earth rumbled, and a giant centipede burst forth at my feet. It towered over me, clicking its mandibles and hissing. It snatched me up in its blades, whipping me from side to side, and sliced me in two at the waist. My lower half fell away, but the centipede grabbed me in a dozen short arms. It changed colors, from bright green to dull orange. Mucus dripped from its wriggling mouth. Then it hacked into my neck. There was the gush of blood, the pain of tearing flesh, and my head bounced to the ground where it came to a rolling stop.

The chimera, unable to hold its centipede form, melted and shifted once again. It became a large, two-legged toad with a face that was all mouth. It opened its jaws, showing rows of jagged teeth.

I could feel my body, but it was as if my neck was a thousand miles long. Giving direction to my limbs was a distant, deliberate affair. I was largely helpless. Penelope was not.

The toad pounced at my head only to be swatted down by my broom. The chimera shook its head clear and screeched at her. She moved in small circles before striking again in a full, wide arc. The force cracked her handle and sent the chimera tumbling away. It jumped to its feet, already shifting again. It sprouted feathers and a single enormous eye. Penelope shot forward and speared it in that eye. The chimera collapsed, very dead.

My broom wasted no time. She tugged free of her opponent and floated to my side. She swept my head back to my torso. It took a few moments for me to get my hands to shove my head back into place. The flesh of my neck knit back together, but even my powers of regeneration were limited so that it was a loose fit. A hard nod or a sudden jerk and it would fall off again.

I pushed myself up and studied the fight. Gwurm's chimera was now a thing with dozens of tentacles. The troll struggled, but he was wrapped in its smothering coils. He gasped just before his body surrendered to the pressure and fell apart. The troll pieces slipped from the chimera's hold. The beast became a badger with a peacock tail and kicked around Gwurm's parts, looking for a vulnerable portion.

I found a stone and threw it at the beast. It whirled, slobbering, teeth bared, and scrambled in my direction. The badger shape grew roughly human as it seized me in clawed hands. It expanded to tremendous size and parted its jaws to swallow me whole. At which point, I shoved an arm down its gullet. My curse gives me a knack for tearing flesh, and the malleable flesh of the chimera proved vulnerable. I punched through the back of its mouth and wrapped my fingers around something squishy and warm and hopefully vital. Although with chimera, this was mostly a matter of chance. The monster bit off my arm just as I squeezed. The chimera gurgled, staggered, and fell over. I was buried beneath its enormous form.

With only one arm and no way of freeing myself, I lay beneath the chimera and listened as Wyst battled the last one. There was a lot of grunting and shrieking, and this went on for some time. Finally, there was one last bubbling screech.

Then silence.

The beast atop me swayed. I thought it might still be alive, but then it rolled over. Wyst of the West knelt beside me. Multicolored blood coated his shirt. Sweat glimmered on his dark skin. He wrapped tender arms around me and leaned me against the chimera's corpse.

"Are you hurt?"

"Hurt, but not harmed," I replied. "How is Gwurm?"

"I'm fine, but I lost an eye. Watch for it."

Wyst fetched my legs, and by the way he was walking, I could see he was injured. His White Knight invulnerability must have failed him in some way. Some of the blood on his side was his own.

As I fished around the monster's slackened jaws to retrieve my arm, Wyst retrieved my sack. I reached in for some needle and thread to stitch myself together and instead found Newt. Like all lost things, he was in the last and most obvious place I looked.

19

Our first trial behind us, and none of us being in traveling condition, we camped beside the chimera corpses. Only Newt had escaped injury, and that was only because he'd missed the battle. This annoyed him. He would have rather taken part and been killed than lose an opportunity to fight. He sulked as the rest of us tended our wounds.

My injuries were the least pressing. I'd stitched myself together and within a few hours, I was restored. I liked the way the thick thread felt around my neck, and I imagined I looked quite horrible. But such was my curse that my flesh rejected the intrusive stitching. I was disappointed when it fell out.

Gwurm wasn't hurt much either, but after he'd been reassembled, we'd discovered some missing parts. An ear and a finger were nowhere to be found. He was fortunate enough to have a surplus of fingers in his pouch, but there was no replacement ear. He accepted the loss with his usual good nature, noting that while two ears were better, one would do fine.

Both Penelope and Wyst of the West required my attentions. My broom was very much a living thing now, and her handle would mend itself in time, providing she got enough dust to eat. I merely bound her with some torn cloth so she would heal straight.

Wyst's wound was the most serious. He'd suffered a deep slash to his side by the chimera's tusks. If I'd been able to use magic, it would have been easily treated. But my magics slid off the White Knight, and I had to rely on mundane methods. I wrapped the wound in a poultice to prevent infection. That he had to remove his shirt for treatment proved less distracting than I'd expected. Ghastly Edna had trained me well. Wyst was not a man. He was a patient. Touching his firm flesh, running my fingers across his lean, muscled body meant nothing to me.

Well, perhaps it meant something. But I concentrated on the wound and finished the task without surrendering to carnal impulses. Only after, did I realize the heat built up within me, especially warm in my lips, breast, loins, and, oddly, ears. I limped to the other side of our small camp to clear my head, pretending to study the dead chimera.

Death had merely slowed their shape-shifting pace. The corpses assumed various deceased forms every ten minutes or so, each smaller than the last. I expected them to eventually become dead bugs, then things too small to be seen, then nothing altogether. It seemed a perfectly natural state of decay for such creatures. Presently, the corpses were that of a hare, a wolf with antlers, and a three-armed man.

Newt beheaded the hare with a kick. "They weren't so dangerous. None of you were killed."

"We're all very hard to kill," I replied.

There was truth to Newt's observation. The chimera, terrible monsters in their own right, had never been a serious threat. The sorcerer who'd sent them must have known that. Their purpose had been to delay us, perhaps even kill one of us with some luck, and to take our measure.

"How did they know where to find you anyway?" Newt asked.

"No doubt, the sorcerer told them."

"How did he know?"

"Most likely, the magic told him. Just as it tells me where to find him."

"I thought the magic was on our side."

"Magic doesn't take sides. It mostly watches and waits for something interesting to happen and sometimes, especially when witches and sorcerers find themselves at cross-purposes, it encourages the most interesting things."

"Sounds as if the magic should find itself a hobby."

"Perhaps that is what we are."

Dusk approached. Gwurm went gathering wood, and Newt went hunting for dinner. Though Wyst and I had been gradually drawing closer over our quest, I sat far from him this evening for reasons I couldn't fathom. I often acted in ways I didn't understand when it came to Wyst. I suspected this was normal, and a good witch doesn't need to understand everything. Nor does she expect to.

Wyst squirmed. His pain was obvious, try as he might to hide it. Every shallow breath carried a soft wheeze. Few would have noticed, but I knew Wyst as few did. His pain distressed me more than even being eaten alive by goblings.

Silence crept between us. For the first time in a long while, I felt uneasy with Wyst.

He pressed his fingers to his wound and winced.

"Don't do that," I said.

"It itches."

"It's supposed to."

His hand hovered over the bandage.

"Leave it alone."

He sneered.

It was nice to see the boy beneath the man beneath the

White Knight. I smiled for reasons yet again not entirely clear to me.

Wyst scowled. "We can't all be fortunate enough to be accursed."

"Fortune can be fickle," I agreed. "Much like a White Knight's legendary invulnerability."

"A popular exaggeration," he said.

"So I gathered."

It was then that Wyst shared the limits of his enchanted invincibility. I was honored to be entrusted with the secret, but we'd shared many secrets. Our physical vulnerabilities seemed almost trivial beside secret desires and mortal admissions.

White Knights could be harmed in four ways: magic, drowning, honorable combat, and corruption. None of these were particularly easy. Greater magic can always overcome lesser magic, but magic greater than Wyst's enchantment was a very rare thing. While Wyst could suffocate, his enchantment allowed him to hold his breath for an hour. Honorable combat was a more general weakness. Even Wyst admitted he couldn't know what was honorable and what wasn't until he was actually harmed. Apparently, the chimera had met the magic's qualifications.

The idea of corruption was of special interest to me. A White Knight's virtue fueled his enchantment. When robbed of it, they were as vulnerable as any man. When captured, a White Knight was usually thrown into a dungeon for a month or a year or however long it took for him to fall to a moment of weakness. Even the most chaste soul would succumb to a piece of fresh fruit or a beautiful virgin's kiss. Then it was off to the chopping block or gallows. This method was far from foolproof. Often as not, the Knight lasted long enough to be rescued or escape.

"Wouldn't drowning be easier?" I asked.

"It would, but most assume that if you haven't drowned in ten minutes that you aren't going to." He lay on his back and breathed as little as possible. "And how exactly do undead witches meet death? Or do they?"

"I'm ageless. Not immortal."

I knew of four certain ways I might perish only through Ghastly Edna and her conversations with the magic. First, there was magic itself, but magic greater than my curse came only once every century or so. Fire, as both servant of life and death, could kill me. Except that as a witch, fire and I were very good friends. Only the most enraged flame posed any sort of danger. Being hacked into three or four pieces was perhaps the most effective, providing steps were taken to keep my parts from rejoining for long enough.

"How long?" asked Wyst.

"That largely depends on how many pieces, but a good month at the very least."

He squirmed uncomfortably. "And the last method?"

I hesitated to tell Wyst this. I'd always thought it impossible. Impossible is a concept embraced by mortals to keep their world safe. Yet some things are so unlikely that impossibility is not much of an exaggeration. But I trusted Wyst with my life. And my death.

"To have my heart pierced by someone I love."

There was another brief silence between us. Before either could end it, Gwurm came stomping into camp. He carried an impressive load of branches. Newt returned with a half-dozen squirrels for dinner. Wyst and I said nothing else to each other that evening. And when everyone had finally gone to sleep, I crept away and sat in the comforting dark just outside the campfire's light.

I watched Wyst from the shadows. His sleep was uneasy. His pain was minor, mere discomfort, but his every troublesome breath put a stitch in my side. I wanted to make him feel better. I also wanted to devour him one succulent morsel at a time. Only after he'd taken me in his arms, and I'd tasted his kiss and felt his warm skin against my own.

"You love him."

I was so intent on Wyst I hadn't even noticed Gwurm was awake. The troll sat beside me.

"I don't know," I said: "What is love?"

Gwurm chuckled. "Nobody really knows. It defies explanation in its complex simplicity. Like magic, I think."

The comparison made it easier to understand. Magic didn't require explanation, merely the understanding to know that it was there. So it was with countless other things in this world and beyond.

"I love him."

The admission was easier in the dark. And as Ghastly Edna had been my mother, Gwurm had become my brother. He took my slight hand in his own immense fingers.

I hadn't noticed Newt was awake too. "If the mistress could hear you now." He took a seat at my feet. "Witches and love, it's unnatural."

I ignored him, as I often did. Demons couldn't love. They didn't have the capacity to care about anyone but themselves. And I pitied him, and all demons, for it.

"You should kill him," Newt said. "If you do really love him."

It was typical demon reasoning to destroy a weakness before it destroys you. But I didn't want to kill Wyst of the West. He didn't frighten me. Neither did sorcerers. Or even love. Only one thing did.

My curse. And what it might make me do.

Wyst stirred on the edge of wakefulness. Deep inside, other things stirred in response. Especially my stomach.

20

Death curses are potent things. Only the greatest wizards are capable of them, and there's little point in holding back when you're about to die. Though I'd known this and lived with my curse all my life, I'd never truly understood just how accursed I was until I knew love.

I wanted to kill Wyst, to devour and digest him so that he would always be a part of me. I wanted to gobble him down because I loved him. But for the very same reason, I would do anything to protect him. Especially from myself. The brief pleasure of consuming him, satisfying as it might be, would pale beside the terrible woe of slaying such a great man. But I could never be happy just knowing him. I needed his touch, his warmth. I needed his flesh in a way that I could never have. No matter which I chose, unhappiness would always be the end result. This was the terrible beauty of my curse. It was frustrating, but as a witch, I couldn't help but admire Nasty Larry's handiwork.

If I was to be unsatisfied either way, the practical course of action would be to have my way with Wyst of the West, devour him, and put aside this dilemma. There was risk involved. Wyst could kill me, but death was not so frightening a prospect. If I could have just one kiss before dying, and maybe a tiny nibble of ear, I could think of far worse fates.

I was troubled by another sleepless night. I sat in the shadows and watched Wyst of the West. Sometimes I felt like a woman content to look upon a slumbering lover. Sometimes I felt like a spider studying a fly. Finally, I could resist my desire no longer.

I crept from the dark while the others slept and knelt beside him. My curse made me a shadow to the sleeping mind. I suppose it was an advantage meant to help spirit off slumbering children, but it worked just as well on men. I caressed his cheek with light fingers and ran a thumb across his lips. My fingers danced down his neck and across his chest.

I fell on my hands and held my face over his. Less than an inch but he couldn't sense me. He stirred. His soft, warm breath rose from parted lips. If I were to kiss him as he slept, Wyst would never know. Was one stolen kiss too much to ask? If no one saw it, if only I knew it ever happened, what could be the harm?

My heart quickened. My insides twisted into knots of hunger and nausea.

I couldn't fight my curse forever. If things kept as they were, I knew what must happen. Either for Wyst or myself. I didn't know which, and I decided not to think about it. The decision wouldn't be made this night. But my hunger couldn't be denied. Not entirely.

I lay beside him. I took his hand in mine and held it close to my breast. Even this didn't wake him. I pressed closer and imagined that we were both naked and spent from a night of passion. Not a very witchly imagining. More appropriate thoughts for a love-struck girl on the edge of womanhood. Yet this was what I was. Undead. Accursed. Ageless. And frighteningly innocent in so many ways.

Minutes of lying beside him were almost enough to sate

my hunger. Almost. I rolled against him, pressing against him as much as I dared. A little more, in truth. I turned his dark face to mine. And I kissed him. A light brushing of my lips against his forehead. Even if it was a one-sided affair, it was my first kiss. Unless I counted Newt, and I didn't. A terrific warmth filled me. My mouth went dry. My fingers trembled. My stomach gurgled almost loud enough to wake Wyst. My desires were filled for the time being, and I returned to the comforting darkness.

Wyst half awoke a moment later. Though I was a shadow, there would be a soft memory left behind, easy to mistake for a hazy dream. He rolled on his wounded side, groaned, and went back to sleep.

"You can stop pretending," I said. "I know you saw."

Penelope floated beside me. She laid low at my feet.

"None of that now. I knew you were awake the whole time so you did nothing wrong."

She stood and tilted forward, then back.

"It was very nice."

Penelope prodded me gently.

I grinned. "Wondrous."

With a gleeful hop and twirl, she fell into my hand. I was glad she'd witnessed it. Having someone else see it gave the kiss reality, and I trusted in my broom's silence.

So I sat in the dark, grinning as a witch never should and waiting for the sun to rise.

That moment when the dawn sears away the night was always my least favorite part of the day, but I discovered that the world is a dimmer place when you're in love. The sun and its uncompromising brightness seemed more tolerable this morning.

The memory of my body against his rested somewhere in Wyst's mind. Once, he touched his forehead where I'd kissed him. He smiled, shook his head, and surely dismissed it as a curious dream. Even White Knights must have had those sorts of dreams. Accursed witches certainly did. Sometimes even when I was awake.

We broke camp and continued on our quest. Wyst and I said nothing for the morning. It was our habit to talk little during the day, and almost all of these exchanges were quest-related. His wound was healing nicely, judging by the ease of his movement. My mundane medicine and his enchantment allowed him to recover from injury far quicker than normal. I didn't offer comment on it.

Newt passed the morning by complaining. He had much to complain about, and the demon in him had no trouble letting everyone know how unhappy he was. I found it amusing that a creature without an ounce of compassion should expect sympathy, but it wasn't that strange. Demons do have empathy, even if only for themselves.

I was only too happy to listen to Newt's grievances. I'd found a degree of affection for his flaws as passing time often encourages. I think we'd all missed his grumblings. Even Wyst smiled as Newt vented.

"Where did you send me anyway?"

"It has no name. If it did, it could be found, and if it could be found, then it wouldn't be where lost things go."

"You have no name," Newt said. "And you can be found."

"Perhaps only because I allow it."

He cast one of his customary dubious glances. I must admit, I'd missed them in his absence. "Anyway, wherever it was, it smelled like wet kobold. And it was terribly cluttered with dreadful lighting. And things were always falling from the sky."

Gwurm plucked his ear and moved it to the right side of his head to better hear Newt. "What sort of things?"

"Rings. Grails. A ratty, yellow fleece. There was a mountain of keys and coins and a field of boots, none a matching pair."

"No troll ears?" Gwurm asked.

"Not that I noticed, but it was a very cluttered place. Especially for a place that has no name and can't be found."

"Pity. If you find yourself there again someday, would you mind keeping an eye out for it?" Gwurm chuckled.

Newt bristled at the notion.

"Three trials left," he remarked. "Which one was that anyway? Combat, I imagine."

"It might have been magic," I replied. "Chimera are magical. Or it might have been peril. Chimera are monsters. And it might have been strength, a test of physical might."

Newt sighed. "Don't you know?"

I merely looked onward enigmatically.

"Fine. Three trials left in any case. When is the next one?"

I kept staring into the distance.

"You don't know. Just admit it."

"It doesn't really matter what I know and what I don't. Things will progress in their own way."

"Meaning you don't know."

I wasn't about to admit anything. No one but Newt expected me to, which was precisely why I didn't. I enjoyed tormenting my familiar as much as anyone. Well, perhaps not as much as Gwurm.

Several hours upstream, the River suggested we part company because it no longer knew anything about our quest except that traveling north seemed the right thing to do. Newt couldn't help but point out that we'd been going north before following the River, but quests were traditionally filled with detours. This annoyed him, but so many things did.

"Do you at least have some idea what this sorcerer is up to?" he asked.

I closed my eyes and lowered my head. "I have seen a crush of phantasmal goblings sweeping across the world, cleansing it of all genuine flesh. And in its place, another world has been made. A world of shadows and glass. A perfect but hollow reproduction."

"You make it sound as if it has already come to pass."

"Perhaps it already has." For the first time, I understood what Ghastly Edna had meant by the past that was yet to be. Time was neither now or later, then or after. Time simply was. Tomorrow was found by walking the hours, one minute at a time. None could know for certain what waited farther down the path, not even the magic. The only way to learn was to make the journey.

"But why would anyone want to do that? Destroy the world just to remake it?"

"Sorcery is illusion. It's potent, but never quite real. But in a world of phantoms, illusion is reality."

"Madness," Wyst said.

"Magic and madness often walk together, and sorcerers have always been especially prone. Theirs is an art that blurs reality and illusion, and most eventually stop noticing the difference."

"Can he do it?" Newt said.

"Where great magic is concerned, anything is possible. But in this instance, I wouldn't worry much. The world is not so delicate. If we fail in our quest, then most likely, someone somewhere will stop him."

Newt was disappointed. He wanted to be the world's savior. It would only confirm what the demon in him already knew: that the universe existed only for his glory. This wasn't true, but I offered him a nugget of self-importance.

"We are the first though, and if we fall short, there will be much more death and suffering before his plan is ended."

Newt would have grinned from ear to ear if he'd had ears. He was now the center of the world. Rather, he had always been, and I'd merely confirmed it. He was content to indulge in his hero fantasies. Without doubt, he imagined himself a sorcerer slayer. The rest of us were mere accessories to his destiny, which was really my destiny. He was enjoying himself, so I didn't point that out.

Northward, the forest thinned to a sparse wood, then a grassy field, then hilly plains. I hardly noticed. Wyst of the West occupied my perceptions. Newt may have been the center of his own universe, but the White Knight was the center of mine. I understood little of love, but I thought this normal. The obsession of fresh love. Time would soften its edge to something more manageable. I could only hold it in check by forcing myself to think of other things. I closed my eyes, lowered my head, and muttered nonsense under my breath. Ghastly Edna had often said, "Everyone talks to themselves, but if they truly wanted to learn anything, they would listen. A one-sided conversation rarely does anyone any good."

So I talked, and I listened, though not very well with Wyst so near. Even with my eyes closed, I could see his pleasing face, those dark eyes, those lean shoulders, delectable ears. I could smell his warm breath and feel my fingers running across the short hair atop his head. I could still taste his skin on my lips. My lust was stronger than ever. As was my appetite.

"You know what must be," I whispered.

I glanced at Wyst. He was watching me. Perhaps he had been the whole time. Neither of us turned away. We just stared into each other's eyes. And then, at the exact same moment, we smiled. I would have kissed him or bit off his soft, chewy lips if I'd been close enough. My body spoke to me in a hundred wordless ways, and I knew what I would do . . . what I must do.

I lowered my eyes from Wyst and pushed my lust aside. The ravenous beast was content to lick its lips in anticipation of the meal it knew was coming.

Newt's hero fantasies ceased being distracting. "This sorcerer, does he really have enough power to do that shells and darkness in your vision?"

"Glass and shadows," I corrected. "Potentially, yes."

Newt whistled. "He must be one of the greatest sorcerers alive then."

"He is, I believe, an Incarnate."

Newt was so taken aback that he slipped from my lap and fell to the ground. He hopped to his feet. "An Incarnate! You didn't say anything about an Incarnate!"

"You didn't ask."

There are many who study the ways of magic, and a select few have the talent to be great. Of these elite, there are an even smaller group who have the power to shape history, to alter the world (and sometimes even the universe) in ways that are never forgotten. To become legends that will live until the end of time.

And then, there are the Incarnates. They are magic given flesh. Or flesh given magic, depending on how one looks upon such things. There is only ever one upon the world, and in whatever craft of magic they practice, they are unequaled. Strangely, they were a mixed lot. Many never accomplish anything of great note. Such power doesn't always go to those who have a desire to decimate kingdoms or better the world. The magic chooses its Incarnates by its own reasons, and none are privy to those reasons.

Ghastly Edna had mused on occasion that Nasty Larry might have been an Incarnate. If so, I was all his awesome wizardly might in one accursed form, but I was not an Incarnate.

Gwurm picked Newt up and deposited him on my lap. "A sorcerer Incarnate," my familiar said. "Then it can only be one man."

"Soulless Gustav," said Gwurm.

I hadn't heard the name before, but I didn't need to ask. I only had to listen.

Newt's eyes grew wide and fearful. "Not so loud. He'll hear you."

"That's just a fairy story."

"No, it's not. I knew someone who knew someone who said His name and attracted His attention." Newt spoke with hushed reverence. Apparently, even pronouns weren't safe enough distance from Soulless Gustav.

"And what happened to this friend of a friend?" Gwurm asked.

"What do you think happened? The poor bastard died. Miserably, I might add. His tongue swelled up. His skin turned to maggots. His heart jumped from his chest, grew arms, and beat him to death."

"That is horrible," I agreed.

"Superstitious nonsense," Wyst remarked.

"No it's not!" Newt nodded at me. "Tell them. Tell them an Incarnate can do that."

"I suppose it is possible," I said. "Of course, it's also possible his heart was upset with him for reasons all its own."

Both Wyst and Gwurm laughed. Penelope shook with her own silent giggling.

"I wasn't aware you had so many friends," I said.

"I wasn't always a familiar, or just a duck. There's more to my past than you'll ever know."

I'd never thought about it, but I hadn't been born in Ghastly Edna's tutelage. A demon-infested waterfowl must surely have had as colorful a background as an accursed witch.

"Fair enough. And in that past, I take it you've met this Soulless Gustav."

Newt sputtered. "Don't say His name. Weren't you listening?"

"Skin to maggots," I said to prove I was.

"Swollen tongue," added Wyst.

"Pummeling heart," said Gwurm.

"Exactly. And that's just saying His name. None who have ever seen Him has lived to tell the tale."

"Sounds like a fairy story to me." Gwurm shrugged. "If everyone who's ever seen him has died, then how do you know he exists?"

"Because none of the unfortunate fools died right away. First, they all went mad. Then they stumbled back to civilization before they perished."

"I thought you said no one lived to tell the tale."

Newt rolled his eyes. "That's just a figure of speech. Of course, they lived to tell the tale."

"What about the swollen tongues?" asked Wyst of the West. "Wouldn't the swollen tongues get in the way of the telling?"

"That was just my friend's friend. Everyone perishes in a different way. Sometimes their eyes burst. Or their brains liquefy. Or their intestines strangle them. I've heard of a man who was compelled to chop himself to pieces with a rusty ax. And another who gasped with such terror that his lungs exploded."

"Sounds dreadful," Wyst said.

"Dreadfully horrible." Newt shook out his wings. "Ghastly and gruesome and appalling and any other terrible word you can think of. Which is exactly why we shouldn't even be talking about Him. Even just thinking about Him is dangerous."

"Stuff and nonsense. We trolls don't believe in such foolishness." Gwurm hunched carefully so not to throw me off his shoulders. "I'll be damned if I'll be afraid of a sorcerer who doesn't have better things to do than send strangling intestines after those who say his name. Even if he does exist." He raised his hands in gnarled fashion. The large size and flexibility of troll fingers makes them quite terrifying when held like that. Like great, twisted claws. "Soulless Gustav can scratch my unmentionables."

"Stop saying His name!"

Gwurm fiddled with his little finger, twisting it all the way around. "Who? Soulless Gustav? Do you want me to stop saying Soulless Gustav? Because if you really want me not to say Soulless Gustav anymore, I'll stop saying Soulless Gustav. You just have to ask."

"Stop saying it!"

"What's that?" Gwurm adjusted his ear. "Stop saying what?"

"Stop saying Soulless Gustav!"

Penelope smacked Newt on the bottom with her bristles. Thinking it the sorcerous wrath of Soulless Gustav himself, the duck jumped in the air with a howl. He flapped his wings madly, fell to earth, and jerked tensely upright. His head twisted back and forth, up and down. My undead ears heard his heart thundering.

Gwurm cracked a crooked grin. Penelope shook. Even Wyst chortled ever so lightly.

"Fine. You got me to say it. Very funny. All I'm saying is that even if He's not real, even if He's just a story, there's no point in taking the risk, however negligible it might be."

Gwurm and Penelope decided they'd tormented Newt enough and agreed. But the sorcerer was still a topic of conversation. Though he refused to sit on Gwurm's shoulders, Newt relented to talk about Soulless Gustav as long as the name went unspoken.

"They say he was born without a soul," Newt said. "That's why he's so mad and evil. And that he must feast upon the souls of virgins to survive, like the Lords of Inferno themselves. And that all the unfortunate soulless virgins are kept as his slaves, an army of beautiful, empty flesh. Neither dead nor alive nor undead but something wholly different and unnatural."

"I'd heard the same," said Gwurm. "Only I'd heard it told that he was born with a soul but lost it."

"Sorcerers don't often traffic with demons."

"I didn't say he'd sold it. I said he'd lost it."

Wyst agreed. "They say he was a good man, but one day, he misplaced his soul."

Newt sighed. "That's preposterous."

"It's just what I've heard." Wyst remained serious, and I couldn't tell if he was jesting or not. "It doesn't seem any more preposterous than having one's brain liquefy for merely saying a name."

Gwurm said, "I lost my mother's nose not long after leaving home."

Newt balked. "Her nose."

"It's troll tradition. Something to remember her by. But I lost it, and it drove me quite mad with irritation. Took me weeks to get over it, but in the end, it was just a nose. I remember my mother just as well without it."

He ran a thumb across his wide chin. "But still, it did get to me those weeks. And I would imagine misplacing one's soul would be a thousand times worse. It is your most personal and irreplaceable possession. I think even the greatest man would be driven mad by that. Mad enough to kill those who dared utter his name."

"I still think it makes more sense that he was born without one."

"More sense, perhaps," I agreed, "but magic isn't always sensible."

"You didn't see any souls while you were lost did you?" asked Gwurm. "Good chance if you had it would have been his."

Newt wasn't amused and ignored the question. "Your mother's nose, you say?"

Gwurm nodded. "It was blue with a wart on the end. You didn't come across anything like that either, did you?"

"No. No misplaced souls. No lost ears. No mislaid noses."

"Well, keep an eye out for it next time you're there."

"I will."

He muttered something about eating it should he ever find it.

We came across an old road and followed where it led. In the early evening, the countryside became somehow familiar. I didn't recognize it. I'd seen very little of the world, but a good witch has a sense of the land.

My curiosity got the better of me, and I hopped off Gwurm's shoulders to speak with the road. I knelt low and asked, "Have I been here before?"

He spoke with a rough, dry voice as any neglected, dusty road should.

"Leave me alone."

"I beg your pardon, but I think I've been here before."

"Perhaps you have," he grunted. "Perhaps you haven't. A great many feet have trod upon this old road. I can't be expected to remember them all."

Despite his protests, I knew every road recollected all those who'd traveled upon it. I also knew that such an old, neglected road wouldn't volunteer information freely.

"And how very presumptuous of you," the road added, "to ask me anything after treading so callously on my back."

"I'm sorry, but isn't that what roads are for?"

"Oh, yes. To be walked and rolled across without thought all hours of the day, that is my job. Answering questions is not.

Now on your way. Stomp away with your cruel hooves and clomping troll feet, but stop pestering me with questions."

Not all roads were so bitter. A well-used, well-tended road is a contented beast of burden. All too often, prosperity leads men elsewhere, and the streets are left behind to grow resentful. This particular road could never have been that important to begin with. He didn't even have remembered greatness to ease his ill temperament.

I stood for a moment, saying nothing.

"Off you go," the road growled.

I remained. None of my companions questioned my motives though Newt did clear his throat impatiently.

"Oh, the cruelty of it," the road lamented. "I, who have helped a thousand travelers find their way, can't even flee from a single bothersome witch. Wait as long as you like. I have nothing but time."

I let Penelope go, and she immediately set to sweeping.

"Oh, my. That feels . . ." The road exhaled. Soft clouds of dust rose and fell. ". . . splendid. It's been ages since I've been tended to. That's it. Now to the left. More. More. Just right."

I snapped my fingers, and Penelope returned to my side.

"Don't stop! Don't stop!"

"Answer my question, and I'll allow her to continue."

The road didn't hesitate. "Yes, yes, you've walked with me before."

"When?"

"Years are meaningless to me, but I know it was when I was more well traveled. Long ago. Your promise. Keep your promise."

"Of course."

Penelope was every bit as eager as the road. She danced back and forth as he sighed pleasurably at her tender caress.

He directed her between approving murmurs, and his pleasure drove her into a fervor of sweeping.

"What's wrong with her?" asked Newt.

I climbed back on Gwurm's shoulders.

"Harder," groaned the road. "Oh, yes! That's it. That's the spot!"

Newt squinted curiously.

I covered his eyes. "It's impolite to stare."

We continued. Penelope fell behind, tending to the road. I trusted she would catch up and left her to her passion. It was barely an hour later that a broken-down cottage came into view. Like the land, it was oddly familiar. I ordered a stop.

"What now?" asked Newt.

I gave no explanation as I studied the abandoned house. It was wholly unexceptional. I climbed the porch steps and pushed open the creaking door to find nothing but dust and spiderwebs inside. It had been a long time since anyone called this place home.

Wyst dismounted. "Is something wrong?"

We walked around to the back of the overgrown yard. A door in the earth beckoned. The rusted hinges broke when I opened it. The evening twilight refused to enter the darkened hole.

"Are you feeling well?"

The worry in Wyst's voice meant much of my witchly inscrutability had fallen away. I would've reassured him, but I wasn't certain how I felt. There were so many thoughts and emotions welling up that I couldn't pick out just one. I descended into the earth, and in the darkness, I found the past I'd left behind so long ago. This was the countryside of my birth. I hadn't recognized it because I'd only seen it once while living in Ghastly Edna's charge. I'd worn a cowl then and kept my eyes closed most of the time. Sunlight had bothered me much more then. But I knew this place.

My cellar.

Wyst's shadow filled the door. "Witch?"

I placed my hand against a rotted support beam and found an omen in the splintered grooves. "We camp here tonight."

Newt's silhouette appeared between Wyst's feet. "Here? In the basement?"

"No. You can camp outside."

"But there's at least another hour of daylight," said Newt. "Shouldn't we keep going?"

"Tonight comes the next trial. Here."

"In the basement?"

I wasn't feeling very witchly at the moment and threw him a glare that never climbed out of the darkness.

"And what do you mean another trial?" he said. "Already? We just had one yesterday. Nothing for weeks and then, two trials right atop one another. Where's the sense of pace to this quest?"

I wasn't in the mood for this. And sometimes, when a witch gets properly annoyed, her magic responds unbidden. A breeze swept through the cellar and up the stairs.

"I would think whatever force was in charge of quests would quack quack quack quack."

I smiled. Then I frowned because a witch should never allow herself to do magic by accident. Especially malicious magic.

Newt kept on talking. Or trying. "Quack quack quack." He cleared his throat. "Quack quack quack." He drew in a deep breath and expelled one last disgusted duck call before disappearing from the doorway.

Wyst dared step one foot in the dark that I'd called home so many years. "Witch, are you certain you're well?"

I glanced up at that handsome face. In the darkness, his eyes seemed to shine. "Certain? Can anyone be certain of anything?" It sounded vaguely witchful, but I was off my game. I decided not to settle.

"Certainty is for fools and death." I liked that, even if I didn't really understand it myself. The phrase reminded me of what it was to be a good witch.

I stepped deeper into the dark, where the shadows enveloped me. "We camp here. Now leave me."

He hesitated.

My voice grew soft and scratchy. "Leave me."

Something must've reminded Wyst of what it was to be a White Knight because he withdrew. His face went blank, and he vanished from the door.

Magic didn't act on its own. It acted on the will and desires of others, and I had to wonder whose will had guided me here. It could've been Nasty Larry or Ghastly Edna from beyond the grave. Or Soulless Gustav. Or even myself. I didn't know the who or why of it, but I trusted to discover it in time.

I stood alone for some time. The light filtering through the door faded. It was an overcast night, and my cellar became a black emptiness. A hole in the ground filled with nothing, just a scarcity of memories.

My childhood hadn't been much to remember. There was the spot at the bottom of the stairs where I'd waited for my meals to be thrown to me. There was the corner where I'd eaten those meals. And there was the other corner where I'd sat and slept between those meals. Countless days, but really the same day over and over and over. This place meant little to me now. It hadn't meant much to me before. I couldn't even remember my family. My life truly began the day Ghastly Edna had pulled me from this hole.

In another world, another time, an explorer of this cellar might easily find a hideous, terrified creature huddling in the dark, abandoned by her family and too frightened to leave this dusty void. A beast to be feared, despised, and pitied. The me that never was but so easily could have been.

Harsh light burned away the dark. Wyst of the West descended the creaking stairs. I kept my back to him. I only knew it was him by scent. I had a predator's nose when it came to men. They were my curse's meal of choice.

The shadows fought against the invading lantern. It had been a long time since their sanctuary had been challenged, but they could only hiss and writhe and fight among themselves.

"Witch?"

I didn't turn to face the White Knight. "Yes?"

"Will you be spending the night down here?"

I lowered my head and closed my eyes. "Perhaps I will."

He moved to the left, judging by the shifting light. I turned my head away. The lantern seemed so terribly bright.

"And the trial, are you certain we face it tonight?" asked Wyst.

"We do not face a trial tonight." I raised a hand and watched the silhouette play against the wall. "I do alone."

"By yourself?"

I offered no reply as none was needed.

Wyst stepped closer. I covered my eyes.

"But . . ." He stammered. I'd never heard him stammer. ". . . aren't we . . . working together?"

"We are, but this next trial is one that only I can defeat. You, the others, will only get in my way."

"But . . ."

I turned my face to him and forced my eyes open. I could only squint, but I hoped it was a mysterious squint. "There are things which must be."

He raised his lantern higher. The rabid shadows refused to fall across his pleasing face. Wyst of the West held out a hand. He closed it into a fist. Then opened it. Then put it atop his head and shrugged. He turned and moved toward the stairs.

"Wyst." As much time as we'd spent together, this was the first time I'd spoken his name.

"Yes?"

"I have a favor to ask you."

The cellar grew so quiet, I could hear the shadows whispering. I was very close to forgetting the whole affair, but he offered me courage.

"You only have to ask."

I couldn't look directly at him. "Could you hold me?"

Wyst remained rigid and silent. I tried to read his face and found only earnest sobriety.

I suddenly felt very foolish.

"I'm sorry. But I have glimpsed the creature I might have been, and I was hoping to find the mortal woman I should have been. If only for a moment. But I should've known even simple embraces are against your oath."

"They are"—He set down his lantern and clasped his hands together—"discouraged."

"I shouldn't have asked. My apologies."

He moved before me and put a hand on my shoulder. "Discouraged. Not forbidden."

And just like that, he took me in his arms. Gingerly at first. I had little experience in physical affection, and he was presumably out of practice. But it wasn't so complicated. We leaned into each other. His arms circled just above my waist. My hands rubbed his back in small circles. I nuzzled his neck. My hat fell off, and I didn't care.

The shadows ceased muttering at the sight.

Wyst was so warm, and his touch triggered the heat within my cold, undead flesh. The cellar seemed a frozen hollow. My heart beat faster. My skin tingled. My stomach twisted.

This was what my curse denied me. I could savor it for only a moment. The trust. The warmth. The imperceptible made tangible, given form in this man. I suspected nothing could be better than this. Except for possibly ripping out his throat and lapping at the sweet blood gushing forth. Probably not even that.

My stomach rumbled loud as thunder. At least, it seemed so to me. I was reminded of what I was. I pulled away. It wasn't so easy. My arms let go with great reluctance, and I sensed some resistance from Wyst. Or maybe only imagined it.

The invisible mark on his forehead flickered, and I knew I hadn't. Wyst's purity remained intact, but beneath the White Knight was a mortal man. Unfortunately, I'd rediscovered the accursed fiend within me as well.

He said nothing. He turned, picked up his lantern, and stared up the stairs.

"Wyst, thank you."

He paused at the door and spoke so softly I barely heard him over the chattering shadows. "You're welcome."

Then he was gone, and I was left in the basement again. I wasn't alone anymore. On one side hunched the creature I might have been. On the other stood the woman I should have been. In this forsaken place, both were as real as the witch between them, but there was another world atop those stairs. A world where only one of us was true. So I bid them good night and many good tomorrows and ascended from this pit into the night.

The others were camped around the front of the cabin. I followed the sound of irritated quacks. Everyone was waiting there but Wyst, who was nowhere to be seen. But his horse was still here. He couldn't have gone far.

Penelope dragged herself to my side. Her tryst with the road had left her exhausted.

"Enjoy yourself?" I asked.

She raised into the air and bobbed.

"Very good, dear, but you should learn to pace yourself. Now go rest."

No sooner had she floated away then Newt stood before me. He quacked once and glared.

"I vote to leave him like that," remarked Gwurm.

Newt shouted something rude at the troll. Though I was fluent in duck, I didn't bother translating.

"He's been like this all night. Persnickety and foul-tempered. More so than usual. Maybe you should change him back after all."

I waved a hand. Newt belched and instantly began questioning me. Demons don't learn lessons easily. "What did you do to the White Knight? He didn't say a word after coming out of that basement. Strangest look on his face. I don't like it. You shouldn't be consorting with him by yourself. It's dangerous."

I smiled. "Life often is."

"Where's your hat?"

"I must have left it in the cellar." Absently, I ran my fingers through my silken hair. "I don't need it right now." I glanced into the overcast sky, just bright enough for my un-dead eyes.

New scowled. "And when is the next trial anyway? I'm get-ting tired of waiting. Does the magic think we have nothing better to do than sit here all night?"

I put a finger to my lips and shushed him. He bit his tongue. I guess he'd learned his lesson after all.

"My apologies, mistress."

"Quite all right. Now, if you'll excuse me, I'm off to face the next trial."

"By yourself?" asked Gwurm.

I nodded.

Newt stood in my way. "But, mistress, I'm your familiar. My place is by your side."

"Not this time."

I stepped around the duck.

"What happened to your limp?" he asked.

I hesitated at the edge of darkness. "Oh, that. I don't need that either. Wait here. I'll be back shortly. Or not at all."

I slipped into the night and went in search of my trial. My thoughts were elsewhere, but an omen in the clouds told me I wouldn't be looking for long. It was already waiting for me in the overgrown fields.

Two shadows rose from the grass. One was a skulking ghoul. The other was a slip of a young girl. The creature that I might have been and the woman I should have been. Reflec-tions given substance through powerful sorcery.

"You didn't really think to leave us in that basement?" asked the ghoul.

"We will always be with you," said the woman. "We have always been."

"I know. We all carry many selves, but in the end, these are just phantoms of possibility, nothing more than ghosts of broken destinies."

The ghoul cackled. "Ghosts no more."

"So I see. But even the greatest sorcery can't serve three fates from a single portion of destiny."

"Yes," said the woman. "And that is why only one of us will walk from this field."

"And I shall be that one," hissed the ghoul.

"We shall see, sister," replied the woman.

None of us could kill the other because, at this moment, none were true enough to die. This was why neither Wyst, Newt, nor Gwurm could be of any help. Only I could return my shadows to the nether from which they'd been summoned, and I could only do this by keeping them from snatching away my identity. Reality was on my side. Yet this might not be enough. Reality was a fickle ally at best.

The ghoul struck first. She was my curse unchecked by Ghastly Edna's witchly lessons of patience. The woman stood back, smiling as if victory were already hers.

The ghoul leaped, hands outstretched to wrap around my throat. As if she could throttle her existence from me. As if I could be slain by strangling. Her technique was instinctive and direct, but I was her match in speed. I struck her across the jaw with a backhanded fist. She fell to one knee.

The ghoul raised her head, grinning. Blood dribbled down her chin. "Very good, witch. You stand revealed for what you are. A creature of strength and power. Do you not feel the gush within your undead heart when you call upon your curse? Do you see now that all your magic is just a trifle? It will let you down one day. But your curse, that shall always be there for you. For me."

The ghoul darted to one side faster than I could follow.

Raking claws tore open my face. I raised a hand to defend myself, but she ducked aside. Her first attack had been a feint. She was quicker than she'd let on.

A fist smashed into my back and knocked the wind from lungs that didn't really need air. "Surprised, witch? Fast as you are, deadly as you are, I am far deadlier." She latched on to my throat and squeezed until vertebrae cracked. "I am your physical power developed to its ultimate. Beside me, you are a weakling. Where is your magic now?" She dropped me into the grass.

I sat up. My breath was ragged. My face was bloodied, and a terrible rage growled within.

"You can't deny it. You want to be me, to feel the certainty that I feel. To know your purpose without question. To seduce and slaughter and glut yourself on delectable mortal flesh. Your conscience is your misery. It is a burden that I don't have, and a burden you yearn to be rid of."

I was tempted, and I felt my reality trickle into the ghoul. Her murky body thickened as mine darkened. I could see her now. Truly see her. She was a hideous creature, every bit as flawless as I, but there was more to beauty than full breasts and green eyes. Her movements were jerking. Her eyes were full of fiendish hunger. Her lips ever snarled, even as she grinned. Her hair was a shimmering black tangle falling like a cape across her back.

I ran fingers across my stinging knuckles and torn face. There was truth in her words, but it was a small truth.

"Conscience is my burden, but all worthwhile gifts have their price."

She shuddered. The stream of existence reversed, and she began to fade.

"But it could be so simple," the ghoul hissed. "Why hold on to that which only makes your life difficult?"

"Because life is complicated and difficult. Anyone who says otherwise hasn't truly lived."

She melted into the earth, but not without one last gasp. "I'll be back. No one can resist their nature forever."

I didn't deny this. To do so would have been arrogant, and arrogance would have been the first step toward her prediction.

"One day, witch, you will wake up to discover I have become you."

"Maybe one day. But not tonight."

The ghoul faded away to a black spot on the ground.

"She never had a chance," said the woman.

"She had a chance." My wounds disappeared. They had never been real. "Just not much of one."

The woman stepped before me. "I, on the other hand, have already won."

"I know."

The stream rushed into the woman. My stolen substance filled her. She was a pretty creature, not nearly as beautiful as I. But I could see myself in her slightly plumper figure and soft brown eyes.

She lowered her head. "I'm sorry."

"You only take what I offer."

It was a strange thing. I didn't surrender myself to her because I hated what I was or because mortality was all that tempting a fate. I liked being a witch, and I'd grown accustomed to my curse. It denied me little. Nothing but the one desire I couldn't ignore anymore.

"He won't love me," she said. "I may be you, but I am not the you he knows."

It was true, but it didn't make any difference. I loved Wyst, and my heart fantasized that as a woman, he could love me back. It was an unlikely dream. Even if I weren't undead, he would still be a White Knight. Dreams are rarely founded on truth, and this sorcery drew on my deepest wishes. I couldn't change those. Even with magic.

"I'm sorry." The woman wiped a tear from her eye.

I sank into the dark earth and for an instant I knew what it was to be a ghost of destiny. But it was brief, even for an instant.

Magic, not my own, crackled through the air. The earth spit me out, and I snapped back into truth. The woman fell at my feet. I felt a terrible pity for her, but she just smiled ever so softly before fading into oblivion. The second trial was finished. Once again, I was alone.

The woman may have been my heart's desire, but my curse was more powerful than this sorcery and my innermost yearnings. Nasty Larry denied my escape even through altered destiny.

I could've become the ghoul. The curse wouldn't have minded, but Ghastly Edna had saved me from that. Her education had given me more than magic. If she'd been here, I would have thanked her.

She would have most certainly replied, "We all save ourselves, child, even if we are fortunate enough to have help along the way."

Smiling, I offered her silent thanks anyway and headed back to the camp.

23

*U*pon my return, *Wyst* was still gone, and I worried. I didn't fear for his safety. He could take care of himself well enough. But I'd sensed our brief embrace had shaken his virtue, and a White Knight's virtue was his greatest possession, his defining quality. Though he'd agreed to the minor violation, I never should have put him in the position to make it. Terrible errors are rarely made all at once. Usually they are performed one small misstep at a time. It had been wrong to ask, but I couldn't make myself feel bad about what had happened in my cellar. This wasn't surprising. The wrong thing often feels right. Such is the nature of temptation.

I took my place beside the campfire without saying a word. Gwurm handed me some bloody flesh to chew upon. Newt couldn't contain his impatience.

"Well?"

I sucked on my fingers. "It's done."

"Just like that?"

"Just like that."

"You defeated the second trial?"

I chuckled. "Me? No, I'm afraid not." Ghastly Edna and Nasty Larry had overcome the trial.

"So you lost?"

"No."

Newt grunted. "I miss the old bat. She may not have told me everything, but I don't remember her being so confounding."

I realized that as much as I loved Ghastly Edna, we were two very different witches. She'd lived by herself with a duck and a cursed girl, both of which did whatever she told them to without question. She might offer a verbal riddle here or there, but she'd spoken little. I was part of a much larger world and demands were made on my witchliness that I'd never seen my mistress face. I liked playing with words, watching how they might say so much and so little at once.

"Is the second trial over then?" Newt dared ask.

I nodded.

"Good. Two more then?"

I nodded again.

"Any idea when the next one is?"

I didn't answer.

"Forget I asked." He put aside his confusion. I'd given him enough practice at it.

Nothing was said after that. Newt and Gwurm went to sleep, but I wasn't tired. I contemplated the overcast night. A soft breeze swept across the fields, and my hair frolicked in the air. It had been a long time since it had been free to dance with the wind.

"I knew you were going to be trouble," said Wyst's horse.

His unsolicited comment surprised me. Up to now, the beast and I hadn't spoken. He'd been spurning me, and I hadn't given it much thought.

He didn't look at me and rocked his head. "Trouble."

I walked over and tried to pet his muzzle. He pulled away.

"Hello."

The horse snorted.

"Have I done something to offend you?"

He strode a few paces away and turned his head to look at me with one brown eye. "You're a witch. That alone should be enough."

"Ah, so you don't like witches."

He flicked his tail in my direction. "I've nothing against them exactly, but I am the loyal steed of a White Knight. It doesn't seem right to speak with one, even a mostly harmless witch."

I paced a wide circle to get around to his front without drawing too close. "Mostly harmless, am I?"

"Did I say mostly." The horse smacked his loose lips. "I meant largely."

"Is there a difference?"

He closed his eyes and kicked the grass. "Leave me alone. I'm trying to sleep."

"As you wish." I turned away.

"You'll be the end of him, and he was such a fine champion."

I stopped. "I would never harm him."

The horse neighed a mirthless chuckle. "You've already done him harm. You've started him down the path of corruption. Once a White Knight starts down that road . . ."

I lowered my head. "I never intended . . ."

"What you intended is hardly relevant. What did you do to him in that basement?"

"Nothing." I whispered to soften the lie.

The horse trotted behind me and nudged my shoulder. "It's not your fault. I know you can't help how you feel any more than he can. That's why it's happening. Do you think you're the first temptation we've come across? There have been others. More than I can count. Wyst has drawn his share of lovely admirers. Why shouldn't he? He's virtuous and brave, handsome and gallant, everything a woman might want. But all the others loved the Knight, not the man. You're different. You see him as none have, and he sees that you see. How can anyone not love someone who loves them for who they are? Especially someone more beautiful than all the others combined."

I reached out and stroked between his eyes. "I didn't want it to happen."

"Neither did he, but it did. And it will."

"Perhaps not."

He stuck out his tongue. "I've been his boon companion for a very long time. I know Wyst better than anyone. Sometimes, better than he knows himself. He's out in the fields now, meditating, struggling to clear his mind of these urges. They teach White Knights to suppress their baser desires. But even a great Knight such as Wyst can't stifle his love."

So great was my surprise that even a lifetime of witchly training couldn't hide it. Agape, I stepped away from the horse.

"He loves me?"

The horse shook his head. His lips turned in a sardonic grin. "Very much so. More than even he suspects."

I struggled to contain my excitement and mostly succeeded. The only trace of my joy came in a soft smile and a spontaneous sprouting of sunflowers at my feet.

"Do you love him?" asked the horse.

I answered without hesitation. "Yes." A pair of silver butterflies materialized in my palm. I let them into the air with a wave of my hand.

"That's it then," sighed the horse. "He's doomed."

"I would never hurt him."

"There are more dooms than death. A White Knight touched by love is ruined. They can't return to a life of virtue after that."

"You don't understand. I'm cursed. I can't love him, not as a mortal woman loves a man."

He nervously nibbled on the tall grass. He chewed a mouthful and spat it out. "You can. And you do."

I wanted to argue. More than anything, I wanted to correct the horse of this notion, but everything I might say would be a lie. Since neither of us would believe any untruth I could offer, I didn't bother. Instead, I seized on a comment I hadn't noticed before.

"Beautiful. You said, I was beautiful?"

The horse gulped down more grass and spoke with his mouth full. "Did I? I don't recall."

"Yes, you did. More beautiful than all of Wyst's former admirers combined, that's what you said."

"Are you certain?" He chewed on his far shoulder to avoid looking at me. I waited for him to grow bored ignoring me.

"Oh, yes, yes. I did say that." He lifted and pawed each hoof twice. "We saw you bathing in the lake, months before we came to Fort Stalwart. Wyst had lost track of the gobling horde, it was very elusive for a horde, and while trailing it through a patch of woods, we saw you."

I'd forgotten my last day with Ghastly Edna and my bath at the lake. I'd known someone had been watching. Now I knew who. And I had only been down there because my mistress had ordered me to. There could only be one reason behind it. Ghastly Edna had wanted me spied upon. It was against the witch's code to be seen in so vulnerable a state, and I couldn't fathom the reason. Even long dead, my mistress could confuse me. There had always been a lesson somewhere to be learned, and I assumed this would be no different.

"Personally, I don't know what makes a woman desirable," remarked the horse. "I've always liked a strong back and sturdy haunches, a nice mane. You've got the mane at least. And whatever women are supposed to have, I presume you have that as well. Because I felt Wyst's lust rise the moment he laid eyes upon you."

I frowned. I didn't want Wyst's lust. I was a beautiful creature, supernaturally so, and men couldn't help but desire my flesh. If the only reason Wyst couldn't resist me was my curse, then I would rather he feel nothing at all.

The horse shook his head. "You still don't understand, do you? It was merely lust at first. A stronger lust than usual perhaps, but lust nonetheless. Wyst was its master. Then this quest started, and over the days, it became something more. And it's all your fault. If only you'd been a proper witch and kept your distance."

I almost argued that Wyst was just as responsible, but even if it was true, everyone is only responsible for their own actions. The blame was mine. And still I couldn't make myself feel bad about any of this.

Because Wyst loved me.

"Shame," said the horse. "He was such a terrific champion of virtue."

I laid by the campfire, closed my eyes, and tried to get some rest. I couldn't even stop from smiling.

Wyst returned sometime later. I pretended to sleep and watched him by magic through closed eyes. He stood over me for a long while, just looking. Then he bent down and barely touched my cheek. I wanted to wrap my arms around him and kiss and nibble him. But I didn't. This wasn't the right place or time, and something in my eyes told me Wyst wasn't ready. But he would be, and I could wait until he was.

Wyst laid down, a mere arm's length away. He didn't go to sleep. A sweet smile across his lips, he just kept looking, and with him watching over me, I had no trouble getting the rest I needed.

"Trouble," snorted the horse just before I fell into a peaceful slumber.

I'd always been the first to wake in the morning, if I got any rest at all. But my sleepless nights must've finally caught up with me, and I slumbered, nestled in dreams of Wyst of the West. I'd dreamed of him before, but never like this. The previous had been carnal in nature, fantasies of fleshly and carnivorous desires. This night, I dreamed of nothing more than being held in his strong arms. It was the loveliest dream, over and over again throughout the night. On the surface, it was very innocent, but I knew it was more serious than all my other fantasies. When the time to leave the dreaming world came, I was reluctant to do so.

Morning light usually disturbs my deepest slumber. When it finally did just that, the sun was already halfway over the horizon. I sat up and shielded my eyes from the sun. I couldn't look at it directly, but it was a very pretty morning.

"I retrieved your hat from the cellar," said Newt. "Thought you might need it." He held it up in his bill. I took the pointed, black hat and pulled it low over my head to shade my eyes. I didn't tuck my hair away, and Newt glowered at the shimmering strands.

I bent down and rubbed a handful of dirt on my face. Not as much as I should, but this was mostly an exercise of habit.

All my companions knew I was beautiful. There was little point in hiding it.

I tried wiping away my slight smile with little success. I could only hope it came across as ambiguous. Not the smile of a woman in love, but the knowing grin of a witch listening to the whisper of magic.

I glanced over at Wyst of the West. He looked back at me, and neither of us shied away. He climbed onto his horse without turning his eyes from mine. We both smiled, softly for most people, but beaming for a witch and White Knight.

Newt said something, but I didn't catch the words.

I pulled my gaze from Wyst and down to my familiar. "Pardon?"

"I asked which way now, mistress?" The question came with an impertinent tone. Especially the last word. I was in much too good a mood to be troubled by it now.

Gwurm boosted me onto his shoulder as I replied, "We follow the road."

Penelope floated into my hand, and Newt took his place on my lap. And we started on our way. As the cabin shrank away, I tucked away its memory. It was worth remembering, not for the quietly miserable childhood but for that brief moment when Wyst and I held each other. That embrace made the highly probable into an unavoidable certainty.

We journeyed in a silence of words but with a great chatter of glances. Wyst and I would steal sidelong peeks, but we weren't fooling anyone. Gwurm and Penelope were polite enough to ignore them. Newt voiced his objections with snarls and grimaces and one exceptionally displeased glower. And the miles passed away.

Late in the morning, Wyst's horse became uneasy. He stopped without warning.

Wyst patted his mount's neck. "What's wrong?"

"This isn't right," snorted the horse.

"How so?" I asked.

The horse blinked three times very deliberately. "Up ahead. The countryside is wrong. Not right at all."

I hopped from Gwurm's shoulder and cleared my head. Beasts possess senses even witches lack, but now I knew to look for something. It took a few long moments of careful study to spot the horse's observation.

Nature is chaotic. Even a tranquil field of flowers is full of disarray, even if it is subtly so. But the landscape before us was a picture of perfect order. The first thing I noticed was the trees. There were four ahead, and yet each was the same in every detail with a bending trunk and an exact arrangement of branches. Even the bark was the same shade and texture with the same knot in the trunk of each.

I noticed the stones scattered ahead next. They were more varied, coming in three different shapes and sizes. Only three. Once I saw it for what it was, I even noticed the grass was arranged in uniform rows with the deliberate patterned arrangement of three short blades, a taller blade, and two mid-size. This wasn't nature. It was only an incredible simulation.

The horde of phantom goblings was one thing, but to re-create the world so completely was an act of unparalleled sorcerous might. It was also the product of a madman. This sorcerer didn't want to remake the world in his own image. He just wanted to remake it for no other reason than he could. Sorcery for sorcery's sake, a grand experiment intended to wipe away the heart of the world.

Only now did I understand just how insidious such a design was. Only now did I truly grasp the power I faced. I was afraid, fearful that my magic wouldn't be a match for it.

Fear is only a bad thing when it provokes poor decisions. Otherwise, a little dread can be healthy. I held my trepidation close. When the time came, it would serve me to keep from underestimating what I might face.

"What is it?" Newt asked.

"A dream of madness."

I left it at that. None of the others could understand. Nor did they need to. Wyst spurred his horse onward. The steed hesitated, but as the boon companion of a White Knight, he had the courage to cross into this sorcerous reflection.

There was a stillness to this false world, and even its small movements were calculated. The fields swayed with unerring predictability. The tree branches bobbed in unison. The clouds overhead swirled in precise, lazy shapes. The phantom kingdom acknowledged our presence with a minimum of response. Our footfalls kicked up small dust clouds, each identical regardless whether spurred by hoof or troll foot. The grass parted, only to snap back into rank and file.

I was horribly uncomfortable. We all were, but I could feel the void in this land. There wasn't life in any of this. I couldn't talk to the grass or speak with the trees. They were dead, empty things. If this was how mortal men saw the world, what a cold, dark place they lived in. I understood why they gathered together so obsessively now.

We must've been close to the end of our quest, but this was only a guess. I couldn't find a single omen in this empty land, and any whispers of the magic were muffled beneath the smothering sorcery. I was so ill at ease that I didn't see the first spontaneous movement in the land until Gwurm pointed it out.

"That's a strange-looking cloud."

A white puff broke formation and darkened. Small pockets of lightning sizzled within, creating two glowing, electric orbs. The cloud leered with its sparkling eyes. A mouth parted in its rumbling billows, and it chuckled. It was an all-too-human chuckle, too soft to be heard all the way on the ground, but we heard it anyway.

Wyst drew his sword.

"Oh, my," said the cloud. "Tell me, my good Knight, just how do you plan on slaying a cloud with that blade, assuming you possess some method of reaching me way up here in the first place?"

The voice was flat and even. It sounded as if spoken gently in my ears, as if this cloud were beside me. But space was a triviality in a place that didn't truly exist.

The cloud squinted. Rather, its eyes dimmed. "Now let's see what we have here. A White Knight, a troll, a duck, and a witch. An odd assortment of adversaries, I must say. What a pleasure it is to finally meet you face-to-face, so to speak."

I tipped my hat to the cloud. "And you must be Soulless Gustav."

"If I must. My reputation precedes me." The puff resumed its part in the lifeless dance, and the face disappeared. It reappeared in the tall grass. Purple flowers bloomed for its eyes.

"There really is a Soulless Gustav?" whispered Newt.

He was heard. I suspected everything unusual was heard by this realm's master. "Well, I would certainly hope so. Who else could send out those plagues of strangling intestines and melting brains?"

"You really do that?" Newt asked.

The grass split into a wry grin. "On occasion. When it suits my purpose. Or when it strikes me as amusing. Or when I just feel bored and in the mood to sow some terror. Not so nearly as often as people claim, but that is the advantage of a well-cultivated reputation. After a while, it does its own work."

One purple bud closed in a wink.

"You've done well to get here. Of course, I expected you would. My magic is not so strong in that place you would call reality, but you've crossed into my kingdom now. Foolish mistake, that. I'd tell you to turn back, but it's too late."

Wyst struggled with his uneasy horse for a moment. He put away his sword. "Hear me now, sorcerer. I am Wyst of the West, Defender of the Weak, Destroyer of the Foul, Sworn Champion of Decency, Avowed Foe of Evil, and by the Order of White Knights, I shall see your madness ended."

"Firstly, my good Knight, my madness ends when I say it does. Secondly, I could argue that anyone who threatens grass is perhaps grappling with madness himself." Soulless Gustav moved from the field to a tree. "Thirdly, the lifestyle you have taken upon yourself is surely a sign of a far more twisted mind than my own. Tell me. Do you ever wonder what sort of man sacrifices even the simplest joys for the good of the world?"

It was a trick question. I would've answered it with a barbed response, but Wyst was no witch.

"A man with a great passion for justice!" he shouted.

The tree rattled its branches. "A great passion, yes, but isn't too great a passion madness in and of itself?"

Wyst fell deeper into the trap. "Not if that passion is righteous."

"Well, there you have it. Righteousness is a great moral quandary, isn't it? Such debates are for scholars and learned men who have nothing better to do but sit around and talk about life rather than live it. I am merely a legendary sorcerer, and you, a virtuous, quite possibly mad, White Knight. My point is, both of us have our goals, and both of us are willing to do whatever we must to achieve those goals. You've given up everything worthwhile in your quest for justice. I've seen thousands devoured by my phantom gobling horde. I see very little difference in the two, save for mine is a lot more fun."

Wyst drew his sword and snarled. "Come forward and face me, sorcerer. Or are you frightened because you know your doom is upon you?"

"Ah, there it is. The bravado, the fervor, and fury. How heroic. How courageous. How inane. Wyst of the West, you are no doubt a great White Knight, judging by your perfect banality. But you are also a great boorish simpleton. Afraid? Of you? My dear, dear Wyst, you really have no idea what you're up against. Well, courage is merely equal parts over-confidence and idiocy."

"I'm not the one hiding in trees and grass."

"I'm through talking with you, Wyst. You are of no consequence."

He left the tree. A whirlwind of dust kicked up before us and congealed into a man of sand. He was tall and thin, wearing a robe of gravel. His face was gaunt with a pointed chin, and he had polished jade for eyes. This was Soulless Gustav, if not quite in the flesh.

He walked to Gwurm. "Did you know, I've always had a fondness for trolls. In fact, my horde of goblings was nearly a crush of trolls."

"Nearly?" asked Gwurm.

"Unfeasible at this stage, I'm afraid. I've yet to craft a phantom troll to my liking. It's the dignity, I think. Your race has a quality, a grace that is rare in such loathsome creatures."

"I've often thought so."

"Goblings, they're easy. Malicious, slobbering, one-dimensional beasts. Wrap an illusion around a ravenous hunger and you're done. Don't worry though, my friend. I'll get it right. Your race will not be forgotten in my new world."

Gwurm smiled without a hint of sarcasm. "Good to know."

"Care for a walk, witch? I would have a word with you."

I hopped from Gwurm's shoulder. Wyst spurred his horse forward. Soulless Gustav smiled with teeth of shining quartz.

"There are things this witch and I must discuss. Things you wouldn't understand, Wyst, as they have nothing to do with poking villains with swords or impotent blustering."

Wyst jumped from his horse and ran Soulless Gustav through. The sorcerer shook his head. "All that righteous fury and not a blessed thing you can do with it. Pity. I can imagine your frustration."

I put a hand on Wyst's arm. "He's right. We must speak of things that only sorcerers and witches can. Stay here." I set down Newt. Much to my surprise, he didn't protest being left behind. I took Penelope along. Having my broom made me feel a better witch.

Soulless Gustav and I walked away from the others. Every step covered the space of four by the sorcerer's will, and they were soon figures on the horizon.

"It seems rude that you should know my name, and I, not yours," he remarked.

"I have no name."

"Everything has a name, even if it is unspoken. But suit yourself." He shrugged, and dust and stone fell from his shoulders. "So now that we have finally met, am I everything you expect? No. Don't bother answering. I know what you're going to say before you say it. You weren't expecting anything?"

"Up to this moment, I hadn't given you much thought."

"You cut me to the quick."

I lowered my hat. "It wasn't an insult. You were only an idea before. More of a notion, really. Important, yes, but not worth excess consideration."

"And now?"

"And now you are more. And still not worth excess consideration because I have seen you for what you are."

Soulless Gustav frowned. "Is that not another insult?"

"Merely an observation. Only you can decide whether to take offense or not."

He ran a flat gray stone of a tongue across his sandy lips. "In that case, I believe I shall."

"As you wish." I turned my back on him. It was both witchly and a mark of confidence. I didn't fear the sorcerer just now. There was a way to these matters.

"I certainly was not expecting you," said Soulless Gustav. "The magic told me a witch was coming, and I knew you to possess notable talent to have defeated my horde. So naturally, I was expecting an old crone, warts and hunch and missing teeth. But you are such a lovely, lovely creature."

I wasn't surprised he saw me as I was. He was a master of illusion.

"I am cursed."

He laughed. "So I see. Afflicted with perky bosoms and soft lips and a nice, firm bottom. I generally prefer my woman plumper, but I must confess, I've never been more attracted. I assume the desire is part of your curse."

"It is."

"Excellent work then. My compliments to its maker."

A wind swept beneath me, raising my skirt. A stream of dust flowed between my feet to re-form into Soulless Gustav before me. "Nice legs too. Slender and supple thighs. Glorious calves. Never underestimate the appeal of a well-formed calf."

"Life is in the details." I wasn't about to let him know he'd struck a sore spot.

It was his turn to put his back to me. "You've come a long way to die, witch. Care to tell me why?"

I thought of Ghastly Edna, and this was surely the man who had taken her from me. My anger rose, but it didn't get the better of me. "Reasons are of little consequence. They are justifications for doing what we would do anyway. And who's to say I've come all this way to die?"

"The magic has shared its secrets with me. I have taken care of any obstacles to my better world before they could become a bother."

"The magic has shared a few secrets with me as well."

"Perhaps an exchange would be in order."

I stepped close behind him. "Perhaps not. If the magic really wanted us to know, it would've already told us."

"Excellent point, but you can't seriously expect to defeat me. My will is law here. That's the perfection of my dream. The old world is a turmoil, a jumble of a thousand thousand parts thrown together. My world shall be a marvelous unity. A creation of one will with one purpose: to serve me." He turned back on me. A sapphire tear rolled down his cheek. "Surely, you can see the beauty in that."

"Harmony, perhaps. Beauty, no. The world is a mess, chaotic and unpredictable and often infuriatingly uncertain." I glanced to the horizon at the troll, duck, and White Knight. Each has his place in my life, and each had become important in ways I never could have fathomed. That was why I valued them so.

"And one beautiful chaos," I said, "is worth a thousand spiritless dreams."

I thrust my hand into Soulless Gustav's sandy body and wrapped my fingers around the hard lump of his heart. His jade eyes popped from his face. I pulled his ruby heart from his chest. His body collapsed into a mound of dirt and stone. I crushed the ruby into glittering shards.

"You didn't think to kill me that easily?" asked a patch of moss.

I didn't, but it did show me what I needed to know. My magic worked even in Soulless Gustav's world. Even more importantly, he could be taken by surprise here. He may have been lord of the realm, but I was not of his realm. I seemed a speck of truth in a universe of phantoms, but his perfect world was now infected with imperfect reality.

"Good day, witch with the unspoken name," said Soulless Gustav from the moss. "If we meet again, I promise to kill you quickly because I like you."

"We shall." I grinned. "And I shall kill you quickly because I have better things to do."

He chuckled as he disappeared.

I stopped to pluck a flower for no other reason than to prove I could disrupt his grand, flawless order. Then I headed back to the others.

25

*W*yst *handled his humbling* encounter very poorly. It didn't show in an obvious way. Anyone else would've seen only a brooding, determined champion, but I felt his sullen annoyance with his own powerlessness. He stared straight ahead, eyes squinted into slits, lips pursed tightly, jaw throbbing. All subtle signs. But to my eyes, his moping was impossible to miss. I would've reassured him, but he was right. He was no threat to Soulless Gustav.

A Sorcerer Incarnate need not fear an army of White Knights. I wasn't certain he should even fear me. Soulless Gustav wasn't invulnerable. Nor did his terrible madness have much chance of spreading across the whole world. Magic did rather enjoy the world, and the magic was stronger than Soulless Gustav, Incarnate or not. I assumed even now, fate was preparing for another to confront the sorcerer should I meet the horrible death Ghastly Edna had prophesied. And another should my successor do the same. Destiny was constantly setting designs in motion, most of which would never achieve fruition. Fate was an energetic child with a short attention span.

"What I don't understand," remarked Gwurm, "is that if this is all Soulless Gustav's illusion, then why doesn't he just turn it all to quicksand or a volcano or something like that and kill us right now?"

"Don't give him any ideas," Newt said.

"It isn't as simple as that," I replied. "The sorcery that crafted this is powerful, but such a creation is delicate by its very nature. Right now, it is a flea on the dragon of reality. As long as the flea remains unnoticed, it can slowly sap the dragon's strength. Should its sting be felt, it will be crushed with casual impunity.

"Every bit of sorcery takes that chance. Soulless Gustav is a great sorcerer. He has created a phantom realm most could never comprehend. But his world is a bloated, hungry parasite, and I imagine a tremendous amount of his magic is spent whispering lullabies in the dragon's ear. It would only take one mistake, one phantom too many at the wrong moment, to wake reality and bring all his plans to a crushing end. His power is at its most dangerous here, but it is also at its most vulnerable."

"It can't be both," Newt said.

"Magic thrives on contradiction."

"Like accursed beauty, for example."

His observation didn't bother me as much as I would've expected. I didn't want to be beautiful, but I found I didn't mind as I once had.

Newt balked. "I don't believe it. He didn't act like a man with a lot to fear."

"That's because he doesn't have a lot to fear. We are only a small threat."

Wyst of the West exhaled sharply.

"That's comforting to know," said Newt.

"The truth is rarely comforting. If it were, lies would not be as well received as they usually are."

"So why didn't you just do us a favor and lie?"

"Witches often don't tell the whole truth, but we don't lie."

"Maybe you should think about making an exception."

"Very well. Soulless Gustav is an overrated sorcerer. His power pales beside my own. Even now, he is surely trembling in his iron tower, assuming he has one, and contemplating throwing himself on a sword." I stroked Newt's neck with my thumb. "Feel better?"

"Not really."

"Actually, I do," replied Gwurm. "Thanks."

"You're welcome."

The landscape in Soulless Gustav's kingdom slowly began to change. I imagined sorcerers, like witches, were never in complete control of their magic, and everything around us was merely Soulless Gustav's will given substance. Steadily, the world grew more menacing. The grass yellowed. Twisted, sinister grimaces appeared in trees. Heaving, gray clouds darkened the sky. A chill wind swept across the plains. I was grateful for the dark and the cold, but there was no mistaking Soulless Gustav's hostility reflected in his creation. I thought some time on whether this hostility was founded in genuine fear or mere offense that we'd dared to disturb his empty empire. I didn't decide which.

The road came to a sudden end. It grew dark as dusk. We traveled onward, and the fields thickened. When the grass reached Gwurm's shoulder, I sensed the approach of our third trial. It wasn't found in an omen, but in good judgment. Soulless Gustav wouldn't tolerate our presence for long. We were an affront to his power just by being here.

"I don't like this," said Wyst. "Perhaps we should turn back and find an easier route."

"There is no easier route," I explained. "There is only one way to Soulless Gustav, and that is the way he has given us."

The sharp blades scraped my legs. It was fortunate that trolls possessed thick skin as Gwurm didn't seem to notice. Wyst's horse trotted on with only an annoyed snort. The field reached my shoulder atop Gwurm's back and was soon over my head. If Soulless Gustav was intending to separate us then we would be separated. But as we emerged from the grass, I knew this wasn't his plan. The fields ended without warning into a circle of bare earth.

On the opposite end, figures broke through the grass. I recognized them immediately for they were us. They were akin to the shadows that had tried to steal my reality, but Soulless Gustav wasn't resorting to the same trick as before. Magic dislikes repetition as I was certain any self-respecting sorcerer did.

We stopped, and our doubles halted. They were exactly like us in formation and stance, every nuance of movement. But they were gray, lifeless duplicates, possessed of lusterless color and a certain lack of detail. I noticed it in Wyst's pleasing face and its absence in his copy. The features were still there: the chewy lips, the nibblesome ears, the bitable nose. But they were somehow not the same. It had much to do with his expressions or the lack of them. All the doubles wore blank faces. Even Penelope's copy carried its bristles in a limp, languid manner.

Wyst drew his sword. His duplicate did the same. I climbed from Gwurm's shoulders as my double descended from his double.

"What manner of sorcery is this?" asked Wyst.

I closed my eyes and listened to the magic. It whispered ever so softly, despite Soulless Gustav's desire to suppress it. We were to be given a fighting chance.

"Effigies. They've been sent to be killed by us."

"Now isn't the time for riddles," said Newt.

"No riddles. They're reflections of sorcery, but we are also reflections of them. If they die, we die."

"You're saying we can't kill them?"

"We certainly can, but we'll be taking our own lives."

"This is a cowardly assault." Wyst jumped from his horse. His double reproduced the move exactly, yet somehow lacking the grace. "Come out and face us, sorcerer! Unless you are afraid!"

Despite Wyst's heartfelt valor, Soulless Gustav didn't materialize to meet the challenge.

We stood there for some time. We watched our effigies. They, in turn, watched us.

"Maybe we can get around them," suggested Gwurm, but this idea was quickly put aside. The effigies matched us move for move, as perfect as a mirror. They couldn't be outmaneuvered. As long as we didn't advance, neither did they, and it gave us time to think on the problem.

"What if we just maim them?" asked Newt. "Would we be maimed in return?"

"They will not be maimed. Injuries which we could survive will kill them. They're made to die."

"I've got it," said Gwurm. "If we don't attack them, they won't attack us. Right?"

I shook my head. "They have been sent to be killed."

"How are we supposed to defeat foes made to be defeated?" asked Newt.

"We let them defeat us?" theorized Gwurm.

Again, I shook my head. "They will kill us if they can."

"Can't you do something with your magic?" Newt said. "Like make them just disappear."

"Such sorcery is beyond simple unmaking."

A perceptible tension rose in my companions except for Gwurm, who accepted the situation with his usual pragmatism. The troll could've been a splendid witch. Wyst dealt with his stress as he always did: silent, steely resolve. Newt, however, wasn't about to allow his annoyance to go unspoken.

"Well, this is just unfair."

The observation seemed absurd coming from a demon, yet it was perfectly understandable. To demons, anything they dislike is unfair. He'd made similar remarks about such diverse injustices as not being able to fly and not being allowed to slay any mortal that struck him wrong. Which was every mortal. Like all these perceived inequities, he was mistaken. I wanted to kill Soulless Gustav. He wanted to kill me. There were no rules beyond that, and even if I found myself confronted with an apparently unbeatable trial, I couldn't fault him for that.

Out of frustration and boredom, Newt and Gwurm experimented with our effigies. My familiar did a silly dance just to watch his duplicate do the same. The troll exchanged his feet and hands and walked around upside-down. They taunted the effigies with crossed eyes and stuck out tongues. The faces were the only element not copied, remaining blank. Wyst did nothing. He just stood there, weapon in hand, jaw clenched, and full of heroic determination and a pinch of moping.

Newt snarled. "I don't really walk like that, do I?"

"Not quite," Gwurm replied. "There's an impalpable oddity that the effigy can't quite duplicate."

The duck sat. "So if they kill us, we die, but if we kill them, we die. I'm out of ideas."

"Not every problem can be solved through violence."

He turned up his bill. "Most can. It's the rare dilemma that can't find resolution with a quick disemboweling."

"If you'd care to go and disembowel yourself," suggested Gwurm, "go right ahead. We'll just stand here and watch."

"I don't see you coming up with any solutions."

Gwurm shrugged. "Alas, I'm mostly a problem basher myself."

Newt grinned smugly, finding vindication in Gwurm's admission.

Soulless Gustav may have finally come up with a trial to end my quest. I pondered if death by effigy qualified as horrible. I didn't think so, but there was an undeniable awfulness to the paradox the sorcerer had put us in. We could either sit here forever or go and meet our deaths.

"You're the witch," said Newt. "You're supposed to handle obstacles of this sort. Don't you have any ideas?"

"Perhaps I do. Stay here."

"Where are you going?" asked Newt and Wyst simultaneously.

"To have a talk with myself."

I walked forward, and my effigy moved to meet me in the center of our arena. When she got closer, I observed a flatness in her. She seemed not quite three-dimensional, and when we came within scant feet, I noticed a shiny quality, almost as if she were made of colored glass.

Penelope slipped from my hand. She angled a threatening tilt at her duplicate.

I greeted my effigy with a slight smile. "Hello."

She remained expressionless. "You should never have come. You should have left Fort Stalwart to die." She didn't possess my voice. Hers was a dry monotone, neither high nor deep, and lacking anything in the way of character.

"Is that me or Soulless Gustav speaking?" I asked.

"You. Or rather the you that finds reflection in me."

"If you are me in any fashion, then you know I couldn't do that."

"I am more you than even Soulless Gustav intended." And she smiled though only for a moment.

It made perfect sense. The sorcerer's power was at its most dangerous but also its most vulnerable. My effigy was so well constructed that it carried some of my own magic. Once again, his false world was tainted with reality.

"But I was still made to kill or be killed," she said, "and I must do what I was made for."

"That, I know. But I also expect that as my effigy, you know how I can destroy you."

"I do, but why do you think I would tell you?"

"Because witches don't lie, and I think you are enough my duplicate that you don't either."

She looked into the angry sky in a slight display of independent movement. "But we often don't tell the whole truth."

"Yes, but it is a witch's trade to offer wisdom."

"Even to her enemies?"

"Especially to her enemies."

We shared a chuckle, even if hers was a lifeless, empty chortle.

"The answer is obvious," she said.

"Most answers are."

"You know the solution already."

"I expect I do since you do. But your counsel would be appreciated."

"And if I should trick you?" she asked.

"Then I would perish with pride for what could be a greater accomplishment for any witch than to be tricked by herself?"

She smiled. "But yours is to be a horrible death."

"One doesn't necessarily exclude the other."

We turned away from one another.

"We are made to die, and we die easily." My effigy arched an eyebrow. I assume she did, since I did. "Beneath the right hands."

Penelope returned to my hand. "Thank you."

"No need for that. You have only yourself to thank. And Soulless Gustav for being perhaps too great a sorcerer."

I returned to my companions, and she, to hers.

"Well?" asked Newt.

"I think I told myself what we must do."

"You think? You aren't certain?"

"Certainty is for death and fools."

I'd used the line before, but I felt it appropriate to the situation and worth repeating. Then I explained what we were to do.

Newt was skeptical. "That's it? That's all?"

"Yes."

"But we'll still be killing them."

"No. We'll be destroying them. We may be reflections of one another, but we are true while the effigies are false. Even in this land of glass and shadow, the magic knows the difference."

"And if you're wrong?"

"We die."

A flutter filled my chest. I didn't fear death, but I wasn't ready to face my end quite yet. I glided to Wyst's side. He was so intent on the effigies, he didn't notice. I reached up and put a palm against his dark face. And I kissed him. On the cheek. As close to his lips as I dared.

Newt gasped.

Wyst pulled away from me. Only a step. He placed fingers

where I'd kissed him. He didn't smile, but he didn't frown either.

"Why did you do that?"

"Because I might be wrong."

I almost apologized, but I didn't regret it. Neither did Wyst, I thought. Though the mark on his forehead dimmed momentarily, his chastity remained intact. The kiss hadn't damaged his virtue. White Knights lived by a strict code, but even his enchantment couldn't fault him for a kiss he hadn't asked for.

I led my companions forward, and we stood before our effigies. We drew close, but we didn't touch. The first contact between us would free our doubles to move on their own and begin a battle we couldn't win.

Newt lowered his head and eyed his double. "How are we going to test this theory of yours?"

My reply was a swift, hard kick to his rear. The effigies duplicated the maneuver among themselves. Newt popped into the air and landed on his back. His effigy exploded in a puff of feathers.

Newt, the true Newt, remained whole, though with bruises to his bottom and ego.

It had worked. The effigies were intentionally fragile phantoms, but they could only be killed by the hands of their originals. Yet they could be undone by turning the sorcery that had created them against itself. The pile of feathers around an agape bill was proof of that.

"Are you mad?" Newt growled. "What if you'd been wrong? You could've killed me."

"You are my familiar. It's your duty to die for me."

"That's true, but it's supposed to be a bloody, violent death. Not demise by booting."

"That's not your choice to make."

"I'd prefer it."

"I'll see what I can do."

Their weakness exposed, the effigies were simple to undo. The could only mimic whatever actions we performed, and they expired easily. The only curiosity was that each passed in its unique fashion.

Penelope smacked Gwurm between the eyes barely hard enough to be felt. The troll's effigy's head caved in like a hollow rind and its entire body shriveled into a wrinkled skin. Wyst nicked his horse along the shoulder. The effigy dissolved into a watery gray puddle with bits of fur floating atop. I bent Penelope with light force. My double snapped her broom and shattered the effigy into crystalline shards.

The last two, Wyst and mine, were to destroy themselves together. Wyst put his sword to my belly in preparation.

I turned to my effigy. "I'm sorry."

"Don't be. This is what I was made for, and though my existence was brief, at least I knew its purpose."

Wyst drove his blade through my abdomen at the same moment I struck a hard slap across his cheek. His duplicate's head popped off. The decapitated body fell over, leaking a putrid white puss from the neck, and with a wide, unwitchly grin, my effigy dissolved into nothing.

"I still don't understand how that was different from killing them," said Newt.

"You don't need to understand. Would you mind, Wyst?"

He pulled his sword from my stomach. A foot higher and an inch to the right, he would've pierced my heart. But the hole in my belly, even delivered by the man I loved, was a minor ache to my undead flesh.

Wyst wiggled his jaw. He'd known my slap was coming, and I suppose that made it honorable. Honorable enough to leave a small discoloration on his cheek.

"You're bleeding," he said.

"It's nothing." The wound would close on its own, but I could see it distressed him. I pressed my hand to the hole and seared it shut. It made him feel better, and I enjoyed the stench of burning flesh.

His enchanted sword repelled tarnishes, but a few smudges of dark syrup were left behind. "Allow me." I wiped the blade with the loose hem of my skirt. The garment was already covered with mysterious stains, but I was always looking to freshen them. It gave me an excuse to get close to Wyst again. He didn't move away.

"I hope I didn't strike you too hard."

He rubbed the bruise and smiled. It was an open, honest smile. The first real grin I'd seen upon his face. I turned from his eyes and glanced at the blade. It was clean, and I polished the gleaming steel.

"Thank you." He returned the weapon to its sheath.

I caressed his bruise with the back of my fingers. Then he leaned in and graced my cheek with a soft kiss. I hadn't expected it, but I was witch enough to hide my surprise.

"What was that for?"

"For being right."

He squeezed my hand, and for a moment, we weren't a witch and a knight. The obstacles between us, my curse, his chastity, were almost forgotten.

"My good Knight, perhaps you are not so mad after all." Our destroyed effigies were gone, replaced by a red cloud cast in Soulless Gustav's shape.

Wyst let go of my hand and drew his sword.

"Oh, let's not bother with all that again," said Soulless Gustav.

Wyst of the West slashed the cloud without effect. He didn't seem surprised, but he was too much a White Knight not to try. He put away his sword and stepped aside.

Soulless Gustav billowed toward me. "That was very good. Defeating my effigies and corrupting a White Knight. You are a credit to witches everywhere."

"I can't take all the credit. I was taught well."

"I see now that I'll have to deal with you myself." He waved. The grass parted. "Follow this path, and you'll find a cottage where you can spend the night. Enjoy it with my compliments. For tomorrow, I'll put an end to your troublesome, accursed life."

"Thank you for your hospitality."

"Mortal enemies need not be impolite. Civility is what separates us from the animals." He shot into the sky and away.

"I'm offended by that remark," Newt said.

"You aren't really an animal," commented Gwurm.

"I'm animal enough."

"Maybe, but you aren't all that civil either."

Newt almost said something rude but reconsidered. I wondered how long his new manners might last.

"No one asked you anyway, you big, loathsome oaf."

Longer than I'd expected.

26

Soulless Gustav's cottage was more of a two-story wooden palace, simple in design but impressive nonetheless. It was early evening by the time we reached it. This was mostly a guess. I have trouble measuring time in the real world, much less a place where night and day came at a sorcerer's whim. Soft light shone from the cabin's windows. The large, crescent-shaped pane over the door sparkled in a rainbow of colors.

"I vote we keep going," said Newt. "Why give the sorcerer more time to prepare?"

I laughed, and realized how much more I was doing that. There wasn't anything wrong with it. A laugh can be very witchy when soft and throaty. "This quest will not be decided by a few passing hours, and I doubt Soulless Gustav is preparing anything."

"What if this is a trick?"

"It isn't."

This didn't comfort his suspicious mind. "How do you know it's not a trick?"

I could've explained to him that my vision told me everything I needed to know. Four trials made our quest. The chimera had been trial by combat. My ghosts of destiny had been trial by strength of self. Trial by peril had been found in our effigies. Trial by magic was the only one remaining, and this could be nothing but the final duel between Soulless Gustav and myself. I could've told Newt this. But I didn't.

The cottage door opened when we drew near. A scar-faced man stepped onto the porch. I recognized him as one of the men that had killed Ghastly Edna or, more accurately, an illusion cast in the exact same form. This one was clean and unarmed. It made it all the easier for Newt to cut off the man's head with a single swipe of razor sharp wings. The corpse fell over and sizzled away.

A fresh servant, same as the last, stepped into the doorway. Newt moved to kill this one too, but I stopped him with a clearing of my throat.

"I'm at your service." The phantom spoke with perfect enunciation. Too perfect. The words sounded as if chopped from other sentences and pasted together. "A warm meal awaits you all in the dining room." He stepped out of the doorway to allow us to enter. "And there is an excellent stable just around the corner, good master Knight. Shall I take your horse?"

Wyst refused to hand over the reins.

"Very good, sir. Allow me to escort you so that you might inspect its quality."

He looked to me for approval. Unlike Newt, Wyst trusted my judgment. It was a great honor. A White Knight's loyal steed was his most valued possession, next to his virtue.

I smiled and nodded.

He nodded back and patted his horse's neck. "I'll find it myself." He disappeared around the corner.

"I'm telling you," said Newt, "the second we step inside, it's going to become a giant serpent head and swallow us all."

"I was thinking something subtler," said Gwurm. "Like perhaps it would shrink until we were all smashed to a pulp."

"So you agree then."

"I might if I weren't so hungry." He was the first to walk through the doorway. "Is that roast boar I smell?"

"Fresh off the spit, sir," intoned the servant. "I do hope you like it tender. The meat is practically falling off the bone."

I followed, catching the scent of a tantalizing variety of raw flesh. "Coming, Newt? Or would you rather stay outside with Penelope?"

My broom had immediately taken it upon herself to scour the porch of every offensive speck and mote, no doubt left there for her by Soulless Gustav's considerate sorcery. Even for a cleaning implement, she could be terribly obsessive when it came to dust. She swept by Newt and hopped at him to get out of her way.

"I still say this is a trap," grumbled the duck as he followed me inside.

The cabin was well lit by dozens of lamps, but not too bright even for my undead eyes. I'd never seen such exquisite tapestries and rugs. Then again, I'd never seen tapestries and rugs, save for the worn, utilitarian carpets of Fort Stalwart. I had an eye for stitching, and their quality was obvious. Had they been real and made by mortal hands, they would've taken years to craft. The one with an embroidered image of Soulless Gustav, standing tall and smugly grinning, was especially impressive. It was so vivid, it could be mistaken for the genuine article. Its eyes even seemed to follow us. It added a touch of dread to the cozy atmosphere. I admired the sorcerer's sense of style.

A banquet was set before us on a long table by the hearth. It was a wide table, but there wasn't an empty space. Soulless Gustav knew his guests. It was mostly meat, mostly raw or blood rare. A small bowl of fruit was present for appearance, and a loaf of fresh bread waited for Wyst. The food was all genuine, not illusion. A most thoughtful importance as a phantom feast would sate our hunger without nourishment. Where Soulless Gustav found reality in this phantom realm was a mystery I didn't give much thought.

Gwurm and Newt warmed themselves by the hearth. I kept away from it and enjoyed the remaining chill of evening.

The servant gestured to a staircase. "You'll find your sleeping accommodations upstairs. I'm certain they'll be to your liking, but should you need anything, please clap for me. Now unless you'll be needing me for anything . . ."

"No. We're fine." I noticed the tremendous crystal chandelier over our heads. It caught every beam of candlelight and reflected it in a cascade of colors.

The servant dismissed himself as Wyst returned from the stable. He seated himself beside the bread, folded his arms, and studied the loaf.

Gwurm prodded the roast boar with his fingers, which he then licked. Newt eyed the troll.

"Well? It's poisonous, isn't it? It has to be poisonous."

Gwurm took a rib and sucked the meat off it. He rolled the flesh from cheek to cheek, poking it with his tongue while chewing. He shrugged, swallowed, and gobbled down the bone. "Seems fine." He sat and tore off the boar's snout. "Excellent, just the proper chewiness."

Newt turned his back to the table. "I'm not eating any of it. If it's not poisoned, it's something worse. Your guts will probably rot away now."

"Some things are worth the risk." Gwurm swallowed a juicy red apple and an uncooked rabbit in one bite. He must've liked the two together because he tried an orange and hen combination next. It met with a satisfied grin.

"You're going to regret eating that," muttered Newt.

"Probably," said Gwurm. "Boar gives me heartburn. Pass some of that goose over, would you, please?"

Newt perked up. "Did you say goose?" He hopped onto the table and licked his bill over the succulent bird.

"You eat goose?" Gwurm stuck out his tongue.

"It's my second favorite."

"But you're a duck."

Newt closed his eyes and inhaled the goose's tempting aroma. "A carnivorous duck."

"Yes, but, well, it just doesn't seem right."

"Birds eat birds every day."

"Big birds eat little birds," said Gwurm. "That goose is twice your size."

"And perfectly seared." Newt smacked his bill. Demons are suspicious by nature but they're also easily tempted. He stood poised over the goose indecisively.

I did him a favor and helped him make up his mind. It was an inevitable decision anyway.

"Is that duck I smell?" I asked.

"Duck? Where?" He found his prey, a raw bird on a platter, and attacked. He tore off a wing and gulped it down.

Gwurm grimaced. "Now that is definitely just wrong."

Newt was far too busy tearing into his meal to bother with a curt response.

I took the bread and cut a thick slice that I offered to Wyst. He accepted it with a smile and passed a plate of raw turkey strips. We ate in silence, save for the crackle of the fire and the tearing and crunching of duck frenetically feasting upon duck.

"I'll say this for Soulless Gustav." Newt belched. "He knows how to treat a guest."

"He's mad," I said, "not rude."

Wyst excused himself. "I want to be rested for tomorrow."

I didn't contradict him, but he wouldn't be facing Soulless Gustav. Not if I had any say in the matter. After he'd climbed the stairs, I clapped once.

"Yes, mistress?" The servant was just there suddenly. Not materializing from nothing. More like he'd always been there, just unnoticed.

"I'll need a bath drawn. And a change of clothes."

I paused, expecting Newt to say something discouraging. He was too contented to bother with even a displeased glare.

My bath waited in a room on the first floor. Like the servant, the room seemed to have not been there before and yet perfectly in place. The long tub was filled with ice-cold water, just as I liked my baths. I stripped naked before the phantom and slid into the water. The servant pointed out the variety of soaps and perfumes and a wardrobe that should possess whatever clothes I needed. Then he was gone again, back to his unnoticed oblivion.

I didn't bathe often. I didn't really need to. My accursed nature did enough to keep me beautiful, but I enjoyed a nice, chilly bath every so often. It'd been too long since I'd had one. Not since I'd dipped myself in the lake the day Ghastly Edna had died.

The recollection made me smile. I missed Ghastly Edna, but she'd sent me to that lake with a purpose. I now knew that purpose. She'd known Wyst of the West would spy me, and that this would be laying the seeds of desire in his heart. Tonight would be her last gift to me.

I enjoyed my bath for an hour. I waited for the water to wrinkle my fingers. It didn't. It never did. I pulled myself from the tub and picked through the perfumed oils. They were all quite lovely, but none could match my own natural scent, a subtle mix of flowers and strawberries along with a new aroma: fresh bread. No doubt added by the magic because Wyst would like it.

I studied my form in a full-length mirror. I hadn't looked at myself, really looked, for a long time. I'd forgotten just how beautiful I was. My flawless, smooth skin was without a freckle. My figure was lean, yet blessed with the soft curves men wanted. My eyes sparkled. I was perfect, and even if a man's desires leaned toward blondes or short women, my curse made up for that.

I found exactly what I wanted in the wardrobe. The silky gown couldn't be more unwitchly. It was soft and sheer and hid little. I slipped it on and smiled, despite myself. Even if I couldn't be a mortal woman, it was nice to indulge in those pleasures I normally denied myself.

I wasn't quite ready to go upstairs yet. I crept outside. Both Newt and Gwurm sat by the fire and didn't notice. Penelope waited on the immaculate porch. She tilted to one side, then the other. Then floated a circle around me. She gave her approval with a hop and a twirl.

"Thank you."

"So are you going to mate with him or eat him?"

The gray fox sat at the bottom of the steps.

"I'm surprised you followed us into this false land," I said.

"I'd come too far to turn back now. Not when things were getting interesting." She grinned. "I only regret that as a simple fox, I can't appreciate it all."

I looked to the moon and pondered whether it was genuine or merely a reproduction.

"You didn't answer my question," said the fox.

"How do you know I want to do either?"

The fox laughed. "I may only be a beast, but if there are two things we beasts know, it's eating and mating. I've watched the way you look at that man. Sometimes, it's with the desire of a female for a male. Sometimes, it's with the gnawing of an empty stomach. Sometimes, it's both."

"I didn't think it was that obvious."

"Everything is obvious when you look for it. So is it mating season for witches? I think he'd father excellent offspring."

As did I. "I can't bear children."

"Neither can I," she said. "But when the season rolls around, I seek out a mate anyway. Even if I haven't birthed a litter in three seasons."

"Too bad," I said. "The world could use more clever foxes."

"The world could use a great many things."

I descended the short stairs and sat beside the fox. "I don't know what I'm going to do. I think I might do both."

She nibbled at an itch in her tail. "I've never been one to play with my food. Although I do enjoy batting around the occasional field mouse."

I stroked her between the ears. "I don't want to kill him."

"I suppose if you just bit off a few less necessary parts, but that would be more of a snack than a meal."

My stomach whimpered.

"Can I offer some advice?" said the fox. "I've never had anything I wanted to both eat and mate, but the logical thing to do would be to mate first, then eat. That way you get both pleasures."

"I don't want to eat him."

"Ah, I know the feeling. I once stole an egg that I didn't want to crack because once I ate it, it would be gone. But

I knew I couldn't be happy just looking at it." She settled her head on my lap. "That's the question you should ask yourself. Can you be happy just having him?"

"I don't know, but I think it's time to find out."

I invited the fox in for a bite to eat, and she accepted. I introduced her to Newt and Gwurm. Newt was more interested in my unwitchly raiment.

"What are you wearing? You can see . . . all your . . . naughty bits."

Penelope threw herself between Newt and me. I didn't need her defense and gently nudged her aside.

I grabbed a sharp knife from the table. "I'm going upstairs. Behave yourselves." I used the plural, but I looked at Newt.

"Good luck," said Newt.

"Remember," added the fox, "mate first. Eat second."

"Rip out his throat," grumbled Newt.

Penelope followed me upstairs. Each footfall seemed heavier than the last. I didn't understand exactly what trepidation gripped me, but as I neared Wyst's room, it grew. Ghastly Edna had taught me not to fear failure or horrible death, but she'd never prepared me for this. She'd once said, "It's easy to defeat life-or-death ordeals. Such tribulations demand success. It's the small tests that require something more from us. When we can turn and walk away is when we find what we're made of."

I stopped at Wyst's door. I reached for the knob but stopped short. I considered turning back. So long as I didn't open that door, I could always live with not knowing.

Penelope nudged my elbow.

I stood there frozen. I even stopped breathing. I ran it over and over through my mind. Could I really live without knowing? What if he turned me away? What if I killed him? What if he was forced to kill me? There were so many questions, and every answer seemed wrong. I was no closer to making the decision when Penelope finally made it for me.

She rapped on the door twice and floated behind me as it opened. Wyst stood there. He didn't say anything. His face remained blank, save for the soft arch of his eyebrows.

I suddenly felt very self-conscious. I didn't mind being practically nude before anyone. Anyone but this man. I was a creature of flawless, accursed beauty, and he loved me. Knowing didn't seem to make any difference. I wanted my thick, black frock. Maybe a hat. Even a shawl to drape across my shoulders would've been nice.

I kept my hands by my side, resisting the urge to hide my body behind folded arms. I swallowed a lump in my throat.

"May I come in?"

His eyebrows rose another notch. He glanced down the hall, back to his room, and back at me before moving aside. I stepped into his room. Penelope stayed in the hall. I whispered a thank you to my broom as I closed the door.

His room was cozy. I was too distracted to notice anything but the bed and a folded blanket lying on the floor.

"I hope I'm not interrupting anything."

"I was only meditating."

The meditation of White Knights must've been a strenuous practice. He was slightly out of breath. Sweat beaded on his forehead, and his entire body was tense. Or maybe these were due to my presence. He could only look at me from the corner of his eye.

It was terribly hot in this room. I paced to the window and opened it a crack. Wyst was reflected in the spotless glass. He studied my back, unaware I could see his glance wander up and down my body. I put my fingers to the window and traced the image of his strong, pleasing face.

"Is something wrong, witch?" He spoke softly. The first time I'd ever heard him mumble.

I was woefully inexperienced, but I was a creature made to seduce. I trusted my instincts. I turned slowly, allowing Wyst to enjoy my form from all angles. Then I glided to him, literally floating a hairsbreadth off the floor. My gown billowed upward, revealing my perfect legs. His already tense body tightened. I drew close but didn't touch him.

He turned his face from me. "What are you doing?"

I put a palm to his cheek and turned his face back. He closed his eyes.

"I can't do this."

Words could say much, and they said all the more when there were so few. He hadn't said he wouldn't. He'd said he couldn't. Can't is for things you mustn't do, yet you know you will.

He put a hand to my hand as if to pull it away. "I've taken a vow, a sacred vow."

I ran my thumb across his soft lips. "Tell me to leave, and I will." I did my best to sound as if this wouldn't bother me.

"I need my virtue," he whispered. "Without it, I'll be no match for the sorcerer."

"With it, you are still no match."

He withdrew half a step. "I can't let you face him alone. I have to protect you."

Again, his words said much. His resistance didn't come from his vows of purity. It stemmed from his love, his desire to keep me from harm. I understood more than he knew. We were so much alike, but unlike my burden, his could be put aside.

"You can't protect me from my fate, Wyst. And you won't meet Soulless Gustav tomorrow. That is my battle alone. You've done everything you can for me. There is only one favor I have left to ask of you . . ."

I moved as close as I could without touching him. The heat of his body washed over me. The lanterns flared with my rising desire. I wanted to throw him down and force him to love me. But it was his decision to make.

He stared into my eyes and bit his lower lip.

"When I meet my destiny tomorrow, Wyst, I will greet it gladly, without regrets. Save one. Unless you see fit to grant me one last favor."

"I can't."

I put a finger to his lips. The lanterns dimmed.

"They're just words, Wyst. They say much and mean nothing. Empty syllables carried on whispers, that's all they are. If you can deny me, deny yourself, without them, I'll go."

He ran his fingers through my hair and smiled sweetly. "I can't . . ."

"No words."

We drew closer.

"But . . ." He sounded parched.

I put my hands on his chest and felt the pounding of his heart. The warmth of his flesh seared my palms. His hand slipped down my neck and slid the gown from my shoulders. I ran my calf along his thigh. Strange, how natural it all was. As if I'd done this a thousand times before.

We kissed. I couldn't remember who kissed who. We just suddenly were. My stomach grumbled. The fiend within wanted to bite off his tongue. I could feel the gush of tangled veins in his throat, just begging to be ripped out.

I pulled away, and it was his turn to be puzzled. "I have to warn you. I might kill you."

I handed him the knife.

"If you feel you must, drive this blade in my heart and save yourself."

The knife clattered to the floor. He took me in his arms and kissed my neck. He whispered softly in my ear.

"Some things are worth the risk."

27

Wyst's *blood tasted* even sweeter than I'd expected.

I enjoyed a drop, gained in a moment when my passion and carnivorous lusts caught me unaware, and I'd nibbled his ear too sharply. It was the only slip. Though at the heights of our rapture, visions of rent flesh did flash through my mind. The carnal pleasures overwhelmed my appetite. Mostly.

Wyst put a hand to my grumbling stomach. The dark of his fingers against my alabaster skin seemed a perfect contradiction. We were so different on the surface, yet so much alike.

"Do you regret it?" I asked. "The loss of your virtue?"

He put fingers to my chin and raised my face to his. "If I'd regretted it, I would've stopped after the first time. And my virtue isn't lost, only my chastity."

His lips graced my forehead. I kissed him and my hand danced down his thigh.

"Again? You really will kill me."

I smiled. He didn't know how right he was. With my curse, I could do just that. I could hold him in this bed and stoke his fires over and over again until every last ounce of his life burned away. The danger of that was a long way off. Wyst was a healthy specimen, possessed of enough stamina to survive a week or two in my dangerous embrace.

I slipped over him and nibbled on his lower lip. He wrapped his arms around me and pressed me tight against him. My stomach roared, no longer to be neglected. I found the strength to roll away. It was easier knowing he would still be here when I got back. I put on my gown and paused at the door just long enough to cast a sidelong glance at him lying there. Any more would have been too much temptation.

Penelope waited in the hall. She didn't say anything, not in her unspoken way, but she did peek in the room to make sure Wyst was still alive. My shadow danced along the walls. It twirled and frolicked, often leaving my feet to caper playfully along the ceiling.

Downstairs, Gwurm was asleep by the fire. The fox dozed in his lap. Newt sat on the table, nestled among gnawed duck bones. He raised his head and frowned.

"As you're not covered in blood, I assume you didn't kill him."

"Sorry to disappoint you." I took a seat and glutted myself on every piece of uncooked meat I could reach. I was hungrier than I'd realized. Absolutely ravenous. This wasn't the meal my appetite desired, but flesh was flesh.

"What's the sense of robbing a White Knight of his purity if you don't bother killing him?" said Newt. "It's like running down a deer and then letting it go. I hope it was worth it, throwing aside your witchly ethics."

I finished sucking down a turkey leg. "I have seduced a White Knight, exposed the mortal man for all the world to see, and he doesn't resent me for it. Not only that, but I've tasted forbidden pleasures of the flesh and learned something about myself. I can't think of anything more witchful than this."

"Your mistress would disagree."

"I doubt that very much. It was by her design that this night came to pass."

"Vengeance is our quest."

I laughed. "Vengeance or death lay at the end of this journey, but not every journey is about the destination."

He yawned and perked up his head. "Can I kill him then?"

He already knew the answer.

"Senseless," he grumbled.

The tapestry of Soulless Gustav spoke up. "I quite agree." The sorcerer stepped from the cloth. He kept his flatness. It suited him as even in three dimensions he was a slight figure. "Didn't mean to eavesdrop, but I have to go with the duck. It's bad form to not take advantage of a White Knight after you've, well, after you've taken advantage of him. It's expected."

"A good witch does the unexpected."

"Excellent point, my dear witch with the unspoken name." He strolled to a chair and folded himself into a sitting position. "Although when the morning comes, I expect you will die."

My only response was a wry grin. I expected him correct, but then again, a great witch can even surprise herself on occasion.

"Speaking of morning." Soulless Gustav waved his hand, and hard light poured through the windows. "You'll excuse my impatience, but I'd like to get this over with."

"No."

"I beg your pardon."

"Not yet."

He glared. "I am master of this realm. You dare to give me commands."

"Not a command. A request. You've been a most gracious host, and I would appeal to your generosity one last time."

His glares softened. "Of course. Forgive me." He returned to the tapestry. "I'll grant you two more hours. As they shall be your last on this world, I suggest you make good use of them."

"I shall. And thank you."

"The laws of hospitality apply to all men, lowly peasant and legendary sorcerer alike." Soulless Gustav resumed his silent watch over the room as darkness buried the morning.

I allowed myself a few minutes to settle my full stomach.

"What did you learn about yourself?" asked Newt. "You said you'd learned something."

"I learned that I can never love a man. Not as a woman."

"You seem to be doing an excellent job so far."

I smiled without mirth. "A temporary indulgence. No matter what, I am accursed. My love will always be doomed."

My shadow stopped dancing.

The jagged truth tore at my witchly veil. Newt averted his eyes and fidgeted in the awkward silence. Penelope leaned against my shoulder.

"Life isn't about the things you can't have," I said. "It is about those blessings you do find along the way." Though the truth is rarely a comfort, I found some solace in this. I couldn't love Wyst for a lifetime, but I could love him for a short while more.

My shadow skipped around the fireplace as I moved toward the stairs.

Newt snorted. "You aren't fooling me. I know why you robbed him of his virtue. You made him vulnerable to protect him."

"Did I?"

"Oh, stop pretending to be mysterious. I see through it all. Wyst may not have been a match for Soulless Gustav on his own, but he could've helped you. And you need every advantage you can get. But now, he's just a man. You've made him useless. You've taken him out of the game because you weren't willing to risk his life for your own."

"Figure that out all on your own?" I asked.

"You're admitting it then?"

I only grinned.

"It is very witchful," he said. "To save a man's life by stealing his invulnerability. Your mistress would be proud." He didn't like acknowledging that and scowled.

A good witch admits to nothing. I ascended the stairs without saying another word and entered Wyst's room. He lay on the bed. My eyes lingered on his lean, dark body. He smiled and held out a hand.

He traced my lips with his fingers. "You are beautiful."

I already knew this, but there was something in the way he said it. Something in his eyes as well. He saw more than my cursed flesh. He saw the mortal woman hidden inside that even I could forget was there. But in his arms, it was different. In his arms, I could almost forget the fiend.

He kissed me, and his flavorful lips stirred my twin hungers. The ghoul hissed and fidgeted, but she was smothered beneath the indulgences of the woman.

Newt was wrong. Even without his enchantments, Wyst was more than a man. Much more.

He slipped off my gown and drew me onto the bed.

And he was far from useless.

28

There was a benefit to being ageless. Time meant nothing to me, a vague abstraction. Two hours in Wyst's bed might pass as slowly as I perceived it. It could never last as long as I wanted, but I could draw out every moment, enough for a lifetime that might reach into infinity. If I survived the next day, and still walked this world a thousand years from now, this night would always remain with me. When the dawn finally came, I was ready to meet either death or eternity.

Soulless Gustav allowed me a slow sunrise. The light slipped through the windows, and I pulled myself from Wyst's arms. I reached for my silken gown but thought better of it. It would have to be left in this room, like so many things. I wrapped a heavy blanket over my body. I leaned over Wyst and kissed his eyes, an earlobe, and finally his lips. Part of me wanted to wake him, but this was best. This was the only way it could be. I turned to the door.

"Where are you going?"

I'd hoped to steal away unnoticed. It would've made everything so much easier.

I closed my eyes and didn't look back at him. "It's time."

"I'll get my things."

"You're no longer enchanted," I said. "Soulless Gustav would kill you even easier than he would have before."

"I won't let you face him alone."

"I know."

I glided to his side and enfolded him in my blanket to enjoy the feel of his skin against mine.

"You won't talk me out of this," he said softly.

"I know. You're a stubborn man, but I think you are very tired. I think you should go back to bed." I batted my eyelashes at him. His lids slipped half-closed.

"What are you doing?" He yawned. He fell limp in my arms. I had no trouble holding him up. "Don't do this." He nodded off and jerked alert. "I have to protect you. I have to . . ."

"You can't protect me as tired as you are." I covered his mind in sleep. Magic that would've burned away against his invulnerable aura only hours ago now proved more than his match.

"Forgive me, Wyst."

I lowered him onto the bed. His slumber was peaceful, save for a soft frown across his lips.

I descended the stairs. My companions sat ready by the table. I wasted no time on politeness and got dressed. Soulless Gustav had given me my hours. I wouldn't be rude and keep him waiting any longer.

"Gwurm, you'll find Wyst upstairs. Dress him and take him from this place. Penelope, you'll go with them."

"And me?" asked Newt.

"You'll be coming with me."

He squinted with surprise. "I will?"

"You are my familiar, aren't you? Your place is by my side, isn't it?"

"Well, yes . . ."

"Good then. We'll see about that violent death you were hoping for. Although I make no promises."

"Yes, mistress." He beamed.

"And me?" asked the gray fox.

"You can do whatever you like," I said.

"Then I shall come along too."

Gwurm went to fetch Wyst, and Penelope tried to force herself into my hand.

"None of that. You'll go with Gwurm. I'll most likely be dead very soon, and he'll need a friend. I'm trusting you to take care of him."

She stood straight and bobbed once.

"Good girl." I turned to Newt. "It's time to go."

He couldn't resist smirking at Penelope, even though all he'd really earned was almost certain doom.

The phantom servant materialized by the front door. "Right this way, madam. The master is expecting you."

Gwurm descended the stairs with Wyst over his shoulder. "Good luck."

I glanced back at my troll, broom, and slumbering White Knight. "Tell him I'm sorry."

"He'll understand."

I wasn't so sure. Wyst was a proud man. He would've chosen to die by my side, and I was wrong to not allow him that.

"Tell him . . ." I found the words very hard to say. I should've told Wyst in the bedroom. Now, I couldn't.

"He already knows," said Gwurm. "Just as you know."

"Are we going or not?"

The servant directed us onto a cobblestone path that led up to a tall hill. Penelope and Gwurm with Wyst and steed in tow headed the other direction. I didn't know if they'd make it, but accompanying me was certain death. Now they had a chance.

I put aside the distraction as we marched up the path.

Magic is everywhere in all things and all places, but there is more magic in some things than others. Accursed witches and Incarnate sorcerers draw arcane power like lodestones. As we drew closer, that power crackled in the air. The magic knew a terrible battle was about to begin, and it offered all its potency before us to ensure a colorful struggle.

Witch magic is a subtle art. I may have been out of my element, but Ghastly Edna had prepared me. "Remember, child, that magic follows no rules other than its own. Many of its followers fail to understand this. They fail to adapt when the magic demands it. Mostly because they've grown set in their ways. But a good witch knows her place, and a great witch understands that experience can as often be a burden as a gift."

To defeat Soulless Gustav, I only had to forget everything I'd learned, but unlearning was a witch's greatest talent. Perhaps I wasn't as far out of my element as I thought.

I was expecting everything and nothing on the other side of the hill, but the landscape remained unexceptional phantom fields of grass. The cobblestones came to an end at a gleaming silver cube.

"What is it?" asked Newt.

"The heart of a world that doesn't exist," I replied.

The shape of Soulless Gustav's face pressed through the shimmering surface. "You should be honored. You'll be the first to glimpse the beautiful fate that shall replace this universe." He glanced to my companions. "I expected you alone."

"The duck is my familiar. The fox is merely an observer."

"For posterity, eh? An excellent idea. Enter and witness my glory."

His face melted into the cube, and I stepped into its impalpable surface. It wasn't so much that I entered it as it expanded around my perceptions. First came the illusion of time to distinguish one moment from another. Then came the fantasy of space. Then came the other details of Soulless Gustav's creation. The countless lesser particulars that make up a phantom universe fell into place. I stood on the threshold of a miniature cosmos. Dozens of tiny planets swirled amid an endlessness of stars. Neither Newt nor the fox were with me.

Soulless Gustav stood at the center of his universe. "Beautiful, isn't it?"

I remained properly inscrutable. "I suppose it is. In much the same way a painting of a flower can almost be as beautiful as the flower itself."

He glowered. Then sighed and smiled in a passable imitation of good humor. "Forgive me, witch. I've forgotten that you lack the vision to see what I've shown you."

His solar system wound to a slow halt. A tiny planet ceased its orbit before me that I might glimpse its continents and oceans. If I looked close enough, I could no doubt see mountain ranges, forests, and deserts as well as villages and cities teeming with millions of phantom inhabitants.

"Mine is a flawless re-creation. This is the universe, my universe. A small thing now, but it shall grow like a seed. And one day, mine will overthrow that flawed jumble you call reality."

I slapped the planet and started it spinning again. "How sad that you think this is a dream worth fighting for. You have my pity."

His worlds twirled faster. He walked forward between the speeding spheres. "You have courage, witch. I'll grant you that. This isn't your reality. Nor is it even that impure realm of sorcery outside this cube. This is my power, pure and undiluted. Here, I am a living god, and you are absolutely nothing."

"Perhaps. But I am a good witch, even here. And you are still a very poor sorcerer, even here."

The only sign of Soulless Gustav's rage came in a clenched fist. "Your bravado doesn't fool me, woman. I sense your fear, your awe."

"You've lived too long among glass and shadows. You sense only those illusions you desire."

He raised his hand. An inch-high double of me stood in his palm. He waved his other hand over them, and it writhed and dissolved into moldering paste amid tortured shrieks.

I smiled. "Most impressive. If I were a phantom, I would be most terrified."

"How dare you . . ."

"I dare. I confess to once having some dread over facing you, but that disappeared the moment you showed me your dream." I reached out and plucked a passing moon. "All that power at your disposal, and this is the best you could do."

"All that I can do!" Soulless Gustav snarled. His voice echoed from one end of eternity to the other as his civility crumbled at the edges. "I have remade a universe!"

I shook my head and balanced the moon on my fingertips. "There is already a perfectly good universe out there. Remaking it is a waste of magic, an exercise in futility."

The orbit of his worlds grew erratic. They zipped about, barely missing one another.

"You dare mock my power."

"Your power, never. It is awesome without question. It is your vision that I find lacking. You have the gift to create whatever your will desires, to make the unreal real. Yet you choose to make something that already is. You lack the one thing every great sorcerer should possess: imagination. Without that, all the magic in this universe and a thousand others counts for naught."

Soulless Gustav's anger was a cataclysm on his creation. Worlds smashed into each other. Stars flashed, only to burn away in moments. The moon on my fingertips cracked in two.

"You don't honestly think you can defeat me?" he said softly through clenched teeth.

"Probably not," I agreed, "but even if I lose, what difference does it make? Even if you succeed in your dream, what does it matter? Either way, this universe continues. Whether genuine or unimaginative illusion, I fail to notice the difference."

Soulless Gustav drew in a deep, calming breath. "Mine shall have one less accursed witch."

"Details. Unimportant trivialities. Pity though." I smiled wide. "I've heard accursed witches can grow on you."

Soulless Gustav's universe exploded. I didn't think it intentional, but this cosmos was a reflection of his will. I understood now why he'd allowed me into the heart of his madness. He wanted my approval in the shape of fear and wonder. I was flattered my reaction meant so much to him, but it wasn't because he respected me as a witch. It had been so long since he'd been criticized, I don't think he could've taken it from anyone. Such was the price of living in an empty dream. He'd forgotten that reality wasn't always to one's liking.

We hovered among the glittering shards of unreality for but a moment. They collected together. An ocean of sparkling blue water formed under our feet. A soft red sky grew over our heads. We stood on the surface without sinking. Thousands of colorful fish swam beneath us. An immense, black eel parted the rainbow schools and sent soft waves across the ocean. Nothing serious enough to disturb our balance.

Soulless Gustav folded his arms tightly across his chest. "What do you think of my sorcery now?"

I knelt and pushed my hand through the depths. A fish swam right into my grasp. I pulled it out, holding it by the tail as it twitched. Its gills gulped for water as its mouth gaped. "As impressive and pointless as before." I threw the phantom back into its home.

Soulless Gustav scowled. "You are starting to try my patience, witch."

"To be honest, mine is wearing thin as well. Shall we get on with it?"

"Eager to die, are you?"

"If death means leaving behind your vainglorious chatter, I welcome it." A witch rarely is so direct, but I couldn't resist jabbing at his narcissism. It was such an easy target.

"You can't win, you know. Would you like to know why?" he asked.

"Not really."

The ocean churned and bubbled, forcing me to shift to keep my balance. Dark things with lumpish shapes surged beneath the waves.

"The magic told me that I had only one person to fear," he said. "Only one who might pose any threat to me. A witch, ironically enough. It even told me where to find her. So I struck her down while she was unaware." He grinned. "Very easily too, I might add."

Now I understood those mysteries I'd almost given up on. Ghastly Edna had known what was happening that final day because the magic had spoken with her too. She could've saved herself, but she chose instead to be killed. She'd given her life to protect me. A witch was to die there that day. It wasn't unavoidable, but it was the most practical solution. Even in death, Ghastly Edna had been a great witch.

I wiped the beginnings of a tear from my eye. "Did perhaps the magic mention something of two witches living in the same cabin?"

Soulless Gustav's smug grin fell away as his ocean grew deathly calm. The shapeless things ceased their swimming.

He squinted. "What?"

"You killed the wrong witch. You took away the most precious thing in my life, and for that, I will kill you. But you have also given me a most precious gift, even if unintentionally." I smiled. "And for that, I shall kill you quickly."

I reached out with my magic and found the two pieces of reality floating in Soulless Gustav's madness. They shone like beacons. I plucked them from wherever they were and drew them to my side. Newt and the gray fox materialized beside me.

"You've forgotten a few." Soulless Gustav waved his arms. An eel broke the surface and spat up four others. Though coated with slime, Gwurm, Wyst, Penelope, and the horse appeared startled but unharmed.

"They aren't part of this, Gustav," I growled.

"On the contrary, everyone and everything are part of this. They do belong to the old universe."

Wyst of the West drew his sword. "Prepare to die, sorcerer!"

"Brave and tired words, White Knight."

Soulless Gustav put a thumb to his chin. Angry red magic surged at Wyst. I sent a billowing tide of warm, blue power against it. They sizzled away against each other. The battle had begun, and none of the others knew, unable to sense the raw magic gathering around Soulless Gustav and myself.

A cloud of glittering dark blazed around the sorcerer. Strange things swam in the furious, blood-soaked reds and bottomless, devouring blacks.

A chorus of greens, blues, and blacks entered my breast. Oranges, purples, and grays added to the mix. The magic rolled down my arms and collected into shimmering power at my fingertips.

I flicked a portion at my companions, wrapping them in a bubble of whites and yellows with a dash of crimson to give the defensive magic teeth.

Soulless Gustav sent inky tendrils against the shield. They burned away in invisible sparks, but the defense would fall beneath stronger assaults.

"You'll never defeat me if you waste your power protecting these specks. Then again, you won't defeat me even with all your power."

"Tell me, sorcerer. Who will you bore with your endless blather in your new universe?"

This was my first direct confrontation with a disciple of magic, but Ghastly Edna had educated me on what to expect. To those with eyes to see it, it would start as a clash of color. Fragments of raw magic molded themselves to one's will, only to be unmade by the other before becoming anything more than possibilities. Dozens of potential magics were thrown between us in mere seconds. Blues collided with greens. Reds shattered oranges. Purples devoured whites. Unsuccessful magic still had some effect. The sea froze. The sky split open into geysers of steam and fire. It was always like this in the beginning. Until one magic finally found its way into being and gave its maker the advantage. As in most battles, duels of magic were usually decided by the first blow.

I held my ground. Better than I'd expected, in truth, but I was slipping. That part I'd given to protect my companions left me the lesser. It was all I could do to unmake Soulless Gustav's sorceries. Soon I was on the defensive, straining against the flood that must come.

It was a span of seconds. Wyst didn't understand what was happening, and he couldn't hold himself back any longer. Some might have called it bravery. Others, foolishness. Still others, frustration. All would've been right. He raised his sword and charged. My protection clung to him, but it wouldn't be enough.

Soulless Gustav thrust a palm at Wyst. Screaming blue oblivion surged forward. A sliver punched through my protection. Wyst staggered and clutched his chest.

"I'm impressed, witch. That should've burst his heart. Now, I'll finish the job. Unless you care to sacrifice yourself for him." He held an orb of blue death in one hand, an ebony spiked chaos in the other. "You can only stop one. Choose wisely."

He hurled the orb at Wyst and the darkness at me. There wasn't any time to think, only react. I tossed a bolt of white in Wyst's defense while raising a wall against the dark. Neither effort was entirely successful. Wyst gaped, fell to his knees. His dark skin paled.

My flesh withered beneath Soulless Gustav's magic. Veins throbbed along my right arm. Muscles shriveled. The limb turned to sludge and dripped from my shoulder. Newt side-stepped the slime.

Soulless Gustav twirled his hands. A serpent of golden power writhed over his head. "I didn't think witches practiced such direct magic."

"There are many things that you don't know." I drew from the incredible power available. My curse did the rest. A fresh arm sprang anew.

I kept my eyes on the sorcerer and did my best not to think of Wyst. He was going to die. I couldn't save him. Or the others. Any magic in their defense would only make me vulnerable. When I died, Soulless Gustav would kill everyone else. The practical thing to do would be leaving them all to perish. Their lives were meaningless in the larger scheme, but Soulless Gustav had already robbed me of someone I'd loved. He wouldn't take another.

Fortunately, only Wyst was headstrong enough to antagonize the sorcerer. Gwurm and Penelope stayed put. Newt sat impatiently at my side, but he wouldn't move until given permission.

The darkness around Soulless Gustav grew and grew. It hissed and throbbed, a living thing with him at its heart. It was as if he'd tapped into a hidden well of bottomless magic I couldn't even sense. Magic was infinite, but there were limits to how much could be safely harnessed. He seemed not even to strain as the dark cloud surged and billowed about him. The sheer metaphysical bulk of it should have crushed him. Yet there he stood, not just unharmed, but its master. Even containing boundless rage didn't keep him from his endless, irksome prattling.

"Fear suits you, witch. I see it across your face. I am everything here. The beginning and end. Yesterday and tomorrow. I am absolute and unconquerable."

If I was to have any chance, I needed to strike now. I threw everything at him without subtlety or restraint. A whirlwind of deadly magic that would've transformed legions into swine, turned rivers into shrieking bile, and driven kingdoms into riotous madness. It was a work of legend, a spell worthy of Nasty Larry himself. And it did nothing.

The dark storm overwhelmed the whirlwind. All my magic shriveled away beneath such unknowable power. I stood naked and impotent before the sorcerer.

"That's it?" He frowned. "That's all you have?"

I said nothing. I'd expected to lose. Now came my horrible death.

Newt quacked with all his demon rage and rushed at Soulless Gustav. I could only watch as the sorcerer turned my familiar inside-out with a snap of his fingers. I closed my eyes and turned from the steaming mound of blood and feathers.

"Let them go. Kill me, but let them go." It was a foolish request. I now understood just how horrible my death was to be. I was to watch everyone I cared for die and be powerless to stop it. It was a destiny more terrible than I'd been prepared for, but fate has a way of surprising one.

A gray fog curled around me. Invisible claws dug at my flesh. Blood trickled from my nose and eyes. Things pulled out my hair in clumps.

Gwurm and Penelope rose to my defense and suffered for it. A swarm of winged mouths poured from Soulless Gustav's sleeves. They snatched away Gwurm, piece by piece. Before he could even yell out, they disappeared into the sky. Only his ear was left behind. Then Soulless Gustav simply drained Penelope of her animation. The slain broom clattered at his feet.

Soulless Gustav clasped his hands together. Pressure crushed my ribs and liquefied my organs, but I didn't die. Such was my curse.

"Where are all your wry words now, witch? Your subtle wit? Your mysterious wisdom? It seems they have abandoned you, like your magic."

I found the will to speak with pulverized lungs and a throat full of blood. "Kill me and be done with it."

"Those are your final words then? Not very memorable, but to the point." He grinned, and the sea of ice swallowed up Wyst's loyal steed. "Patience, my dear. The relief of death will come soon enough. I'm afraid you'll have to endure my vainglorious chatter just a while longer."

He knelt beside the fox. "I think I'll let you live. Perhaps even after I've remade the universe. As a reminder of this polluted yesterday."

He petted her muzzle, and the fox bit his hand. He yelped and shook her loose. Blood dribbled down his palm. She grinned as only a fox facing death could. Snarling, he sent a wisp of cold black, and she was a moldering skeleton.

Soulless Gustav released me from my agony but held me immobile. I floated behind him as he walked to Wyst of the West. I couldn't watch, but I couldn't close my eyes.

Wyst pushed himself to his feet, steadying himself with his sword. He wheezed. It seemed a miracle he could even stand. His every breath was labored. Sweat soaked his skin. "Let her go, sorcerer."

I reached out for magic and found none. All power in this universe served Soulless Gustav, but this seemed a contradiction. Magic served no one. Even in this unreal place, the magic had to be real.

Wyst raised his sword in a trembling hand, standing on shaking knees. He didn't have any strength left. "You won't kill her while I draw breath."

"Quite correct, but only because I want her to watch you die." Soulless Gustav raised his bloody palm, and Wyst floated into the air. The sorcerer rotated his thumb. Wyst's arm snapped, but he didn't yell out. Soulless Gustav wiggled a finger. Wyst's legs twisted. He gasped. Tears streamed down his face.

"This isn't your fault," he whispered.

Even dying, he still thought of me. I wanted to reach out and touch him. To know his kiss one last time would almost make my horrible death tolerable. A current of magic trickled to my call, and I was free for the briefest of moments. Soulless Gustav raised an eyebrow and chains shackled me to the frozen ground.

"Perhaps you've suffered enough, witch. Time to end this game before it grows tiresome." A coil of black entwined around the Knight's throat.

He smiled painfully at me. "I love you."

"Now those are excellent last words."

Wyst's neck broke with a soft crunch. His corpse collapsed in a heap.

I didn't believe it. I couldn't accept it. The trickle of magic slipped from my heart and onto the dead Knight. Oddly enough, Soulless Gustav seemed not to notice.

"Ah, love. Think about it. You can't touch it. You can't see it. You can't really even describe it. Not without a fountain of ambiguous, pretty words. If you think about it, it's the greatest illusion there is."

Behind him, magic filled Wyst's body. The white and greens danced along his broken form. His shattered arm straightened. Soulless Gustav seemed oblivious to it, and I wondered how he could be. It might've been because his own power was so great. Like a giant, unaware of the gnats buzzing at his feet.

More magic gathered at my fingertips. I sent it against the chains that held me. They rusted away.

"So there's a little fight left in you yet."

Wyst stirred. I didn't know how. I couldn't raise the dead without touching them, and I couldn't heal them. He seemed perfectly whole. He stood, very surprised to be alive. Not nearly so surprised as Soulless Gustav.

Then I grasped it. I hadn't restored Wyst's life. I'd unbelieved his death, and the dribble of magic running through me was different from what I'd called upon before because it was genuine.

Soulless Gustav brought a portion of his incredible might down upon my head. I thrust a cone of red around myself and all that power splashed away without touching me.

I passed my hand at Newt's body. With a slurp and gurgle, skin and feathers wrapped around his organs. He raised his head and glanced at his wings.

Soulless Gustav gaped. "How did you . . ." He couldn't finish the question, so strong was his confusion.

Penelope hopped to life as the icy depths spit Wyst's horse to the surface. Flesh sprang onto the gray fox's bones. Finally, Gwurm's parts rained from the sky, falling into perfect arrangement. All were unbelieved back to life with just a few dollops of magic. Real magic.

"It's done, Gustav. You've lost, and you've only yourself to blame."

"Oh, no, witch." His deep, raging voice rumbled, sending cracks through the ice. "Now you shall behold me as I really am."

"I already do," I replied softly. Too softly to be heard over his blustering.

He threw up his arms. Great monoliths of ice thrust their way to the sky. A downpour of steaming rain sizzled the air. The sorcerer grew fifty feet tall. His flesh turned to glittering silver, and his eyes became crackling lightning.

I draped a golden dome over myself and my companions to keep the unpleasant rain at bay. "I take back what I said before, Gustav. You have more imagination than I gave you credit for. Too much. You've forgotten that this isn't real. That was your first mistake, and I think you made it long ago."

Ice transformed into sand and rock. Clouds parted to reveal a swirling void. Chunks of earth were ripped from the ground and swallowed into it. Not a hair on any of our heads moved. I wished my friends away from this crumbling madness. They faded, leaving only Soulless Gustav and myself.

"I am a god here!" growled Soulless Gustav.

"God of a dream. A master of glass and shadows. Lord of nothing." I laughed. I shouldn't have, but I was too amused. "Here, in this place, your power is at its greatest. But here, in this place, your power is at its most vulnerable. Out there, in the true world, your illusions touch reality, and through that, gain substance. A man killed by a phantom gobling dies because even death can be fooled when the sorcery is potent enough. But here, death is merely a dream. To be accepted or disregarded at one's whim. And I don't accept it. I deny it all."

I clasped my hands together and released a wave of magic and unbelief. Soulless Gustav's universe ceased to exist. It was too fragile to stand against even the smallest skepticism. Soulless Gustav had foolishly allowed me in, and it was far too easy to unmake it from the inside. It was like waking from someone else's dream. Black surrounded us. A tiny fountain of colors stood between us. The legendary sorcerer was reduced to his normal stature, a little shorter in fact. A dull aura of power surrounded him, far less than godhood. He knelt beside the fountain.

"This is all the magic of your realm," I explained. "This is the well of life from which your universe drew existence. Everything else, even your godhood, was merely a delusion. Delusions stacked upon figments piled upon fancies on the shoulders of phantasms. A house of cards."

The sadness on his face stirred my sympathy. "Your first mistake was allowing me inside. Your second was in bringing the others. I was prepared for my death. I would've believed it, but I couldn't accept it for them. Their deaths, false though they were, showed me the truth."

I passed my fingers through the fountain and pressed them to my lips. The raw magic tasted of blood and lemons. The fount was just a trickle, a drop borrowed from the real world to fuel a shattered cosmos. I almost felt sorry for Soulless Gustav as I plugged it with my toe and starved away the remnants of his world.

The darkness fell away. We stood amid the field of his impure sorcery, that place where reality and illusion mingled. A flood of power filled me when we crossed the threshold. Soulless Gustav hadn't lost complete touch with true magic. It swelled around him, but he was a broken man. Dreams he could no longer believe in surrounded him, and he wept.

My companions stood by my side. None could look at the fallen sorcerer save Newt.

"Do you want to kill him? Or can I?"

"There's no need."

"But your vengeance. Surely, you're not going to let him live."

"Death would be a mercy. Now he lives, forsaken and miserable, without hope or joy or even the hollow fantasies of such. This is my vengeance."

"Now that is just cruel." He smiled at me. "The mistress would be proud."

"And what about this place?" asked Wyst.

"I could unmake it, but there's no need. It will fade on its own in time, and the world will never know it was here."

I cast one last glance at Soulless Gustav, sobbing. My vengeance was more than I could bear to witness any longer. I turned and planned on walking away without looking back.

"You dare turn your back on me!" He growled. His voice cracked. I felt the surge of magic as he called upon it. "You won't be able to unbelieve death here, witch."

My companions moved to my defense. Their protection was unnecessary but appreciated.

All Soulless Gustav's subtlety was gone. His anger made his sorcery an obscene, vulgar effort. He molded it into a beast of fangs and claws and glaring red eyes of no discernible form. It was too hideous to be genuine, too grotesque and shapeless to be accepted by the universe. It was the final phantom, the stinging bite that woke the dragon. Soulless Gustav unleashed his own doom.

I'd only meant the dragon as a metaphor, but the magic must've enjoyed the notion. The earth trembled as a black and red serpent parted the clouds and filled the sky. It couldn't be seen entirely in its vastness. It opened terrible jaws and a cleansing, white flame washed across the sorcerous kingdom. Save for the rumbling earth, it made no sound. The purifying blaze burned without even a crackle. The scorched landscape turned to ash, then nothing. The fire seared my companions without touching them. We were real. I didn't even feel its heat. Soulless Gustav wasn't so fortunate. Twisted and blackened, he lay on the barren earth. Soulless Gustav was soulless after all. He'd been living among illusions too long. Somewhere along the way, he'd become a phantom himself.

He drew an agonized breath. "I curse you, witch with the unspoken name. From this day forth—"

"Oh, do shut up."

His eyes widened. It was a breach of etiquette to interrupt, but the death curse I now carried was quite enough.

"Well, how rude."

He crumbled away. Penelope couldn't help but sweep his ashen remains into a neat pile.

The dragon disappeared. A portion of one massive golden wing was the last to fade. The figment of space was the last illusion to fade from Soulless Gustav's realm. The field of bare earth shrank and shrank until it was but a patch barely two feet across, the last monument to the foolish dreams of the greatest sorcerer that had ever lived.

"That's all it was?" asked Newt.

"Doesn't seem like much," agreed Gwurm.

"Just because it became this," I said, "doesn't make it less than it was."

A gust carried away the ashes.

"So that's it?" said Newt. "It's over?"

"Not quite."

I knelt low and put a palm to the earth. Fresh green grass sprouted over Soulless Gustav's monument.

"Some dreams are best forgotten."

I'd hoped not to have to do this final thing. Truth be told, I'd expected to be dead and not have to. Every victory comes at a price, and this was mine. I took Wyst away, where the others couldn't overhear. Nothing had changed between us, but everything else had.

"I should be angry with you." He took my hand. "But you saved my life."

I smiled. "No. You saved mine."

He took me in his arms. It felt so right, so perfect, but it could never be.

"Wyst . . ."

He held me tighter. "We were meant to be together."

It was a romantic notion. I would expect no less from a White Knight. A force beyond our control had indeed brought us together. Her name had been Ghastly Edna. But another power kept us apart, and his name was Nasty Larry.

"I'm never going to let you go," he whispered.

I listened to his heartbeat. I could feel every throb of veins, every gush of blood. His embrace was a wonderful fantasy, and I enjoyed it just a moment more. Then I pushed him away. He couldn't hold me. I was much stronger than he was.

I wanted to hide my eyes, but I looked him in the face. "We are what we are, Wyst. We can't be anything else."

"I can."

"No, you can't. You are a champion of righteousness, and this world needs you far more than I do."

He put a hand on my shoulder. "This world will get along just fine without me."

"This can only end badly, Wyst. I am accursed. Every day my appetite grows. One day, maybe tomorrow, maybe a year from now, I will devour you. Or you will be required to kill me."

"I could never kill you."

"I know. That's why this can never be." I put a palm against his chest to keep him from drawing closer. This was harder than I'd fathomed. "One day, I would kill you, and I would become everything my curse intended me to be."

Wyst cupped my chin. "You won't."

"I would. Unless you promise to kill me when the time comes."

He closed his eyes. "I could. If I had to."

"If only I could believe that." I kissed his cheek. "You've given me a wonderful gift, but even if you could change who you are, I would always be what I am."

The truth was a jagged barb. I wanted to believe he would kill me. I wanted to believe that devouring him wouldn't be so terrible a thing. I was too good a witch to believe a lie.

Wyst had no more arguments. I think, like me, he'd known this was the only way it could end. Though he might deny it, Wyst was a White Knight body and soul, and White Knights were defined by their sacrifices.

"There isn't a place for us in this world. Only in that phantasmal kingdom that no longer exists." I took his hand and gave him my moldy squirrel hide. "This was a gift from the first person who ever meant something to me. I pass it onto you. To remember me by."

The hide smelled of dust, and most of the fur had been worn away. Wyst rubbed it between his fingers with a soft smile.

And then, I kissed him one last time. A soft touch of closed lips. Anything more, and neither of us would have been able to walk away.

He wanted to argue, to find a justification, some hidden truth that would make this possible. I desperately wanted him to, but even all the magic in this world couldn't keep us together. It was difficult, but the both of us had faced difficult truths before. We were certain to face many more in the future. None so difficult as this last one for a good long while, I hoped.

He closed his eyes and drew in a soft breath. "I'll always love you."

"I know." I turned away. "I'll always love you too." It was a whisper, but he heard.

"Wait." Wyst of the West stood straight and inscrutable, every bit the stolid White Knight. "I'd like to give you something."

"You've given me enough already."

Our eyes met for the last time. Neither of us smiled. We were a witch and White Knight again.

"One last thing," he said. "To remember me by."

"I'd like that."

He gave me my gift. He took his horse by the reins and went in search of his lost purity. The gray fox met me halfway back to my companions.

"Off on your own again?" I asked.

"No, I'm going with the Knight. I think he has interesting possibilities."

"Watch over him for me."

"I will because you can't."

I stroked her muzzle and bestowed her with a touch of magic, a small enchantment to extend her years and allow her to speak with one White Knight. "Thank you."

She grinned as sly and canny as a clever, curious fox could. "It's the least I can do for allowing me to share such an entertaining journey." She ran after Wyst. He slowed that she might catch up.

It may have been morning in Soulless Gustav's dream, but it was a little past midday in the real world. I noticed the sun for the first time in all its vulgar brightness and pulled my hat low over my eyes. Somewhere in that small distance to my companions, I left behind the trappings of mortal womanhood. Only the trappings. Everything important, all the feelings and joys and memories, those would always stay with me.

I allowed myself one last unwitchly smile.

I said nothing as I met my companions and kept on walking. They knew enough to follow without being told. Penelope floated beside me and gently nudged herself into my hand. She held herself tense in my grip.

"I'm fine, dear. You don't need to worry."

She relaxed.

"You aren't limping," observed Newt, "and you should tuck away your hair."

I chuckled silently. I'd just defeated the greatest sorcerer alive, and my familiar still felt compelled to instruct me in what it was to be a good witch. I should've shown him his place, but I decided to be charitable.

"Where are we going?" asked Newt.

"Back to Fort Stalwart." I listened, and I heard the magic

for the first time. It was a soft, gentle voice, full of mischief. "They will have need of a good witch again. And soon."

"Will there be bloodshed?"

"Mayhem and danger, certainly. Bloodshed, perhaps."

The promise of such was enough to satisfy him.

"So what did Wyst give you?" asked Gwurm.

"How did you know he gave me something?" I said.

"Just a feeling. You gave him your squirrel."

"He didn't give her anything," said Newt. "You were watching."

"On the contrary, he gave me many things, both ordinary and beautiful. But perhaps, least importantly, he gave me a name."

Newt perked up. "What is it?"

I smiled.

"You aren't going to tell us."

Silence was my only reply.

I didn't expect him to understand, but it was enough to have the name. Letting others hear it would have robbed it of its worth, made it a mundane, ordinary thing. I didn't want to share it. I wanted it all for myself. Now I truly was The Witch with the Unspoken Name. Or, more truthfully, the Witch with the Name That Had Been Spoken Once. But that was a bit long and awkward, even for a good witch.

"I still don't see what good an unspoken name is," said Newt.

"Then you've never heard the story of Nameless Walter," said Gwurm.

"Wait a minute. If his name is Nameless Walter, then he can't be nameless."

Gwurm chuckled. "Ah, but therein lies the tale . . ."

I only half listened as my troll began the story. It was an

amusing and colorful fable, but my mind lay elsewhere. Some part of me still wanted to turn back and run to Wyst, but being with him would only make me into the monster I was supposed to be. In the end, it would destroy everything worthwhile he'd given me. Knowing this made it less difficult to walk away, but it didn't make it easier.

I wanted to glance one last time over my shoulder, but there was no reason to. Looking behind would only show me the things I'd seen, and everything of importance I could always see. Every time I smelled fresh bread. Whenever I closed my eyes. Or the caress of a breeze on my lips.

And every time my name was never spoken.

Turn the page for a preview of

TOO MANY CURSES

A. LEE MARTINEZ

Available in September 2008

 TOR®   A TOR PAPERBACK

ISBN-13: 978-0-7653-1835-0   ISBN-10: 0-7653-1835-0

1

Margle the Horrendous had a habit of collecting things. There were his books on various subjects of study arcane and lore obscure. His castle was filled with various monsters, or pieces of monsters, for purposes only wizards might fathom. Other chambers were filled with jewels, enchanted knick-knacks, gold and other precious things, and all the peculiar odds and ends that ultimately meant little to wizards yet which they insisted on hoarding. He also had a great assortment of enemies who he had gathered over the years. Margle rarely killed his foes. Death rarely amused him. Instead, he kept them close, a grand collection of old rivals and fallen heroes. And as with all his collections, it was Nessy's task to take care of them.

Margle was an exceptionally generous master, meaning that he was generally too busy to bother yelling at her, and when he did, he usually threw things not dangerously hard or sharp and missed more often than not. And Margle was frequently absent from the castle, leaving Nessy the run of the place—or at least the rooms that weren't forbidden to her, where she wasn't interested in going anyway because there were certainly many horrors waiting in Margle's castle. There were even one or two rooms the wizard himself never went into. And one place, The Door At The End Of The Hall, that even he avoided going anywhere near.

Nessy enjoyed maintaining Margle's vast library. And if she should take a peek at a secret volume or two while alphabetizing the shelves, Margle had yet to notice or care. She'd even picked up a handful of magic tricks. Nothing serious, but small spells of practical use. Feeding the horrors in the bestiary was the worst of her tasks, but even that she did without complaint. It was honest work and gave her a roof over her head and food in her belly, and though she knew that one day Margle would certainly kill her in a fit of rage or for some fiendish experiment or maybe just because it would amuse him to do so, she was glad to have it.

Except for the occasional overly chatty gargoyle.

"Did I ever tell you about the time I slew three ogres while armed with only a wet towel?" Gareth asked.

"Yes." Nessy polished his stone head with a rag as the gargoyle continued.

"Well, it was a terrible struggle. . . ." He blathered on for some time, and Nessy nodded as if listening. She pitied the poor soul trapped in a stone demon perched over an archway. Such was the fate of Margle's enemies. At least this particular enemy.

"Are you listening?" Gareth sighed.

"No." Nessy was ruthlessly honest, not so much because she valued the virtue as because she seldom considered lying before she spoke.

"I was a great hero, you know."

"I know." She spat in his eye and wiped away the dust.

"I hate when you do that."

"Would you rather have dirt in your eyes?"

"No."

"Well then . . ." She nimbly climbed onto his back and shined his horns. Gareth didn't move, couldn't move. He could only talk, and talk a lot. And stare down the corridor at The Door At The End Of The Hall.

"Ever wonder what's in there?" he asked as he always did when being polished.

"Best not to imagine."

"Maybe for you. That's all I can do."

"Well, maybe if you were quieter you'd get more visitors."

Gareth grumbled, "The others are just jealous of my legendary feats."

A disembodied voice spoke up. "Ah, yes, that's it. Certainly nothing to do with your personality. Or lack thereof."

"Hello, Echo," said Nessy. Margle had taken away everything but Echo's voice. While she lacked anything in form, she was at least free to roam the castle.

"He's back."

Nessy's tall, fuzzy ears cocked. She heard the distant thunder that always signaled her master's return. "Thank you, Echo."

The voice didn't reply. Or she was gone. It was impossible to know, but one was never really alone in Margle's castle. Nessy jumped to the floor.

"You aren't finished," protested Gareth.

"I'll be back. And you can tell me all about that time you died and had to wrestle the lords of the underworld to return from the grave."

"That is a good one. See, I'd just been slain while fighting an army of lizard men. I'd defeated them, but at the cost of my very life. . . ."

Nessy walked away. He continued. Gareth enjoyed hearing his stories more than anyone else. An audience was mostly a technicality.

"What a bore," said Echo, somewhere over Nessy's right shoulder.

"You could listen to him occasionally," Nessy said. "He gets lonely."

"Oh, I do. I'll ask him about one of his tales of adventure, and then I'll go find something to amuse myself, leaving him to prattle."

"That's not very nice."

"Well, I'm invisible. You only know I'm around when I'm talking, and he never lets anyone else speak. So he never knows. Sometimes, I come back later, and he's still going on. Then I pretend I've been listening the whole time. If I do it right, I can keep him amused for days without ever really having to listen to him."

This struck Nessy as a touch unethical even if she couldn't see the harm. But she had to admit that she didn't polish the gargoyle as much as she should because there were times she wasn't in the mood.

A small bat swept down and landed on her shoulder. "Are ye lasses speaking of the old gray blowhard? Can't stand the lad meself. His stories are all fuss and bluster."

"Hello, Thedeus," said Echo.

"Sir Thedeus!" squealed the four-inch bat.

Like all the castle's fallen heroes, he was stubborn about letting go of his greatness. They were all alike. Gareth was only a little worse.

The hallway torches flared. Margle liked a bright castle. It was expected that Nessy be in the tower to greet him on his arrival. If not, he'd threaten to shave her fur or throw her into the bottomless pit in the castle bowels. He wouldn't do it. Probably wouldn't, she corrected, knowing that he would kill her one day. She also knew that when he did, it would have little to do with anything she'd done. But there was no sense in making him mad. Her stubby kobold legs gave her a slow walk. She dropped to all fours and scampered at a brisk trot.

Sir Thedeus disliked the bumpy ride and took flight. "Given any thought to me suggestion, lass?"

"Not that again," said Echo. For a bodiless voice, she sounded curiously out of breath.

"Aye, it's high time we kill that evil bastard."

"And how exactly do we do that?" asked Echo.

"All I need is an opening, a moment of weakness. Then I pounce from the shadows and rip out his throat."

"You're a fruit bat."

"I've still teeth, lass."

"Nessy has to peel oranges before she gives them to you."

"Ach, have ye ever tried nipping an orange rind?" said Sir Thedeus. "I'm telling ye, it canna be done."

"Nessy does it."

"Fine. She can rip out the foul bastard's throat then. I don't care. As long as he dies and the spell is broken. Don't ye want to be a person again?"

Nessy pulled farther ahead. At full speed, she could outrun Echo and Sir Thedeus. She darted through the labyrinth of corridors. Margle was close, but she took the long way. She wasn't worried enough to go near the Wailing Woman today.

A clap of thunder told her that Margle's arrival was imminent. She bolted up the stairs, having lost Echo and Thedeus somewhere along the way.

An apparition rattled his chains at her. He howled pitifully.

"Not now, Richard."

She ran through him without pausing and reached the top of the tower not a moment too soon.

A great, black bird flew through the tower window. It

clutched a stone the size of a kobold's head in one talon. It glared at Nessy with burning red eyes and shrank into Margle's shape. He was tall and thin, rather bony even for a wizard. His billowing robes only made him look more fragile. In Nessy's experience, a wizard's mystical powers were inversely proportional to his physical presence. Margle was a powerful wizard and a slight man. Sir Thedeus's teeth might just be able to bite the scrawny wizard's head off if the bat put his mind to it.

Margle's glare strengthened. "Where's my wine, dog?"

Nessy lowered her head, covered her muzzle with her hands, and tucked her tail between her legs. "I'm sorry, master."

He wrung his hands. His stringy forearms tightened. "And I thought I told you I wanted this floor polished."

"I did polish it, master."

He sneered. "Don't contradict me, beast."

"No, master. But the stones are slick, and I thought they might be too slippery."

"Ah, there you go again. Thinking is not your purpose."

"No, master." She licked her lips. "Yes, master. Sorry, master."

"I should boil you alive for eternity."

"Yes, master."

Margle gritted his sharp teeth. "You're fortunate, dog, that I'm in a good mood."

Nessy peered at the stone in his hand. The shape, color, and markings showed it to be a nurgax seed. She'd read of them in Margle's books but didn't mention that to the master. Nurgaxes were rare beasts, valued by wizards more for their rarity than their power. Nessy remembered the passage in the book. When the seed was broken, the nurgax would spring full grown and devour the first living creature it saw.

It would then imprint on the second living creature it saw, forming a bond that could only be severed by death.

"Shall I put that away for you, master?"

His sneer deepened. "Beast, you're never to touch this. Do so and I'll flay you."

"Yes, master."

"Layer by layer by layer."

"Yes, master."

"Then I shall make a hat from your tanned hide and matching bookends from your bones."

"Yes, master."

Margle was in a threatening frame of mind and kept on for another minute. Nessy nodded and acted appropriately fearful. The threats didn't mean much. When Margle did finally kill her, it would probably be without warning.

". . . And I'll serve your eyes in my soup," he finished.

"Yes, master. Shall I fetch your wine?"

"Wait, beast. I haven't dismissed you yet."

Nessy's fur bristled.

Sir Thedeus flew into the tower and perched on her shoulder again. "Oh now if ever there was a throat needing ripping out," he whispered. "Should I go for it, or would ye like to, lass?"

Margle held up the nurgax seed. The skin on his face tightened. A lock of gray hair fell across his eyes. "Tell me, dog. Tell me how you live to serve me."

"Of course, master."

"Would you die for me?"

"Ach, what a great prat," said Sir Thedeus.

Nessy bowed. The day she'd been waiting for had finally arrived. She was mildly relieved. Good to get it over with and being devoured by a nurgax was a quick death.

Margle repeated the question. "Would you die for me?"

"Yes, master." But only because she had no choice. She looked up at Margle. He was ready to smash the seed on the ground.

"I canna take it any longer." Sir Thedeus hurled himself at Margle's throat. Despite the thinness of the wizard's neck, the small fruit bat merely nipped ineffectively. Unimpressed but startled, Margle backed away. His foot slipped on slick, polished stone, and he tumbled. The nurgax seed broke open and a giant purple monster sprang forth. It had one eye and one horn, tiny wings, and a body that was just a giant snout on two heavy legs.

Nessy scrambled behind a table out of sight.

The nurgax growled curiously.

"No. Stay away!" All the confident malice was gone from Margle's voice. "Stay where you—"

Then came a crunch. And a second crunch. And a slurp. Then a contented purr.

Nessy poked her head out. The nurgax stomped over to her. It licked her once, drenching her fur in its slimy drool.

She laughed. It laughed.

"What did I miss?" asked Echo, her sudden wheezing breath beside Nessy.

Sir Thedeus swooped around in circles. "Nothing much, lass. I just killed the bastard!"

TOR

Award-winning authors
Compelling stories

Please join us at the website
below for more information
about this author and other great
Tor selections, and to sign up for
our monthly newsletter!

www.tor-forge.com